BECKONING CANDLE

A NONFICTION NOVEL

BECKONING CANDLE

A NONFICTION NOVEL

by

RANDY WILLIS

Beckoning Candle
2021 Revised and Expanded Edition
Copyright © 2018 and 2021 by Randy Willis
Registration Numbers
2018 TX 8-659-512
2021 TX 8-943-862 new and revised text

Published by:
American Writers Publishing, LLC
PO Box 111
Wimberley, Texas 78676

www.threewindsblowing.com
512-565-0161
randywillisnovelist@gmail.com

ISBN-13: 978-0-578-40321-2

Library of Congress Control Number: 2021930588

Printed in the United States of America

Dedication

To my three sons
Aaron Joseph Willis
Joshua Randall Willis
Adam Lee Willis

And my five grandchildren
Baylee Coatney Willis
Corbin Randall Willis
Presley Rose Willis
Olivia Grace Willis
Juliette Rebecca Willis
and my future grandchildren

With gratitude and love
Their strength of character has been demonstrated
Many times in how they treat people who can do
nothing for them.

—Randy Willis aka Dad, Grandpa, and PaPaw

"Go now, write it on a tablet for them, inscribe it on a
scroll, that for the days to come it may be an everlasting
witness." Isaiah 30:8 (NIV)

"I will pour My Spirit on your descendants,
And My blessing on your offspring."
Isaiah 44:3 (NKJV)

I've learned much from seeing the world through the
eyes of my grandchildren. Jesus said, "the kingdom of
heaven belongs to such as these." Matthew 19:14 (NIV)

TABLE OF CONTENTS

BECKONING CANDLE

DEDICATION   v
INTRODUCTION   7

PROLOGUE   8
NARRATIVE   16
EPILOGUE   93
CHARACTERS   97

HIDDEN FREE BOOK   112
APPENDIX A   200
APPENDIX B   206
THE STORY OF JOSEPH WILLIS   209
MY FATHER AND ME   250
AUTHOR'S NOTE   253
IN APPRECIATION   263
ABOUT THE AUTHOR   265

INTRODUCTION

I've read that novels don't need an introduction, but *Beckoning Candle* is more than a novel. It is three nonfiction novels. Truman Capote claimed to have invented this genre with his book *In Cold Blood* in 1965.

Beckoning Candle depicts real historical figures and actual events woven together with imaginary conversations using fiction's storytelling techniques.

Beckoning Candle was inspired by true stories handed down by my ancestors. In some instances, it is 100% fiction.

—*Randy Willis,* 2021

"Hardships often prepare ordinary people for an extraordinary destiny." —*C. S. Lewis*

BECKONING CANDLE

a nonfiction novel

"You have enemies? Good. That means you've stood up for something, sometime in your life." —*Winston Churchill*

Prologue

December 25, 1941
The Ole Willis Place
On Barber Creek
Longleaf, Louisiana

Ran Willis arises before sunrise, nestles next to the fireplace, with hot coffee—as alone as the morning star.

The wind whistles through the dogtrot and awakens Julian. He struggles upright, half asleep, and rubs his eyes as he pours a cup of coffee.

"It's our first white Christmas! Grab some firewood—please.

And check on the horses, mules, and the dogs too."

"Yes, sir, Daddy. Merry Christmas!" Julian shivers as he chips through the frozen water trough with a horseshoe. He gathers the firewood, now covered in two feet of snow. Icicles adorn the trees overhanging Barber Creek. It is cold and rather barren, but it has the loveliness of a Christmas card. And, like a Christmas card, it will hold that image in Julian's mind for years to come.

Ran's eldest son, Howard, driving his International Harvester truck, can be heard a mile away as it plows through the snow on the red dirt road. The family knows there will be

8

no snowfall that will prevent Howard from delivering a Christmas tree to the

homestead—a real tree, and not one of those artificial, awkwardly bent imitation trees with no texture, no fragrance, and no fullness.

"That's a big cedar. Let me help." Julian drags the Christmas tree out of the truck bed.

Howard's wife, Zora, cries out, "I need help, too." Ran clasps her. "Ah-ha! All my favorites: freshly baked pies, peach preserves, and okra in mason jars. Oh, my, and even your famous buttermilk pie."

Ran's wife, Lillie, collects each family member's handcrafted decoration for the tree. "Let's hang them." The aroma of cedar, sugared fruit, and gingerbread brings back memories of Christmases past.

Today is Ran and Lillie's grandson Donnie's fourth birthday, to boot. "Can I play with my birthday gifts, Grandpa?"

"Yep, but keep the stick horse at a trot. Let him get used to this colder weather, eh? See what else Santa left you. The new game *Shoot the Moon* and a wooden jigsaw carton puzzle."

Good, long-time neighbors, John and Ruth Duke, and their two kids, Johnnie Ruth and Jerry, arrive with a pumpkin pie and two fruitcakes.

Miss Ruth always spikes her fruitcakes with a little rum. "It's no different from using cooking sherry and, therefore, is not an affront to the Lord," Ruth says. "It provides moisture and helps preserve the cake."

Ran fidgets. "The better part of valor is not to mention that to Lillie. Her definition of what constitutes a mortal sin may be different from ours. Let me taste-test the cake for moisture." He pinches off a nibble and smacks his lips in approval. "Now, indeed, that's the moistest cake ever! I may have another slice or two later."

Johnnie Ruth and Donnie sit on the floor. Donnie prefers *Conflict*, a military board game—Johnnie Ruth, paper dolls. Howard reaches and hangs the star of Bethlehem on the tree.

"It almost touches the ceiling." His brother Herman carved it from a piece of hickory. Christmas stockings, stuffed with nuts, candy, and fruit, hang on every available nail. Earlier, Lillie had placed books, tablets, pencils, wooden soldiers, and even a rockin' horse under the tree.

The children's faces glow from the fireplace. Herman stokes the fire with a piece of pine-kindling.

The sunrise colors glisten in the snow. "Who can paint like the Lord of creation?" Lillie proclaims.

Donnie and Johnnie Ruth grab a shovel, off to go sledding from the barn. They slide down the hill to the banks of Barber Creek.

"You kids, get back up here," Lillie yells. "That's too dangerous.

Ten more feet and you'd both be frozen lollypops!"

Julian blows in his horse's nose to calm him. It's not the first time the animal has experienced snow, but it has been a long time, and any sudden change in the weather makes horses skittish, until they get reassurance from their masters that all is well and everything is still just fine. "The Comanche use to do this in Texas. Helps you bond with the horse."

"I'm going to churn ice cream in my new pewter pot," Lillie promises. She stirs snow, milk, cream, butter, and eggs. She also prepares Ran's favorites, especially dewberry pie, along with a cup of kindness known as Community dark roast coffee.

Ran grins. "I hung some mistletoe."

Lillie looks him in the eyes and kisses him on the cheek. "The kids."

"We have enough to feed Camp Claiborne's 34th Red Bull Infantry," Ran says. The nearby U.S. Army military camp accommodates 30,000 men but does not give Lillie a sense of safety. A world war is still raging, and every American is on alert.

Lillie's eyes sparkle. "Please play my favorite Christmas carol—*O Holy Night*?" Ran's father bought him a fiddle on a cattle drive from East Texas when he was barely twelve. He spent his evenings teaching himself the fingering and bowing techniques.

"How can I refuse a woman of such virtue—and one so beautiful? Our home overflows with your sweet joy."

Lillie hugs him. "Will it be our last Christmas with our sons?"

The snow drifts against the windows and doors, begging entrance into their lives like the events of the previous three weeks. "There's nothing as peaceful as Louisiana Longleaf pines covered in a fresh layer of snow," Ran muses. "Ah, if only the world were that way."

Ran's eighteen-year-old nephew, Robert Willis, Jr., enlisted July 31, 1940, and reported aboard the battleship *USS Arizona*, on October 8, 1940, at Pearl Harbor. A surprise military strike by the Japanese Navy Air Service, on the morning of December 7, 1941, detonated a bomb in a powder magazine. The battleship exploded and sank. Hundreds of marines and sailors were trapped as the ship went down.

The family held out hope, but those hopes were vanquished a week ago, like a shadow darkening all elements of light. Rapides Parish Sheriff, U. T. Downs, and Robert's pastor from First Baptist Church, Pineville, delivered a Western Union telegram to Robert's father.

Downs struggled to speak with tears in his eyes. "It has been confirmed that Robert's entombed in the *USS Arizona* at the bottom of Pearl Harbor. I just can't tell you how grieved I am to bring this news to you, especially so soon after Thanksgiving. This is the part of my job that I dread the most. If there's anything I can do for you folks, just say the word."

Howard and Zora took Donnie to the Pringle Picture Show in Glenmora to see *How Green Was My Valley*. "We need to seem as if nothing has changed for Donnie's sake," Zora insists. "I fear that we will be one of many, many families who will receive telegrams before this war is over. Our hearts are broken, but we must carry on."

Julian now works with the horses and mules—plenty of grain, hay, and water for them. He grooms their coats of hair and checks to see if they are sound and well-shod. He's gentle with horses, the elderly, and children, but as tough as rawhide on men who are no- account. "I wish I could ride you guys into battle, but an airplane will have to do."

Two stray goats, covered with ice, nudge their way into the barn. Julian jumps up to shoo them back outside. "Get out of here. You're going to break Daddy's deer horn hat rack I made. It's his Christmas gift." The goats resist but then yield when Julian gives each a swat.

Herman, quiet and soft-spoken, takes off, without saying a word—impeccably dressed, as always.

Howard and Julian help their father with the firewood.

"It's best you two find him—now! Take my Ford," Ran insists.

They pump ten gallons of gas into Ran's '40 Ford Coupe at Bob Johnson's Grocery Store at Shady Nook. "Where do you think he's at?" Howard asks.

"Charlie's Cafe in Glenmora is the closest—let's try there first."

"He just left, but not until he whipped two men for making fun of his khaki pants," the owner tells them when they arrive. "Did he say anything?" Julian asks.

"He mentioned, he would not be back, ever, and he preferred Boom Town's honky-tonks. Not sure which one, but they're all outside Camp Claiborne's main gate. As long as that base keeps bringing in new boys who are wet behind the ears and willing to waste their pay during a weekend pass, those places will thrive. Check 'em one by one."

This time one man lay on the floor in need of medical attention. "Let's check the Wigwam, in Forest Hill," Julian says, "before

someone kills him or, God forbid, wrinkles his pants. I played pedal steel guitar there several times in Horace Whatley's band. It's a rough joint."

The sounds from the beer joint known for live music and its jukebox shakes the windows as they drive into the parking lot. Chicken wire fencing wraps around the bandstand to keep the band from getting hit with beer bottles.

As they enter, the bartender yells. "Break 'em up before they destroy the place!" Three men are holding Herman while two others are landing repeated punches and kicks. The jukebox blares Jimmie Davis's hit—*I Hung My Head and Cried.*

Herman, bleeding like a stuck pig, calls out, "Are y'all going to help me or just stand there, whistlin' *Dixie*?"

"I'll take the three holding him, you the other two. Use that chair, Howard."

After a melee of about ten minutes, they settle with the barkeeper for fifty bucks in damages and haul Herman outside to his truck. His lip is busted, his nose is bleeding, and one eye is starting to seal shut. He refuses to show any sign of weakness or pain, although he wheezes when drawing in a breath between bruised ribs.

They arrive home in time for a delayed supper. Ran examines Herman's cuts and bruises. "Save all that anger for the Japs and Hitler."

Lillie brings clean towels. "My three sons fighting in the Devil's playground and on Christmas Day! May the Good Lord find mercy to forgive you for such behavior!"

Ran smiles. "At least they didn't go to the Duck Inn…it provides more than liquor." She does not find the humor in his observation, as her grimace reveals.

Lillie pulls her collar up, tightens her scarf, shoves her hands deep into her pockets, turns her face, and walks outside into the biting wind. "I need to gather more snow for the ice cream."

She returns—but with no snow. "It's suppertime." Her words are all that is needed for family and guests to gather around the candlelit table.

As Ran says grace, light dispels the darkness in their hearts just as the Star of Bethlehem did long ago. The reflection in Lillie's face, from the beckoning candle, contradicts the devastating news from Hawaii.

Ran bows his head as everyone joins hands. "Lord, we know the world will still turn, the songbirds will again make their joyful sounds, and this too will pass. Keep our sons in the hollow of Your hand. Bless this food—and bless our nation. In the name above all names—Jesus."

American men from coast to coast step forward to retaliate against the attack on U.S. soil. In the days shortly after Thanksgiving, Julian had enlisted in the U.S. Army Air Corps. And Herman in the ground forces Army after hearing President Roosevelt's words on the radio: "No matter how long it may take us to overcome this premeditated invasion, the American people in their righteous might will win through to absolute victory."

Howard went with his brothers and did his best also to enlist. However, the recruiter didn't even need to wait for the results of a physical to see that Howard had a deformity that would make him 4-F. Howard had a severe head injury caused by a blow from a split rim truck wheel. It had exploded while Howard was filling a tire with air in Glenmora. He tried to disguise the injury by pulling a cap down over his hair and forehead. Still, the recruiter—who was not new to his job—pulled off the cap, surveyed the scar, and motioned a thumb over his shoulder, indicating Howard was "out" of the running. Ran tried to assure Howard he could still be of service to the nation in other ways. For a scrapper and brawler like Howard, those words brought little appeasement.

Now, as they continue to enjoy what will probably be the last Christmas as a united family for perhaps years to come, Howard stokes the flames in the fireplace with a kindling-stick from a busted chiffarobe.

Ran raises his fiddle.

"Join me in the family key."

Everyone joins in.

"O holy night, the stars are brightly shining,
It is the night of the dear Savior's birth;
Long lay the world in sin and error pining,
'Till he appeared and the soul felt its worth.
A thrill of hope the weary world rejoices,
For yonder breaks a new and glorious morn."

Ran leafed through his great-grandfather Joseph Willis's six-inch thick leather-bound journal written long ago as the long day ends.

"What would Joseph Willis do?"

Narrative

1575
Chettle, Dorsetshire
Southern England

Chettle is known as the loveliest village in England. The Willis family lives in the tiny hamlet in a deep valley dotted with a few limestone cottages and a towering church.

"This is a glorious day," Nathaniel's father proclaims, as the entire Willis clan walks to the Church of St. Mary for three-day-old Nathaniel's baptism. "And I'm not talking just about the weather." He smiles as they approach the colossal church.

"How much for his baptism?" Nathaniel's father asks. "Four shillings," the parish priest replies.

"You've gone up a shilling or two!"

"Salvation is worth four shillings, don't you agree?"

"I'll read my Bible tonight and try to find in the Holy Scriptures where four shillings seals the deal with the Good Lord. If the child lives a long life, even four shillings may prove to be a bargain."

"Would you rather Queen Mary's rule? She would have burned us all on a stake. We can bless Queen Elizabeth that our Parish Church of St. Mary is part of the Church of England."

"God bless the Queen, yes. But I am not sure what that has to do with having to pay for a baptism. What else do I have to pay for—autumn?"

1588
Tilbury Camp, England

Time passes quickly, and before anyone can believe it, it's Nathaniel's thirteenth birthday. Thirty years earlier, Elizabeth I succeeded her half-sister, known as Bloody Mary, as Queen of England and Ireland. Mary was responsible for 300 English Protestants' deaths, burned at the stake for heresy. Elizabeth hates Catholicism. She established the English Protestant church when she became the Supreme Governor of the church.

England's little wealth and many enemies entice Spain. As the most powerful country in the world, Spain, with unparalleled wealth coming from the New World, threatens to destroy this small country. With Spain's military might, endless numbers of soldiers, horses, armor, weapons, and ships, it seems invincible.

The Spanish Armada of 130 ships sails in 1588 to escort an army of 55,000 men to invade England. The goal is to overthrow Queen Elizabeth I and crush the spread of Protestantism.

Queen Elizabeth prays all day and night. As the sun rises in the dark clouds over the English Channel, the Queen greets her land forces at Tilbury. Dressed in white with armor, a silver cuirass, and mounted on a grey gelding, Elizabeth addresses her army camp.

"Shortly we shall have a famous victory over the enemies of my God."

The queen rallies her troops. "I am come amongst you, as you see, at this time, not for my recreation and disport, but being resolved, in the midst and heat of the battle, to live and die amongst you all; to lay down for my God, and for my kingdom, and my people, my honor and my blood, even in the dust."

Elizabeth rides tall on her grey gelding. "I know I have the body but of a weak and feeble woman, but I have the heart and stomach of a king, and of a king of England too."

The next day her troops observe a public fast for victory. If Queen Elizabeth ever felt nervous about challenging the most enormous power in the known world, she never showed it. Her men draw courage and find determination from their queen's stance.

The Armada drops anchor. Simultaneously, the Armada waits for news from its army, the English mount a surprise attack. The Armada is caught off-guard. Its massive ships are not maneuverable, making them vulnerable to the speedy, fast-turning English warships. The Spanish fall victim to an English fireship attack. The English launch eight burning ships loaded with timber and gunpowder into the midst of the Spanish fleet. Enemy ships start to burn, become significantly damaged, and drift from the protection of their grouping.

With time, the Spanish Armada signals for a massive retreat and withdraws north, up the coast. But, a mighty wind begins to blow. The storm blows the bulky, unruly Spanish vessels against the coastline. The Armada's army, blockaded in a harbor, cannot come to the rescue.

The English celebrate their victory by giving praise to God. Queen Elizabeth calls for a thanksgiving service to be held at St. Paul's Cathedral in honor of the country's deliverance. A commemorative medal is struck with the inscription, "God blew and they were scattered."

The Spanish Armada was not the only armada sent against England. Others came in 1596 and 1597. However, by God's grace, these fleets, too, were dispersed by storms. Without these victories, England would have reverted to the Catholic faith.

Nathaniel and the entire Willis clan remain faithful to the English Protestant church during Elizabeth's reign. She lives until 1603.

1603
Great Britain

In 1603, the King of Scotland, James, becomes King of England and is the first monarch called King of Great Britain.

The next year King James convenes a conference at Hampton Court for a discussion with representatives of the Church of England, including leading English Puritans. One of the Puritans petitions the king that there might be a new translation of the Bible because others were corrupt. The King jumps on the idea, insisting, "We will name it after me."

In 1607, Nathaniel's son John Willis is born in London. Severe harvest failures had forced the family to move to London.

The King James Bible is completed in 1611 by 47 scholars, all of whom are members of the Church of England.

August 1620
Plymouth, England

"I must leave London to find employment. I have no choice, Father, with our failing economy," John says. "It falls to me to help support you and our family. I grieve over having to leave all of you, but I see little choice in the matter."

"You're only fourteen. If I were a younger man, I'd go with you. You have limited training and experience. What work do you imagine you will find?"

"A bulletin says there's work to be found 150 miles north of London—near Bawtry," John explains. "There is nothing here. I will explore this option and see if work is available elsewhere. Do I have your blessing?"

"I'll agree if you join a church—first thing once you find employment."

John makes the trip, arduous as it proves to be. Jobs are not as abundant as he had hoped, forcing him to take a lowly position, mucking stalls, grooming horses, and feeding animals in a stable. The churches he visits hold no appeal to him, so he does not desire membership.

John enquires about a radical church he has heard the locals talk about in the streets.

"That church is no longer here," a man on a street corner informs him. "They didn't feel welcome in this community. They pulled up stakes and abandoned this town."

"Where did they go?"

"Holland."

John swallows hard. "This is sad news to hear. From what I've learned, this church held views I could relate to and believe in. I reckon that's God's will for me. I want to join the Separatist William Bradford's church."

The stranger looks aghast. "You know he is a radical, refusing the King's law. You join him, and you will get yourself run through with a sword. Are you willing to risk your life?"

"It's not a pleasant thought, but if needed, I am. The challenge is, how do I find this man and join his followers?"

"In that regard, I have news for you. William Bradford will be in Plymouth in a few weeks. It's a port on the southern coast of England—a hard two-week ride on a good horse."

"I don't have a horse."

"You do now."

"You are a Separatist?"

"Perhaps."

"I know that area. My cousins live in Devonshire. Two of my heroes were born there, Sir Francis Drake and Sir Walter Raleigh. They helped Elizabeth defend England against the Spanish Armada. And both explored the New World—America. One day I dream of going there, too."

"Perhaps you can name a colony like Raleigh did Virginia in honor of our late virgin Queen Elizabeth?"

"Who knows? Anything is possible in a new uncharted, wide-open land. Thank you for the use of the horse. It will help me on the first of what will no doubt be many travels in my future."

True to his quest, John arrives in Plymouth on Devon's south coast in less than two weeks and diligently seeks Bradford.

"Sir, I'm John Willis. Please tell me why you attempted to sail for America last month but then canceled your plans?"

"Young man, we would have gone the distance if the *Speedwell* had been seaworthy. Her timbers were rotted, her sails were torn, and her ropes were frayed."

"Why are you risking your life to go there now? If you make it, it will be in the middle of winter!"

"We have no choice. The king wants to kill us for our beliefs."

21

"Why not co-exist with the Church of England like the Puritans?"

"Because the King controls the Church of England. We will have no part of a church headed by a king or a church ruled by a pope. We believe the church should be led by Christ alone. We have no desire to co-exist, but to separate ourselves from any church headed by a man."

"That's why you're called Separatists?"

"I reckon, but followers of Christ is a better name."

"Aye, would that I had the passage and place to join you now.

God speed, sir."

The winds that saved England in 1588 blew again, but this time in the sails of a tiny 110-foot ship named the *Mayflower*. It sets sail two weeks after John Willis's encounter with William Bradford.

Bradford's departing words pierce John's heart. "We will be ruled only by Jesus, the Christ—God Incarnate."

As religious persecution increases, Nathaniel and John Willis become Separatists. They, too, have no desire to co-exist. But what options do they have?

July 1635
Plymouth Colony
The New World

Fifteen years after the *Mayflower* voyage and Nathaniel's death, 29-year-old John Willis sails on the ship *Paul*. John arrived in St. Kitts in the West Indies on April 3, 1635. Within days he made his way to the New World—America—in Plymouth Colony.

The first thing John does is stop a man on a street corner. "Do you know of a man named William Bradford?"

"You're new here, aren't you?"

"Just arrived."

"He's the Governor of Plymouth Colony. He has been for more than a decade. There're only 400 of us. You will not walk far before you trip over him."

John walks two blocks. He sees a man of erect posture and approaches him.

"Excuse me, sir, do you know where I might find the Governor?"

"You have just done so, young man. How may I be of assistance?"

"Sir, I'm John Willis. We met in England two weeks before you sailed for America. I'm a Separatist now because of your words. I have desired to follow you here to this new land, but finances and family circumstances held me back until recently. But, here I am, and as eager as ever to follow your leading."

"Young man, the first thing you need to do is join Plymouth church. We need a deacon—be our guest—my wife has cornmeal pudding and Indian corn on the table by now."

John Willis very soon steps into the role of Deacon John Willis, the first deacon in Plymouth Church. It is the fulfillment of a dream he has had for many, many years.

"A woman's heart should be so hidden in God that a man has to seek Him to find her." —*Joseph Willis* 1784

{6}

1784
Bladen County
North Carolina

Joseph Willis towers over his friends—six-foot, two inches. His slim and muscular build and dark hair, and high cheekbones accent his boyish grin.

Even though he is a recognized Revolutionary War hero—admired by men and women—and the only son of North Carolina's largest plantation owner, he is modest, open, friendly, and patient. He lives out the aspect of gentle in the word gentleman.

In the fall of 1784, Joseph's first-cousin General John Willis begins to plan his annual invitation-only formal debutante ball at his Red Bluff Plantation. It will always be the highlight of the year for the Willis family and friends from far and wide. Autumn in North Carolina brings a kaleidoscope of colors for weeks. The bursts of red, yellow, and gold foliage reach their peak then. Nature puts on a display unrivaled by any human artist.

John responds to a request from a beautiful socialite from Virginia to meet Joseph. With wealth, grace, and charm, she awes most men.

She arrives with a radiant glow. "Pray, Miss, may I introduce my cousin, Joseph Willis," John says, with a slight bow.

"You may, Sir, indeed."

"Miss Cornelia Anne Graham, please meet Joseph Willis."

"Honored, Miss. I'm your humble servant."

"And I am yours, Sir. You're taller than I imagined. I mean, compared to how John described."

Her beribboned black hair in ringlets stands out to him, as does her petite waist.

The two became intrigued with each other. "Would you dance with me, Mr. Willis?"

"Yes, miss, but I have never danced."

"I will teach you—no one will know."

Joseph is most eager to tell his best friend, Rachel Bradford, about his encounter with the intriguing Miss Graham. He has always appreciated Rachel's simple ways and supposes her kind heart, and humility came from her great-great-grandfather, William Bradford.

"I've met an enchanting woman—a beautiful debutante from Virginia. She taught me to dance. Her waist..." Joseph pauses as he sees Rachel's composure suddenly alter. "Are you ill, Rachel? You're as pale as a sheet. Can I get you a cup of water? Please, sit for a moment."

"No, I must go—now," she insists, turning to make a hasty exit.

"Shy as a schoolgirl, as always," Joseph says, as she rushes away.

Rachel walks a mile to Joseph's mother's home. Ahyoka is sitting on her front porch, knitting. She looks up and sees Rachel approaching. She senses some sadness in the younger woman. She holds her arms wide and embraces Rachel, southing her cares.

"Welcome to our home, and thank you for being a loyal friend to my son." Ahyoka's emotion-rich voice gives Rachel newfound confidence.

"That's just it," Rachel confesses, trembling, tears flowing from her eyes. "I want to be more than a friend."

"I know, Dear One."

"How? Miss Ahyoka, how?"

"By the look in your eyes every time you say his name. Do you think I was never young once and in love? I know the stirrings of the heart in matters like this. Truly, I understand."

"I'm so afraid I'll lose him. I do not know how to show I care. I can hardly speak. Do Cherokee women know about such things?

"There's another woman now! He tells me she's beautiful and has charm, grace, and the smallest waist he's ever seen."

"Do you think he loves her? They have only met. Can love arise so quickly?"

"My dear, men are easily deceived by a glance—a gesture—a smile. It's up to you to show him the difference between a passing fancy and lasting love."

"How? I have no experience in the thoughts and ways of men."

"By realizing you have to tell him."

"I'm not sure I can. I become dizzy and weak in my legs and knees just thinking about it. I know I will become tongue-tied and flustered."

"You do not have a choice. I promise Joseph does not know your heart—men never do—tell him. Men like Joseph can plan a battle, organize a plantation, become a master horseman, and speak Latin, but they cannot recognize love when it is staring them in the face."

"Tell me how—tell me now, please do. How can I make my feelings known?"

"Look him straight in his face and tell him the sun and moon rises in his eyes. He will not have a response. Pause a second, and then tenderly and sweetly whisper to him, 'I am in love with you…and only you.' Say nothing more. Just walk away. Give him time to consider your words and behavior."

"But, am I attractive enough to gain Joseph's affection?"

"Attractive enough? There are plenty of pretty ribbons to put in your hair. And, if I know a thing or two, that tiny waist of hers is no doubt the doings of a synched corset imported from Paris. I've heard tell about them. Sounds like a form of torture to me, but it is amazing what some women will do for vanity."

"Can that kind of thing restrict your breathing?"

"We will soon find out!"

Ahyoka smiles with a playful grin. "He will no doubt, come to me for advice. Now, the question is, shall we plan the wedding for now or later? I'm thinking of a dress of white embroidered organza over rose-colored taffeta and white doeskin moccasins. Oh, but listen to me butting in. This will be your wedding, not mine. As long as it is white, you decide what to wear."

"And this blunt honesty will work? You're convinced of it?" Rachel lets out a huge breath. "I cannot thank you enough."

"Men never know what they want." Ahyoka's eyes sparkle. "They have to be helped along."

"What will happen next?"

"Your hearts will lead your love to where it needs to go—after the wedding."

Afraid that if she thought too long about it, she would lose her resolve, Rachel summons up all of her courage and seeks Joseph. She finds him fishing on the banks of the Cape Fear River. Dusk begins to descend, with fireflies and whippoorwills and crickets calling.

Joseph looks up and smiles as he sees Rachel approach. Unlike earlier that day, she is no longer shaking, nor pale. There seems to be a determination in her step and bearing.

"Hello, Rachel, happy to see you. You look much better than when we last talked. Come closer. I have much to tell you—hold on a moment. I have to see if this is the biggest catfish in North Carolina's history."

Rachel, excitement in her voice and teeth biting on her bottom lip, looks him straight in the eyes. "Before you speak, I have something I must tell you. I've hesitated too long. Excuse my bluntness, but this cannot be postponed." She squares her shoulders and leans slightly forward. "Joseph Willis, I love you, and if you're too stupid not to see that, you two deserve each other! And, I'm not wearing any corset, no matter *what*, in this lifetime or the next."

Having said her piece, Rachel pivots and marches off with a downturned face. Joseph is dumbfounded both by her behavior and her words. Absentmindedly, he drops his cane pole and stands there. He stares down at the catfish, whose expression seems to say, "Don't ask me!"

As expected, Joseph goes to his mother for advice. Promptly he is told that to miss a life with someone as devoted and dependable and loving as Rachel would be something he would regret forever. Thus, gaining his mother's approval and spending time contemplating how he had overlooked the charms and grace of Rachel, he makes a formal call on the young woman and proposes marriage. She eagerly accepts, but never in their entire life together does she ever explain what she had meant by the remark about the corset.

"Women…unfathomable," Joseph would simply muse when the remark came to his memory.

Joseph Willis and Rachel Bradford marry on Christmas Day—clandestinely since he is half-Cherokee.

January 1785
Bladen County
North Carolina

Two weeks after her wedding to Joseph, Rachel decides to learn more about her new family. Who better to go to for such information than her patient and wise mother-in-law Ahyoka.

Once the two women find a place of privacy, Ahyoka is honored to have Rachel seek knowledge of Joseph's heritage. Rachel's eyes filled with an inner glow of joy as she says, "Dearest Ahyoka, I know little of you. Tell me when you first knew you loved Joseph's father?"

"It's a story that delights me, and I'm thankful you ask to hear it. Let me begin by offering you a gift that is part of that story. Where do I begin? It was not love at first sight or second glance, or even after careful consideration." The older woman pauses, squints as she drifts back in time, bringing forth memories of bygone days. "I trusted no man—none ever gave me a reason why I should. It would take time, lots of it, intertwined with respect and trust for it to grow into love."

Rachel fiddles with her wedding ring to avoid eye contact. "Did you ever consider divorce?"

"Divorce? Never. Murder? Many times! And you will, too, but it's when love seems to fade like the morning dew that respect and trust will bring you through. And, like the dew, love will reappear."

Rachel smiles with both palms pressed to her heart as she notices the twinkle in Ahyoka's eyes.

"Where was I? Oh, when I was about your age, Agerton made his first trip with his brothers to purchase slaves. It was in Charles Towne in the summer of 1756.

"When Agerton arrived in Charles Towne, with his two older brothers, Daniel and Benjamin, he changed his mind after seeing firsthand the torment of slaves. They were treated like beasts—animals controlled with leg irons and neck collars.

"Agerton turned away when someone handed him a handbill advertising a slave auction in Dorchester. Years later, he gave it to me. I still have it on my mantle.

"Let me read it to you, 'Just imported in the Hare, directly from Sierra Leone, a cargo of Likely and Healthy Female Injun Slaves. To be sold on the 29th day of June.'"

After a pause, Ahyoka continued. "Agerton dreamed the night before of a beautiful young woman drowning in a river. He jumped in and made a daring rescue.

"He decided all he needed was a woman to cook and clean. She would need to be young enough to serve him a long time but old enough to cook well. No slave fitted that description in Charles Towne.

"He told his brothers, 'No! I can't be a part of this. I'll find a cook somewhere else. I can do without field hands.

"'I am going to Dorchester. They have an open market on Tuesdays.' Agerton told me all the details. He shook his head and walked away and took the wagon—without their permission.

"Agerton never gave any thought to what slaves faced before they arrived at his brothers' plantations. According to his brothers, they were benevolent-slave owners. Agerton doubted their assessment.

"During the eighteen-mile journey north to Dorchester, the horseflies buzzing around his head and biting his arms, irritated him even more. Only the gentle flow of the Ashley River finally calmed him.

"When he arrived in Dorchester, he heard men's loud voices as they bought and sold produce, cattle, merchandise—and slaves.

"A small crowd gathered at the opposite end of the market.

Agerton reined in and asked an older man about the commotion.

"'A white man has come to town with a pretty Cherokee slave girl for sale,' he explained. 'Don't normally see Injuns sold around here, especially females. Mostly Negroes. Some men are having a little fun with this.'

"Laughter filled the air as Agerton approached the crowd. Someone had tied up three older Indian women held by Indian men, but no one appeared interested. One Indian man tied a young Indian girl to a white man. Many wanted her.

"A fat man with a scraggly beard poked her with a finger. Her eyes were cast down. She would not look at what was happening.

"When she lifted her head, her dark brown eyes, and beauty caused Agerton's heart to race. Agerton's dream flashed through his mind.

"The white man squeezed her shoulders and grinned at the crowd. 'Strong arms, and that is not all.' He winked as he rubbed her back. 'Yep, she could light the fire in my chimney.' The crowd laughed as his hand started making its way down her back.

"She cried aloud. 'Lord Jesus, help me!'

"Agerton stepped forward and grabbed the man's arm. 'That's enough.'

"'What ya think ya doing, Mister?'

"'Take your hands off my slave.'

"'What ya mean, your slave? She ain't yours.'

"'She's about to be.' Agerton glared at the white man. 'How much do you want for her?'

"'One rifle. Two knives and three hundred dollars. You got that much?'

"'I do. Come with me. The weapons are in my wagon.'

"As they walked toward his wagon, the girl clenched her jaw— muttering. 'Why, Lord—why?' Agerton led her by a rope tied to his left hand, and asked the white man, 'Does she speak English?'

"'She speaks English. I made sure of that. And, she is Cherokee, so you can work her like a mule.'

"Agerton paid him his due and lifted his rifle and two good hunting knives out of the wagon. He raised his eyebrows. 'Is this what you want?'

"'Yep, that will do.'

"Agerton gently directed the girl into the wagon as the white man returned to the auction. He squatted next to her in the wagon bed and untied her.

"He turned to her. 'We're going to Charles Towne to meet my brothers.'

"He cleared his throat. 'What's your name? I'm sorry about how those men treated you, but I won't treat you that way. I promise. You can trust me.'

"'I am known as Bringer of Joy in your language.'

"Slowly, Agerton looked her in the face in an attempt to comprehend who and what she was. He knew she had no advantages in life.

"But, she had a deep-rooted sense of self-respect, quiet dignity, and personal strength for a slave.

"Agerton smiled politely. 'We're not going to see many folks for the next couple of hours. You might as well sit next to me so we can get to know each other.' Her face became flush when out of nowhere, he changed the subject. 'You look very much like the girl in a dream I had.'

"With trembling lips, under her breath, she said, 'Oh, no. He's a crazy one!'

"'How did you become a slave?'

"'That question reminds me of my mother.'

"Agerton reined in the horses and gently touched her arm. 'I shouldn't have asked. I'm sorry.'

"She moved away. 'I've never talked to anyone about it because it makes me cry. She gave me strength. She was my only friend, my only protector, except One other. I am heartbroken over her.'

"Leaning over, Agerton patted her on the shoulder. 'You don't have to talk about it.'

"'Well,' she said, 'maybe he's not crazy,' softly thanking God. "Urging the horses, he looked her in the eyes as if he could see her soul. 'Go on, please go on.'

"'You're my master. Can I talk like this?'

"'I've never owned a slave,' Agerton said with a shrug. 'If it does not make you uncomfortable—why not?'

"'I was a young girl watching mother wash clothes at the river bank while tending to my baby brother. Without warning, the Cherokee warrior, Oconostota, captured us.'

"'Where was your father?'

"'My father, Attakullakulla, was hunting in the mountains." 'Oconostota's warriors took my mother, Nionne Ollie, my infant brother, and me far away to the Little Tennessee River.'

"My mother and brother were adopted by Oconostota's wife. I was sold to a white slave trader because I was young, and she was jealous. To increase my value, I was left chaste and was sent to a school to learn English.

"'The school was owned by Christian missionaries. They taught me about Christ, and how He has a plan for each of us. They said that when everything seems hopeless, Jesus will intervene if we have faith. Even though I prayed every day, it all seemed impossible to me as a slave girl with no family or friends.

"'I was treated by my owner's wife as though I was a cursed outsider. I existed only to work and provide food for their family. As I increased in trade-value, his wife, a gloating white woman with twitching hands, insisted I be sold."

"Agerton, teary-eyed, mumbled. 'You—your mother—your brother.' He cleared his throat. 'Did you ever hear what became of them?'

"'Never. Mother was a caring and strong woman. She told me my future would be with white people.

"'I heard tales of my brother, but I knew they were made up stories to try to make me feel not alone."

"Agerton was so taken by the slave girl that he didn't see an enormous mud hole. As the wagon straightened out, they heard a loud thumping. A broken limb with moss and mud had twisted around a wheel.

"The maiden climbed down while Agerton tied the horses to a tree and tried to free the wagon wheel of the limb.

"He resorted to grabbing a knife from a box in the wagon bed and slicing through the moss to remove the branch.

"He tossed the knife back in the wagon and told her to keep an eye on the horses while he headed to the riverbed to wash his hands."

"'Be careful by the water,' Bringer of Joy called out.

"Agerton laughed, but as he knelt to splash water on his hands, the horses snorted and reared. She screamed. 'Get out! Run! Gator!'

"Agerton saw two enormous eyes atop the water. He only had enough time to yell, 'Oh, God, save me.' The beast lunged and nicked his arm.

"He ran as fast as he could, feeling no pain and seeing no blood until he tripped over a root and found himself on the ground with the gator moving in on him. Agerton screeched in terror when it hissed and roared. Convinced he was about to die, his life flashed before him.

"As the animal edged closer to Agerton, the maiden slipped behind it, her jaw set and eyes ablaze. She lifted her dress to her knees, sprinted, and dove onto its back, forcing its head to the ground. Straddling the alligator in the dirt she shouted at Agerton to run.

"Agerton scrambled to his feet and took off, shaking uncontrollably, blood running down his arm.

"He spun around to return to help but crashed into her instead. They both tumbled to the ground. They laughed and sobbed as they struggled back to their feet. The gator slithered back into the Ashley.

"Agerton took her into his arms. Amidst tears, panting, and trembling hands, he sighed. 'I thought you were a goner. I'm—I'm so thankful! You saved my life.'

"'Let me see your arm,' she insisted, gently pushing him back. 'We have to stop the bleeding.' She tore a sleeve from her dress. 'Lie down.'

"Agerton felt lightheaded as she wrapped the sleeve around his arm. 'You're the girl in my dream,' he whispered and closed his eyes. "After a long pause, she swallowed. 'Here, we go again.'

"When Agerton awoke, she was gone. He eased himself upright. The blood loss had made him weak. He realized he must have been in a state of shock. He had fainted and then gone into a deep sleep.

"Now rested and the blood from his wound stopped, he looked around and realized he was alone. His only vestige of her was the remnant of her torn dress tied tightly around his injury. When he realized the wagon was gone too, he yelled, 'How could you have abandoned me? What about my dream?'

"With no other option, Agerton began trudging toward Charles Towne. Soon he heard a wagon approaching from behind. Desperate for a ride, he waved his only good arm, and his heart leaped as she pulled alongside and helped him into the bench beside her.

"'I thought you had left me.'

"'Never! The alligator spooked the horses, and they pulled free of the tree and ran down the road. I had to leave you to find the wagon before dark.'

"Agerton leaned over, closed his eyes, and turned his face toward her. She quickly thrust the reins into his hands. 'We'd better go.'

"Agerton squirmed. 'Yes, it's getting late.'

Following a lengthy, awkward silence and some wincing, he heard, "The color is returning to your face.' Bringer of Joy assured him he would be all right. 'You're looking better. When we reach your brothers, you should have a doctor look at the gash in your arm. The bleeding has stopped, but he may want to put some stitches there to hasten the healing. It may hurt.'

"Agerton shrugged. 'Not as much as having my arm bitten off.'

"'Yes, well, that is true enough,' she agreed, displaying a wide grin. She bit her lip to keep from laughing.

"'How'd you learn to wrestle an alligator like that? You were amazing.'

"Matter-of-factly, with a crisp nod, she replied, 'My mother was always afraid to be near the water. She said danger hid there and that snakes and alligators lurked nearby. She taught me early about protecting myself from hidden dangers—not only snakes and alligators.'

"'That's why you warned me to be careful?'

"'It was my Mother's words that came out of my mouth.'

"'But it was you who subdued the alligator.'

"'I saw the men of our tribe capture them. It is not as difficult as you think. Once I was on its back, I knew I could control it.'

"'Your mother would have been proud.'

"'Yes, but you and I were fortunate it was not a big one.'

"'It was large enough. You shocked me with your strength and courage.' Agerton touched her hand. She did not move away. 'And thank you for bandaging my wound.'

"'This is my only dress.'

"'I'll buy you a new dress.'

"'With Cherokee colors?'

"'Absolutely.'

"When they reached Charles Towne, Daniel spotted his brothers pulling up to the boarding house. They burst outside and shouted, 'Where have you been? And what happened to your arm?'

"'It's a long story. I'll tell you all about it on the way home, but first I have to buy a dress.'

"Benjamin, pondering why Agerton needed to buy a dress, asked, 'Who is she?'

"'A drowning woman I purchased in Dorchester. We ran into some problems on the way back. She saved my life.'

"Benjamin dared not ask another question.

"Daniel crossed his arms. 'Does she speak English? What's her name?'

"She gazed at him. 'My Cherokee name is Ahyoka.'

"'What does that mean?

"'Bringer of Joy.'

"Agerton whirled around. 'What?' He stared at her for what seemed to be an eternity, completely caught off-guard by her announcement. 'You are a woman of surprises. You told me your name before, but it didn't register with me until now. But, yes, oh, yes, you are Joy—in many ways.'

"He faced his brothers beaming. 'Meet Joy. She will be going home with us.'

"Agerton made good on his word, although he did not buy a dress for me that day. He had one custom made for me. It included a ribbon that wrapped around it from my torn sleeve used as a bandage—with all the Cherokee colors in tack."

"Miss Ahyoka, you were the woman in his dreams?"

"I'm not sure about that. Agerton never saved me—I saved him. "Precious One, the dress is in that wooden box. Would you take it out for me? I've saved it for this day."

"It is beautiful, Miss Ahyoka!"

"It is yours now. Joseph told me he was called to be a preacher. And, you and he made plans to settle in the Louisiana Territory. Would you wear the dress when you reach your new home?"

With a voice choked with tears, Rachel could only nod— yes.

T   H   R   E   E

"Earth's crammed with heaven, and every common bush afire with God. But only he who sees takes off his shoes."—Elizabeth Barrett Browning

{8}

1794
Greenville County
South Carolina

Joseph and Rachel enjoyed planning for a family. Rachel first gives birth to Agerton, named after Joseph's father. Mary Willis and Joseph Willis, Jr. follow in due time.

The family moves to Greenville County, South Carolina, on the south side of the Reedy River.

The delivery of Rachel's namesake does not go well. Proper medical attention is scarce, even in developing territories. Many a seemingly strong wife succumbs to infection, blood loss, and delivery complications.

With a warm voice and a caring tone, Rachel takes Joseph's hand and says, "Go to the Louisiana Territory. God has called you there. It's my dying wish. It is your *destiny.*"

"Not without you."

She closes her eyes and passes to the other side.

"Why, Lord, why?" Joseph prays aloud. "I will not go without her. If you wanted me to do so, why did you let my helpmate die? Why would you call me on an impossible task?"

The days become months, and the months to four years. At age forty and being of mixed-race, with four children yet to care for and feeling abandoned by God, he finally gives up.

"It was a tragedy," Ahyoka reminds him, "that brought us to this point. God was with me when all seemed hopeless, and He is with us now."

"I'm already forty. I must have misunderstood His call."

"Moses was your age when he decided to choose his Hebrew faith."

"Yes, and he spent the next forty years tending sheep for Jethro on the backside of the desert. Am I to wait until I'm eighty for a burning bush? God does not appear in that way anymore. And Moses had Zipporah, a wife, to help him. They will not accept me with my dark skin."

"Zipporah was Ethiopian. She was dark. And, yes, Moses's sister Miriam and Moses's brother Aaron spoke against Moses because of it. You have many reasons why not to go. But will you do as Jesus did when He said, 'Not my will but Thine'?"

Joseph mounted his mule and rode to the banks of the Pee Dee River. "Lord, not my will but Thine." He felt older than his years. Depression set in as he wondered about the ups and downs of his fitful life—the death of a loving wife, the joy of four beautiful children, the harsh life of a backwoods preacher, the encouragement of Ahyoka. His pockets lacked gold. His home was humble. His clothes were frayed. His mule was swaybacked. His muscles were sore. He leaned forward, a broken man, sobbing over his failure to have accomplished anything significant. Tears blurred his vision; his breath came in short gasps, his hands began to shake.

"Lord, someone has set darkness in my path," Joseph cried.

Suddenly, as though in a trance, he looked to Heaven. Was it his imagination? Was it a vision? Was it a dream? Of this, he had no judgment, but of one thing he was clear: Christ appeared to him with an outstretched hand.

"It is I who has called you. Go as I have spoken."

"But, Lord, I have nothing."

"I will be with you—I am all that you need. In your weakness will be my strength."

His shaking stopped. His breathing slowed. His vision cleared. No, this had been no nightmare or magician's trick or illusion or child's make-believe fantasy. He was convinced the Lord Almighty had spoken to him with a directive to spread the Gospel. He would obey.

Slowly, Joseph rides home, meditating on this life-changing experience. Upon arriving home, as has always been his practice, he seeks counsel from this mother.

"Mother, the Lord spoke to me. I am not too old, not too poor, not too timid. He has impressed upon me to do His bidding in spreading His holy word. I must depart."

Ahyoka shows no surprise or shock, nor any sign of disbelief in what Joseph tells her. It has been her fervent prayer that Joseph would recognize his calling and accept his mission. She smiles and says, "Take the dress I gave Rachel. Keep our Cherokee colors with you always as a reminder of our love for you."

"I need you to go with us."

"I will be a burden—the great *I Am* is all you need."

"It was you who reminded me to pray, 'Not my will but Thine.' Will you do the same?"

"I will, but I will be of no use."

"When you were born, you cried and the world rejoiced. Live your life so that when you die, the world cries and you rejoice." —*Cherokee Proverb*

{9}

1798

Holston, Tennessee, Ohio, and Mississippi Rivers

Joseph Willis, his children, and his mother decide to leave South Carolina in the spring, traveling by land to Tennessee's northeastern corner. They build a flatboat. When the Holston River reaches sufficient depth toward the end of the year, they set out for the Louisiana Territory by way of the Holston, Tennessee, Ohio, and Mississippi Rivers.

A month passes before they approach the confluence of the Tennessee and Clinch Rivers. Hostile Indians guard the pass. The Indians captured the family. The children cry out in terror as they are dragged before the Chickamauga Cherokee's preeminent war leader.

With piercing eyes, a flinty face marked by smallpox, the chief's voice declares, "You do not belong to our nation. We do not allow colonists and settlers. The penalty is death!" The chief turns and gives the orders to his warriors. "Take them to the killing ground."

But then he pauses. "Wait!" He feels intrigued by the look in Joseph's mother's eyes.

"You Cherokee?"

"Ii vv," she replied, in Cherokee for yes.

"What is your Cherokee name?"

"Ahyoka."

"What was your Edoda's name?"

"Attakullakulla was my father."

43

"What was your Unitsi's name?"

"Nionne Ollie was my mother."

The chief falls to his knees and looks to the sky and cries out, "Unetlanvhi, wah-doh!" meaning in Cherokee, "Creator, thank you."

He slowly rises, becoming unnaturally still, looking back and forth to the heavens and into Ahyoka's face. "I am Tsiyu Gansini—Dragging Canoe—your brother!"

Akyoka embraces and kisses her brother and motions to Joseph and the children to come closer. "He will do you no harm. Dragging Canoe, they are your family too."

"The boys look like me—uhusti. The girls are distoduhi like our mother."

"Yes, I agree, the boys are handsome. And the girls are beautiful, like our mother."

"Who is the man?"

"Joseph, my son—your nephew."

"He is brave and broken, like me. I see it in his face. He looks like our Father, tall with wisdom in his eyes."

Dragging Canoe stands on a stump and announces to the entire tribe, "My sister, who was dead with the white men, is alive again. Let us celebrate."

The next day Dragging Canoe asks Joseph to walk with him to a hill overlooking the Tennessee and Clinch Rivers. Dragging Canoe tightens his fist. "We use this point as a lookout to guard our land. Our ancestors have lived and hunted here for centuries. The white man tries to steal it. I want you to know this. I want your children to understand this and their children one day.

"Whole Indian nations have melted away like snowballs in the sun before the white man's advance. They leave scarcely the names of our people, except those wrongly recorded by their destroyers. We hoped that the white men would not be willing to travel beyond the mountains. Now that hope is gone. They have passed the mountains, and have settled upon Cherokee land.

"When you cross the Mississippi River, they will hate you because of your Cherokee blood and the color of your skin. You will need a helper. Take another wife there. Be sure she is not ashamed of our heritage."

"I will, Uncle. I know my Rachel would want that too."

"What does the name Joseph mean?"

"It is from the Bible. Joseph was a man in the first part of the Bible—called the Old Testament. In the last part, the New Testament, he was Jesus' step-father."

"Jesus. Yes, I've heard of Him. How can you trust a man or a God whose followers say one thing and do another?"

"His Book never asks us to trust His followers, just Him."

"Why?"

"Because." Before Joseph can finish, Akyoka and the four children arrive.

"Mother, could you have the children sing *Jesus Loves Me*?" With the voices of angels, the children sing.

"Jesus loves me, this I know, For the Bible tells me so.

Little ones to him belong;

They are weak, but he is strong.

Yes, Jesus loves me! Yes, Jesus loves me!

Yes, Jesus loves me! The Bible tells me so."

Dragging Canoe, nods yes with tears in his eyes.

The next day Dragging Canoe's braves load Joseph's flatboat with food and blankets. He instructs young Agerton and Joseph, Jr., "Always carry your canoe."

Joseph, Jr., visibly sweating, lifts one of the canoes over his head. "Like this?"

"That will do. I will call you, Carrying Canoe. I could not lift mine at your age."

Ten Chickamauga Cherokee warriors escort them in their canoes, safely as they travel west on the Tennessee, Ohio, and Mississippi Rivers. They continue with them until they land safely at the mouth of Cole's Creek eighteen miles above Natchez.

Joseph, Jr. insists everyone start calling him Carrying Canoe.

☆   ☆   ☆

1798
Natchez District of Mississippi

Joseph Willis decides to cross the Mississippi River alone into Louisiana Territory because of the unknown dangers. He cannot take the flatboat because his children are too young and his mother too old to navigate the boat back across the treacherous river.

He saddles his mule and walks to the riverbank with the entire family. Joseph then eases into the murky waters on his mule Josh. They swim to the other side, albeit arriving two miles downstream due to the swiftness of the water.

He returns for his family weeks later after being almost killed by a mob in Vermilionville and settles farther north in Bayou Chicot, Louisiana.

In 1798, Joseph Willis preached the first sermon by an Evangelical west of the Mississippi.

The hostile Spanish-controlled Louisiana Territory with Spain's dreaded Code Noir forbids any Protestant minister from preaching Jesus. The penalty is slavery in Mexico's silver mines or death.

Therefore no Protestant minister dares to enter the Louisiana Territory except one—Joseph Willis.

Joseph establishes over twenty churches, and in 1827, settles in "No Man's Land," the lawless disputed area between the Sabine River and Calcasieu River. It is the home of Jean Lafitte and his pirates, runaway slaves, and outlaws. He plants two churches there for them. Antioch in 1827 and Occupy in 1833.

In 1853, he returns to the mighty river at age ninety-five that he swam on his mule more than a half-century before.

June 1853
Steamboat Paul Jones
Two fathoms deep
Mississippi River, near Natchez

Joseph Willis had turned ninety-five in 1853. He decides to see the sights along the Mississippi River one last time. His swimming the mighty river on a mule-days are long since passed. This time he will travel on the Steamboat *Paul Jones* from Natchez to Baton Rouge. A cool breeze breaks up the unrelenting sun. Joseph places a wet towel around his neck to relieve the heat.

The steamboat passes another one loaded with convicts. Joseph sits on the main deck next to a seventeen-year-old boy whom the leadsman called Samuel. They both are watching the colossal paddlewheel churning the muddy waters when the boy turns to Joseph. "How do they navigate in these shallow waters? It looks unsafe!"

Before Joseph can answer, the leadsman throws a knotted rope overboard and yells, "Half twain! Quarter twain! M-a-r-k twain!"

"What does that mean, Mister?" The boy crosses his arms while pushing his glasses up.

Joseph leans forward. "It means it's the second mark on the line, two fathoms—twelve feet deep. That's the safe depth for this steamboat. We're in safe waters now."

Samuel waves an offering of thanks to the leadsman. He also opens up to Joseph, explaining how his father died of pneumonia when Samuel was eleven and how he dreamed of being a steamboatman.

"Tell me more, Samuel."

"I wasn't expected to live when I was born. My brother and sister had already died of childhood diseases. Mother said God spared me because He had plans for me. She made me remember Bible verses. I washed that down with Shakespeare and read everything I could. Mother insisted I never throw a card or drink a drop of liquor, although I did occasionally slip off and smoke my corncob pipe.

"I figured no one was perfect. That is, until a late-night thunderstorm convinced me that God wanted me to mend my ways, so I put my pipe aside.

"My righteousness did not last long, for I developed an aversion to slavery. Our local pulpit said it was in the Bible, and God approved of it. It was a Holy Institution.

"After seeing a dozen men and women chained together to be shipped down the river, I determined that the church and I worshipped a different God. Those slaves had the saddest faces I'd ever seen, and the slave traders were human devils. My Father never laughed, yet he never was as unhappy as those slaves. It all made me want my dream even more."

"Tell me about that dream?"

Samuel's eyes sparkle. "When I was a lad living on the banks of the Mississippi, in Hannibal, I could see the steamboats go up and down the river. I wanted to ride one. One day a big steamer moored up at our little town—this was my chance. After all, I'd already fished away the summer.

"The steamboat advertised it was a 'lifeboat'—I reckoned that meant it was safe and would provide the time of my life. I reckoned wrong—at least about the safe part! It was the kind of lifeboat that wouldn't save anybody.

"I became overjoyed to be on a real sure-enough steamboat, enjoying the motion of the swift-moving craft until it commenced to rain. When it rains in the Mississippi country, it rains. The rain drove me to cover. I realized it was not a lifeboat when the rain was almost my demise. I thought I would die as the red-hot cinders from the big stacks came drifting down and stung my legs and feet. Would I ever see my home again?

"For some reason, Mama's supper came to my mind. I expressed my desire to get off that boat. They put me ashore in Louisiana. I finally made it back home.

"Mister, please excuse me if I was a little edgy when the leadsman yelled mark twain. I thought it meant something bad."

"Just the opposite, son." With a slow smile, Joseph assures him they are safe.

Samuel raises his thick eyebrows. "Where you headed?"

"Only as far as Baton Rouge," Joseph mutters, fanning himself from the heat with one hand. "Seven thousand people have died this year in N'Orleans from the yellow fever epidemic. I want to go to Heaven—but not today. Baton Rouge is far enough."

"Your story of the lifeboat wrongly advertised reminds me of Louisiana's Governor Johnson."

"How's that, Sir?" Samuel asks, scratching his head.

"The good Governor got the great state of Louisiana to build the state prison in Baton Rouge. I'm considering visiting those inmates we passed earlier and tell 'em about a real lifeboat."

"What kind of boat is that, Mister?" Samuel gazes at Joseph.

"One built many years ago by a feller named Noah. His boat was mark twain, too—safe from the dangers that lurked in the murky waters below. That boat had no helm, for human hands did not guide it."

"I love a good story, Sir. I fancy myself as a storyteller. Would tell me the rest of it?"

"Be glad to. God told Noah He was going to destroy the Earth because of its wickedness. But, God was also going to provide a way of protection from His judgment. The Lord told Noah to build a boat—a boat of safety, if you will. The Good Book says Noah found grace in the eyes of the Lord.

"That was the first time that word appeared in the Bible. Noah received the unmerited favor of God. Grace provided deliverance from the Lord's judgment.

"Now, there was a lot to be done. The Lord told Noah to build the boat out of gopher wood. We call it cypress in Louisiana. It will not rot in our lifetime.

"'Put pitch on the inside and outside too,' the Lord insisted. The word pitch in Hebrew means atonement. We need to be in Jesus just as Noah needed to be in that boat. As the storms of God's wrath beat upon the ship, the winds of God's wrath would later beat upon the Lord Jesus. If we are on the inside, not one drop of judgment can come through. We are sealed with that atoning pitch—Christ's atoning blood.

"It took Noah more than 100 years to build it. It takes a lot of faith in the Lord's promise to do that. The boat was built like an ancient coffin. There was no steamboat pilot to guide it—only God.

"The Lord gave precise instructions. 'Set the door of the boat in its side.' There was only one door to pass through to escape God's judgment. Jesus is that one door.

"By faith, Noah and his family entered the boat. Once they were all inside, the Lord shut the door. God sealed the door—not Noah.

'Put a window in the top of the boat, Noah, so you can look to Heaven for all your needs.'

"God had Noah build rooms in the boat. There is a room for me.

There is room for you—for the asking.

"Noah's boat floated many days. It finally landed on Mount Ararat on the seventeenth day of the seventh month. That's our April 17th—the same day Jesus rose from the grave. Noah went into the boat with little, but when he came out, the entire world was his."

"What is your name, Mister?"

"Joseph Willis."

"You should be a preacher."

Joseph smiles at the irony of that statement. "Grace provides our Salvation. Grace provides our Savior. Grace provides our security—grace keeps us. But, we all must choose to put our trust or not to put our trust in God's ark of salvation—Jesus. There's still room in that ark of safety."

"I reckon Heaven goes by favor." Samuel exhales. "If it went by merit, we would stay out, and our dogs would go in."

"That's a clever way to put it. You should be a writer."

Joseph Willis died in 1854, at age ninety-six, in his beloved Louisiana. Forever in the ark of salvation—Christ.

"Never let your horse drink water you wouldn't."
—*Daniel Hubbard Willis, Jr.* 1900

{12}

March 10, 1904
On Barber Creek
Near Longleaf, Louisiana

Daniel Hubbard Willis's Narrative

Jeremiah and Jacob Stark are my best friends. They're typical brothers, arguing about almost anything, but Lord help the person who attempts to come between them—and me, too. They are the kind of men you could ride the river with—the river of life that is. I, Daniel Willis, will testify under oath to that fact.

My Grandpa told me when I was only knee-high to a grasshopper, "You have to be present to win." In the cow business, that means the stockyards north of Ft. Worth. It's the center of the world for a cowman. It's known as Cowtown.

Names are important. They should have meaning. My eldest son, Henry Elwa Willis, named his son Kit Carson Willis. During the War of Northern Aggression, I read every dime novel about the great mountain man and Indian scout.

Speaking of the War for Southern Independence, I named my youngest son Randall Lee Willis after my commanding general, Randall Lee Gibson. We call him Ran.

He will be eighteen in two weeks. Hopefully, he will be blessed with a wife like his mother, and they will have at least one boy—maybe two—or three would even be better.

Perhaps one of them will honor General Gibson, too, by naming a boy Randall Lee.

Everyone can call him Ran, also, or perhaps Randy.

My sons, Henry Elwa and Robert Kenneth, base their cattle operations near the Lecompte, Louisiana railyards.

My son, Daniel Oscar, chose a different path after his brother Eugene died of appendicitis because there were no doctors nearby. Daniel Oscar is the only medical doctor in Vernon Parish, in the town of Leesville.

I became a cowman in 1865, near our home—the Ole Willis Place. The fertile, red dirt hills of Louisiana have been good to us.

We live near Babb's Bridge and Longleaf. I first learned the cattle business there on Barber Creek's banks and cattle drives from East Texas. It was on one of these drives I first met Jeremiah and Jacob Stark. I thought I knew everything there was to know about being a cowboy—it would not take long for me to discover just how little I knew.

In December of 1899, the Texas & Pacific passenger depot opened in Ft. Worth. I'd seen a postcard of it. Never had I ever seen a building so grand. I had to see it with my own eyes and perhaps buy a cow or two. But, I would need help.

That help came when the Stark brothers agreed to accompany me to Cowtown.

They said all I had to do was introduce them to my old friend Charlie Goodnight, who had settled 300 miles west of Fort Worth. I agreed. And, of course, I needed to make sure my bride of a half-century was good with it all.

Years before, I met the enterprising Goodnight when we joined in making the gather, after the War of Northern Aggression. We built our herds from gathering Longhorn cattle in Texas that roamed free after the war. He showed me how to build a kitchen on wheels he invented called a chuckwagon. I used it on many a cattle drive from East Texas to Louisiana.

We first met at a Confederate Reunion in Houston. He had been a scout for the Southern cause. Before that, he'd trailed cattle to Louisiana. After telling me all about it, he offered me a cigar, which I declined, but I did accept his advice on improving my herd through cross-breeding with Hereford bulls. I knew I needed to buy more high-grade bulls to build a better herd.

Perhaps, he would sell me one of his prized Herford bulls on this trip.

Years before, Goodnight invited me to the JA Ranch in Palo Duro Canyon, but I got word he no longer managed it. A stomach ailment almost proved fatal to him, so I figured if I ever would visit him, I'd better do it soon. I purposed in my heart if the opportunity ever arose, I would do just that. That opportunity came in '87 when the Fort Worth and Denver City Railway was built through the Texas Panhandle. Goodnight was ranching in Armstrong County near the Fort Worth and Denver City line. I got excited to see him again.

My wife, Julia Ann, did not share my excitement. "Wait until your brothers can go with you." Wrinkling her nose always meant no.

In the *Alexandria Town Talk*, she'd read that Ft. Worth had dance halls with whiskey and rye and woman of ill repute. That kind of lifestyle does not sit well with her or the ladies at Amiable Baptist Church. That's putting it mildly.

I informed her that the newspaper had failed to mention Alex had those vices, too, not to mention N'Orleans. My observation did not diminish her concerns. "And, remember, don't get above your raisin'. The Good Lord don't like that— neither do I," Julia Ann said.

"I know, pride goes before a fall," I said, trying to assure her of my knowledge of the Bible. My words were of little comfort.

"All I'm saying is, don't let the Stark boys pitch your tents toward the cities of the plains," Julia Ann said.

"Cities of the plains. I thought that was Sodom and Gomorrah." "Exactly—exactly my point!"

"My cherished, Julia Ann, where are you getting all of this? Was it from that article in the *Town Talk* by Billy Sunday?"

She smiled.

"Mr. Sunday must have had those heathen Yankees in mind. Nevertheless, my wife had a long talk with the Stark brothers. More like the Spanish Inquisition.

She reminded the Stark brothers and me that the Lord loves the Yankees as much as we Rebels.

"My favorite novelist was a Yankee general, Lewis Wallace. He was inspired to write his second novel by the goading of an agnostic," Julia Ann said.

"Wallace conceived the book after sitting on a train, listening to Colonel Robert Ingersoll for two hours," she explained, and she pulled out an article that described the incident.

I kept that article about it. I'll share here an excerpt. Wallace wrote that Ingersoll poured out "a medley of argument, eloquence, wit, satire, audacity, irreverence, poetry, brilliant antitheses, and pungent excoriation of believers in God, Christ, and Heaven, the like of which I had never heard."

Until then, Wallace had been indifferent to the claims of Jesus. He wrote, "Yet here was I now moved as never before, and by what?

"The most outright denials of all human knowledge of God, Christ, Heaven. Was the Colonel, right? What had I on which to answer yes or no? He had made me ashamed of my ignorance: and then–here is the unexpected of the affair–as I walked on in the cool darkness, I was aroused for the first time in my life to the importance of religion. I thought of the manuscript in my desk. Its closing scene was the child Christ in the cave by Bethlehem: why not go on with the story down to the crucifixion? That would make a book, and compel me to study everything of pertinency; after which, possibly, I would be possessed of opinions of real value."

Wallace subtitled the book, *A Tale of the Christ*. He later wrote, "It only remains to say that I did as resolved, with results— first, the book *Ben Hur*, and second, a conviction amounting to absolute belief in God and the Divinity of Christ."

The next morning Julia Ann packed enough of her famous dewberry pie, smoked ham, and fresh bread to have fed everyone on the train. She included Daniel's Bible and her copy of *Ben Hur*.

I didn't dare mention to her that Ft. Worth's downtown was known as "Hell's Half Acre." Butch Cassidy and the Sundance Kid were said to have roamed Hell's Half Acre streets between robberies. Sam Bass once used the Acre as a hideout, but he was long since dead, and Cassidy and Sundance were rumored to have fled to South America three years ago.

I figured, why mention that since I had no intention of venturing into the Acre. The fact that Jeremiah had a reputation as the fastest man with a gun in East Texas would have been of little comfort to her, too—but it was to me. The one thing we all three agreed on was we did not need Mr. Sunday's approval.

As we boarded the Texas & Pacific Railway in Alexandria, her words and Great-Grandpa Joseph Willis's teachings flooded my mind. The trip from Alexandria on the Iron Horse added to the excitement, with continuous speeds up to 20 miles an hour. Within two days, we approached the Texas & Pacific Railroad passenger depot in Ft. Worth. A porter pointed to one building that was eight stories in height. We marveled at it. It must be the tallest building in the world. The postcard I'd seen, as a boy, did not do the depot justice.

As we deboarded the train, excitement and anticipation hung in the approaching spring air. Ft. Worth's population had grown to more than 26,000. The railroads made possible tremendous growth.

Drovers had trailed more than four million head of cattle through Fort Worth since The War of Northern Aggression.

The railroad and barbed wire had long since ended the great cattle drives north. Northern cattle buyers now established their headquarters in Cowtown. We soon discovered Ft. Worth's slogan, "Where the West Begins," to be true.

Cowtown came of age in 1902 when Armour, Swift, and Libby, McNeill & Libby built their packing houses. It brought a significant influx of new people.

There are horse and mule dealers in abundance too. I needed to replace Father's wagon—an old broken-down wreck—held together with wire, but a good one in its heyday. No doubt about it—this was the place to be for a young cowman trying to better himself in the cattle business.

13

March 11, 1904
Cowtown, Texas

The train chugged into Ft. Worth. "I think that's Miss Tilly's Steakhouse in the distance," I said.

"It has a reputation as the best eatery in Cowtown, and this brochure says it's a short ride on a mule-drawn streetcar."

The sign on the front door read, "No Dancing On Tables With Spurs." Beef steaks were not the only thing on the menu. The second sign confirmed that. "You Must Be 18 or Older to Enter." The hostess seated us at a table in a courtyard out back.

We discovered that the cost of a 28 ounce T-bone was 35 cents. "Who can afford that?" I asked the brothers. They both shook their heads in agreement and shared their opinions.

"We've traveled to Cowtown's Union Stockyards to buy Longhorn cows and maybe a Hereford bull or two later from Goodnight to build your herd, Daniel," Jacob said, justifying the extravagance as the high cost of doing business.

Jeremiah agreed. "This is research, if you will, of your future purchase's quality."

That's how the brothers saw it; that is after I offered to pay for the meals.

As we waited for our meal, Jacob noticed a beautiful stuffed bird on a counter next to a portrait of Robert E. Lee mounted on his horse Traveler. Pointing to the stuffed bird, he inquired of Jeremiah. "What kind of bird is that?"

Jeremiah crossed his arms. "I don't know, but Miss Tilley needs to get a better taxidermist. That's the worst job of stuffing a bird I've ever seen."

"Have you ever known anyone with the gift of criticism? Well, you have it," Jacob said.

Jeremiah smirked. "No, I don't!"

Suddenly, off his perch, the bird flew out a window.

Jacob and I busted out laughing.

"Case settled." Jacob started whistling *Dixie*. I couldn't help but smile in agreement.

As we devoured our research, I asked a feller sitting at the table next to us, "Mister, where's a good place to bed down for the night?"

"The Westbrook Hotel, in the 'hotel block.' It's the most noted boarding house in all of this cow country. Expensive though, at a dollar a day, but I wouldn't go there just yet."

"Why's that?"

"No rooms available, but I heard Frank Fore will be checking out soon. His room should be available within two hours."

"Bless you, Mister. May I be so bold as to ask your name?"

"Jim Miller, but most folks call me Deacon Jim Miller since I'm at the Methodist Church every time the doors are open. I rarely come in here since I don't smoke or drink ardent spirits. I agree with Billy Sunday; they defile the Lord's temple."

"Here we go again," Jeremiah whispered. "Did Julia Ann hire this guy to follow us, or was it Billy Sunday?"

Jeremiah observed Deacon Miller's gun lying under his black frock coat and Stetson with an inquisitive look. "That's a mighty fancy shotgun you have there."

"Thank you. I plan on squirrel hunting a little later." He glanced at his gold pocket watch.

As we walked out the door of Miss Tilly's, Jeremiah seemed enamored. "I feel fortunate that the first person we met is such a Christian gentleman."

"What a pious and kindhearted soul. He reminds me of your Grandpa," Jacob said.

"Not hardly. There's one big difference. My grandpa never talked about how he lived the Christian life; he just did it. He taught me to keep a keen eye on a feller who starts every other sentence with I."

"Ah, Daniel, now you're a pessimist," Jeremiah said, pulling at his ear.

"Do you know what a pessimist is Jeremiah? An optimist with experience."

"Funny, really funny." Jeremiah chuckled.

Two hours later, the room did become available, just as Deacon Miller predicted. Miller had killed Mr. Fore in the washroom of the Westbrook Hotel. The rumor was Miller and Fore did some real estate business in Fort Worth that had gone south. Frank Fore was said to be an honest businessman who threatened to tell a grand jury that Miller was selling lots submerged in the Gulf of Mexico.

Deacon Miller failed to tell us he was also a great actor, in the tradition of John Wilkes Booth. According to the newspaper, people rushed to see what happened. Miller fell over Fore's body, with tears in his eyes, "I did everything I could to keep him from reaching for his gun."

Jeremiah shared Deacon Miller's prediction with Sheriff John T. Honea.

14

March 12, 1904
Cowtown, Texas

"I know all about Deacon Jim Miller. He's a hired assassin. Killed twelve men, some say. That's not the half of it. Unsubstantiated but persistent rumors claim he was only eight when he did away with a troublesome uncle and his grandparents. The first I heard of him was when he killed two men in Midland. Two of my lawmen claim Miller shot Mr. Fore in self-defense. Witnesses always seem to pass away in these cases.

"He usually ambushes his victims. Miller killed a lawyer named James Jarrott two years ago. Miller shot 'im four times in the back while Jarrot watered his horses near his farm.

"Mr. Stark, I know of your reputation with a gun. A Texas Ranger told me of you. If I know your fast, you can bet Miller does too. Now, what I'm about to say, uh, I never said, if you get my drift?"

"Yes, sir, but why doesn't someone arrest him?"

"They have. Miller has a big-time lawyer, and, as I said, the witnesses either lose their memory or mysteriously die.

"Now, what I was about to say is, if I were you, I would call him out before you get it in the back. Your reputation precedes you, Mr. Stark. He's no match for you, at least in a fair fight."

"Thank you, Sheriff."

"For what? We never had this conversation."

To our surprise, Miller agreed to meet Jeremiah in the street in front of Fort Worth's White Elephant. The saloon was an establishment located in the south end of town in the notorious vice district known as "Hell's Half Acre."

There were women everywhere hanging out their windows, dressed as I'd never seen, with porch lights mostly in red.

Miller strolled out the swinging doors of the White Elephant as if he'd just won a considerable poker hand. Jeremiah stood to wait for him in the middle of the street.

"Lord, protect us all. I will never speak ill of your servant Billy Sunday again," I prayed fervently.

They squared off with about 40 feet between them. Miller had no notches in his pistol.

Jeremiah held his hands loosely beside his hips. "You first."

Miller smiled, pulling his gun. Jeremiah followed suit. Miller had not cleared leather when two .45 caliber bullets hit him dead center in his chest. He did not fall. Miller aimed and ripped a shot through Jeremiah's right shoulder. He walked forward, pointing his gun at Jeremiah's head.

As he approached Jeremiah to finish the deed, someone fired a shotgun in the air while yelling, "Dueling is illegal, boys. You're under arrest, Miller. Get this boy a doctor."

Sheriff Honea witnessed it all, from where I do not know. "He started this," Miller said.

"Check under his coat; I know I hit him—twice." Jeremiah was bleeding and shaking. "Did you hear my bullets ricochet?" Sheriff Honea handcuffed Miller but not until he removed his long black frock coat. Underneath was a thick iron plate.

"That's not illegal, Sheriff."

"Maybe not in a Texas court of law, but I'm sure you being a man of God and all, you know it's a sin to deceive anyone in God's court."

"Since when did you become God's Sheriff?"

"The same day, you became a Christian."

After throwing Miller in jail, the Sheriff walked over to the doctor's clinic. "Jeremiah, as soon as you're able, you need to leave town. His lawyer will not be long getting here, with the new railroad."

"I'm not afraid of him."

"I know you're not, but you're a wounded duck. At least go home until you're on the mend. Miller is sure to take advantage of you if you don't."

"This is not over, Sheriff. Will you be all right?"

"Yeah, I didn't make it this far by being stupid. I'll tell the judge, who's my friend, I didn't clearly understand the law in this matter. Miller will no doubt be set free, at least in this court. I doubt he will stay free for long in God's court, although I have no jurisdiction there."

Three days passed. Miller's attorney arrived in Cowtown. We packed our bags and headed to the railroad depot.

"Can't wait to get home." I bounced from foot to foot, missing

Julia Ann.

"Home?" Jeremiah cracked his knuckles? "You promised to introduce us to Charles Goodnight, and I'm going to meet him with or without you!"

"Are you sure? You're frail, not out of the woods yet!"

"I'm well enough. Wasn't Goodnight the scout who tracked down the Comanche war chief Peta Nocona so Texas Ranger Sul Ross could kill him? I read all about the Battle of Pease River in a book."

"Yes, that's what Sul Ross claimed, although others swore Peta Nocona wasn't even there. Goodnight told me once it should be called the Pease River Massacre, not a battle, cause it was mostly Indian woman and children killed."

"I don't care what anyone calls it," Jeremiah retorted with a scathing tone. "He's still the man I want to meet."

"Why?"

"He's the only man I know, or should I say, you know, who can tell me how to track down Jim Miller and hang him from a tree without getting shot again."

I agreed, but only if Jacob would return to Forest Hill and tell Julia Ann why our return trip home had been delayed.

The Stark brothers both agreed that was the best plan since I was the only one who was a friend of Charlie Goodnight.

"Now Jacob, don't burden Julia Ann with the details of the gunfight. I'll tell her later," I pleaded. He nodded his understanding.

I added, "Perhaps we should not burden Charlie Goodnight with the gunfight details either. We could make our way over to the XIT Ranch instead. They sell Longhorn bulls and even Durhams. After all, the railway now makes its way to Channing, Texas, the major shipping point for the XIT. I am sure we can find a few top-grade Longhorn bulls on their three million acres, with more than 150,000 head of cattle."

None of this mattered to Jeremiah. All he could talk about was Jim Miller and Charles Goodnight. He couldn't care less about the XIT or the south end of a northbound cow.

"What kind of person is he?" Jeremiah tightened his fist.

"Is who?"

"Goodnight. I want to know what to expect?"

"He's a cowman. The kind you'd share blanket and bread with. His word is his bond, a handshake his contract. I trust Goodnight.

"He's a Christian gentleman with an affable nature. But like all men, he has feet of clay."

"How do you mean?"

"The flow of his tobacco juice doesn't bother me, but his profanity can be troublesome. His salty language knows no boundaries: women, preachers, animals—it doesn't matter.

"The rumors of him smoking fifty cigars a day are embellished—I've never seen him smoke more than twenty—in a row. He's not a drunkard, although he will have a toddy occasionally. He has an abiding reverence for the Good Lord, but a healthy disdain for organized religion—yet he's paid for two Baptist churches and keeps a room in his home for traveling preachers. He's an enigma."

"I don't know what an enigma is. All I want to know is how to kill Miller without him killing me."

As we pulled into the railhead and departed the train in Goodnight, Texas, we both noticed stacks of the *Fort Worth Star-Telegram* and the *Goodnight New*s with bold headlines, "Gunfighter Kills Deacon Jim Miller."

"Well, Jeremiah, my friend, someone beat you to it. Miller's dead."

"Read, on down the page. They're saying that someone was me. How can that be? You can always believe what you read in newspapers, can't you?"

To that, I rolled my eyes.

"I wish I could find words to express the trueness, the bravery, the hardihood, the sense of honor, the loyalty to their trust and to each other of the old trail hands."
—*Charles Goodnight*

{15}

March 17, 1904
Armstrong County
Goodnight, Texas

Charlie met us at his front door. "Great to see you again, Daniel! I reckon your friend is Jeremiah Stark, the man who shot Jim Miller? The paper said he left Ft. Worth with you to visit me."

"It's me, sir, but he shot me, not me him."

"I can see that. Newspapers never get it right except when they write about how handsome I am." He smiled at his humor.

"Well, come on and see my home. Molly has supper almost ready. She's been over at Goodnight College much of the day. We just chartered the Goodnight Baptist Church to help run the school. Daniel, your great-grandpa, would have liked that."

"Yes, he would have. Glad to hear that, and it's good to know your concern for education."

"Truth is, it was Molly's idea. Don't get me wrong, I believe in education, although I only had six months of formal schooling. If I'd had more, maybe I would not have invested in Mexican gold and silver mining.

"Come, both of you. I want to show you my buffalo, elk, and antelope. Buffalo hunters have almost wiped the bison out! I shipped some to Yellowstone National Park.

They have free-ranging there."

Jeremiah kept a steady eye on the herd. "I'm impressed that you've preserved the bison."

"I got the idea from Molly. Years ago, she heard two bison calves bawling. No doubt, the buffalo hunters had slaughtered their mamas. She convinced me we needed to raise them. Now, look at them.

More than 250 to remind me of what greed can do. Molly saved the buffalo.

"We best head back to the house. Molly should have supper ready.

"After supper, I suspect you'll be wanting to know if all those stories about the Comanche are true?"

"How did you know that, Sir? Was that in the paper too?" Jeremiah looked like he'd just heard one of the Buffalo speak.

"No, son, if you didn't, you'd be the first visitor in forty years who failed to. For decades people have come to hear my stories and experiences. All my life, I've been private, but if these stories can be of any good for future generations, I'll be like a jackass in a hail storm—just stand here and take it. Don't get me wrong, I like telling the stories and showing off the buffalo, but I'd prefer not to be a tourist attraction.

"I almost forgot. A few old friends are joining us for supper."

As they gathered around Molly's table, the aroma of her son-of-gun-stew and the most robust coffee this side of the Sabine filled the room. One old black man with a wind-carved face and a grey-headed Mexican even older joined them.

"Daniel Willis and Jeremiah Stark meet Bose Ikard, as good a cowboy as any Comanche. I trust him farther back than any living man. This feller is Nicholas Martinez, a Comanchero who I once used as a guide when I first came to the Palo Duro. He's since made a fortune in sheep and is here today to attempt to do the same by trading for a few of my cow ponies."

"Mr. Goodnight," the old Comanchero leaned forward. "I saw your remuda today. I bought a few horses like them before."

"Bought them while I slept, you mean!" Goodnight, smiled from ear to ear.

Everyone laughed.

Bose Ikard stood with a dignity that made all of us anticipate his words as he nodded to Goodnight.

"Gentlemen, learn from this man—from his stories of triumph over tragedy—victory over adversity, for the wisdom of others blows where it wishes—like a West Texas wind."

Admiring Goodnight's long white hair, Bose Ikard lifted his glass. "You remind me of Samson. We can see the wisdom in your hair."

"Taking care to keep my hair was my top priority as a young man. It wasn't any Delilah who wanted it, only a few thousand Comanche. Now, today, my concern is how not to let flattering words cause me to lose a dime in a trade."

None of them could contain their laughter. After dining, Molly cleared the table of dishes. Everyone helped. As they walked through the Victorian-style parlor, Jeremiah stopped him to inquire about the photo of his late partner Oliver Loving.

"The bravest man I ever knew. He taught me how to be a cowman." Next to Loving's photo was another of a massive bull buffalo inscribed Old Sikes.

His rifle was in the curves of two buffalo horns above the fireplace mantle. A hewn log above the gun read: "But seek ye first the kingdom of God and his righteousness, and all these things shall be added unto you."

He directed us to the second-floor sleeping porch with spectacular views of the countryside and his bison herd. "Sit a spell, gentleman. We should retire early tonight. I have much to tell you tomorrow on our trip."

"Trip?" I asked.

"In the morning, we'll take the wagon to the canyon rim, and I'll tell all about what you came here to hear. The array of colors in the Palo Duro always bring back memories— good ones—and not so good ones. The red rock cliffs carved out of steep walls remind me of all the bloodshed in vain. Molly will prepare the leftover stew and some buffalo jerky for the trip."

We arose before sunrise. On the trip to the rim of the canyon, curiosity got the best of me. "I noticed the Scripture over your fireplace mantle last night. It's good to see you're planning on Heaven."

"I've given it a lot of thought. I figure if I could take longhorns and cross-breed them into the best cattle in America in only eleven years, what could I do in eleven million?"

"You built several churches. Which one do you belong to?"

He spread his arms wide. "That one!" We stopped to look in awe at the vast Palo Duro Canyon. It stretched for more than 100 miles and was 10 miles wide in some parts and 1000 feet deep.

"There's my cathedral!"

"I have never seen a landscape with so many colors. The steep sides have layers of orange, red, brown, yellow, grey, and maroon," I said. "Look at the prickly pear, yucca, mesquite, and juniper."

"There are thousands of mesquite and juniper trees. Palo Duro is Spanish for hardwood. The canyon's named after those Junipers," Goodnight said.

"I noticed you don't cuss anymore."

"You damned right, I don't."

16

March 18, 1904
The Cathedral
Palo Duro Canyon

Charlie shifted a half-smoked cigar to the right side of his mouth as they paused to survey his church. "Gentleman, have one?"

"Yes, sir," Jeremiah said. "Your cigar has a pleasing aroma."

"I got this one and 50 dozen boxes from the Willis Cigar Factory in Willis, Texas. Any relation, Daniel?

"Never know," Daniel said.

"This here the Sumatra variety. They say it's from the Abajo district of Cuba. Wesley Smith, a veteran of War of Northern Aggression, founded the cigar-manufacturing operations down in Willis, Texas.

"That's why I first started smoking them. Then I discovered those Cubans are on to something. Smith was a former lawman, too, like you, Daniel," Charlie coughed.

"Smith told me they'd won international awards in Chicago and Paris."

"Chicago? That's on the fringes of Dallas, isn't it?" Jeremiah asked.

"Yes, sir, just like Paris in on the outskirts of Natchitoches," Daniel interrupted before Charlie could answer.

Everyone laughed. Charlie shifted his cigar to the other side of his mouth, "It seems every time I'm on my saddle horse riding fence from here to the West Texas sunset. Where was I, Jeremiah, enjoy a Cuban cigar."

Daniel reached for one too. "When did you settle here?" Jeremiah asked. "Got a light?"

"Use my cigar. In the summer of 1876. I drove 1,600 longhorns from Pueblo, Colorado, to the edge of Palo Duro, not far from here."

"Did the Comanche try to stop you?"

"Not then. Ranald Mackenzie led his Fourth United States Cavalry to the canyon two years before and defeated them.

"My involvement with the Comanche began the year I was born. My birth was one day before the siege of the Alamo ended. Two months later, the Comanche kidnapped Cynthia Ann Parker. She was only nine. All this in 1836, the year I was born.

"In the autumn of 1845, I accompanied my family from Illinois to Texas, riding bareback on my white-faced mare Blaze. The Republic of Texas celebrated my arrival by officially being inducted into the United States the next month.

"Much has been written about Cynthia Ann's kidnapping and recapture and my part in the latter. Oh, it all has some truth; the best lies are half-truths."

I nodded slowly. "I read about you and Cynthia Ann in DeShields's biography of her."

"I did, too. DeShields never let the truth get in the way of a good story.

"Damn newspapers. Damn dime novelists. Damn politicians."

17

March 18, 1904
The Cathedral
Palo Duro Canyon

"Charles, there're about twenty Indians headed straight at us and closing in fast. Are they hostile?" I asked, somewhat concerned.

"Hope not."

"Me, too, because they're now 50 yards from us and still riding hard." To my great relief, the Indian riders reined in their ponies but fanned out to encircle us. Charles smiled broadly and lifted his right hand as a peace gesture. The leader of the Indians came forward on a huge Paint Horse stallion and mirrored the peace gesture.

"Daniel and Jeremiah meet the chief of the Quahada Comanche. Correction, the chief of all Comanche. At least that's what the federal government says.

"Chief, meet Daniel Willis and Jeremiah Stark."

The biggest and toughest looking man in Texas dismounted. "Me Quanah. Quanah Parker."

"He's the wealthiest Indian alive and the baddest man I've ever known," Goodnight said.

"I used to be bad man. Now, I citizen of United States. No fight anymore." He paused a moment, then turned his attention to Jeremiah, rubbing his chin and sizing him up.

"Jeremiah Stark? You man who killed Jim Miller?"

"No, sir. The newspapers had that wrong."

"They always wrong."

"I read your father, Peta Naconi, was killed at Peace River by Sul Ross."

"I want to fix some Texas history straight up. Some say Sul Ross and rangers kill my father, Peta Naconi. No, not so. I be eleven year old when they captured my mother, Cynthia Ann Parker, at Peace River fight. She was with party of

Indians hunting buffalo. I never see her again." He paused a moment in contemplation, then continued his narrative.

"Ross no kill my father. He not there. My father sick. I see him die five years later.

"Ross friend, DeShields, wrote that to make him famous. He becomes governor of Texas. Politicians say anything to get elected."

"I read you were living at Fort Sill, Oklahoma. You've come a long way," I noted.

"Here to hunt buffalo on Goodnight's land."

"I thought those days were long gone," Jeremiah said.

"You thought wrong. Thanks to Goodnight."

"He's too busy hunting wolves with President Theodore Roosevelt to make this trip often," Goodnight said.

"Take a couple of my beeves too."

18

March 19, 1904
The Cathedral
Palo Duro Canyon

Charles, Jeremiah, and I headed back to Goodnight's home.

When I was a boy, the Comanche were lords of these plains," I said.

"What happened?"

"The Comanche dominance began in Texas in the 1740s. They blocked French expansion west, from your Louisiana. They drove the Apache into the mountains of northern New Mexico.

"They destroyed the Spanish advance. The Spaniards killed more than a million Mexicans, but they were no match for the Comanche. This victory gave them horses. They became skilled horsemen, like no other people we had ever seen. And one of them could shoot a dozen arrows at you in a matter of minutes, accurately even long-range.

"In 1820, Spain was unable to persuade its citizens to move to Texas because of them. A year later, Mexico achieved its independence. Their citizens also feared to enter Mexican Texas. The Comanche caused Mexico to allow immigration from the United States. The next year, Mexico granted a permit to Moses Austin to settle 300 families in Texas.

"He died, and his son Stephen F. Austin took charge. He brought hundreds of families into Texas on behalf of the Mexican government. They would be the ones who sacrificed their blood fighting against the Comanche to settle in Texas.

"The plan backfired 15 years later, in just 18 minutes, at San Jacinto. Sam Houston made sure of that.

"But, it would take another 40 years before most of Texas, including Palo Duro, could be settled because of the Comanche.

"They were the most powerful Indian tribe in American history. Finally, two enemies arose from the white man they could not defeat, smallpox and cholera, not to mention the greedy buffalo hunters killing off their source of food, shelter, and clothes.

"I started in 1857 and trailed a herd up the Brazos to the Keechi valley in Palo Pinto County. The War of Northern Aggression ended that. After the war, in 1865, Indians ran off 2,000 head of my cattle."

"Tell me more about the man in the photo at your home?" I asked.

Charles answered, "In the spring of 1858, I took on a partner, Oliver Loving. I helped Loving drive a herd through the Indian Territory to the Rocky Mountain's mining camps before the war. In 1867, Loving died from wounds he received in a fight with the Comanche on the Pecos River. With the aid of Mexican traders, he reached Fort Sumner, only to die there of gangrene.

"I assured him that his wish to be buried in his beloved Texas would be carried out. He is buried in Weatherford."

Jeremiah rubbed his chin. "I did not want to ask this while we were with Quanah. Is it true you were the scout that led the Texas Rangers to the Comanche camp where Cynthia Ann Parker was recaptured?"

"That's about the only thing written that is true. What happened was the Texas Rangers massacred a small group of mostly women and children in December of 1860, on the Pease River. It was only newsworthy because Cynthia Ann Parker was there.

"Ranger Sul Ross embellished the story to get himself elected Governor. It worked. He did well as president of an Agricultural and Mechanical College near the post office in College Station.

"Almost thirty years later, I became friends with Cynthia Ann's son Quanah Parker when he came to hunt the scarce buffalo. I made a treaty with him in which I promised two beeves every other day for Quanah's followers, provided they did not disturb my herd."

Jeremiah cocked his head. "Y'all are friends even though you were the scout who led Sul Ross to their Pease River camp. How can that be? Ross said he killed his father and said, you chased his sons, Quanah Parker and his brother. And Cynthia Ann Parker was recaptured and starved herself to death because of the loss of her husband and children."

"That's quite a story. The only problem is, as Quanah said, none of it is true, except the part about Cynthia Ann Parker being found alive. Quanah, his brother Pecos, and his father Peta Nocona were not there. Don't believe everything you read, especially when it's told by a man who wants to be elected to some political office. You can always tell when a politician is lying. Just watch his lips; if they move, he's lying."

"How can you be friends with Quanah Parker after the Comanche killed your partner and the kidnapping of white Cynthia Ann Parker?" Jeremiah asked.

"Vengeance is the Lord's. That's what I have been trying to tell you. God causes all things to work together for good." He crossed his arms as though he was finished speaking, but then another thought came to mind.

"Let God handle Jim Miller. God does not need your help to right this wrong."

Jeremiah narrowed his stance and looked away. I tried to soothe things by smiling and changing the subject. "How did you manage those rough cowboys?"

"The first thing I did was strictly enforce my rules against gambling, drinking, and fighting.

"I don't know if any of this will help you get Jim Miller out of your head, Jeremiah, except to show that God has a way of taking care of an evil man like him.

"Daniel, would you be so kind as to tell me again that story about the XIT? You know the one about the real cowboys. You can leave out the part about my barbwire fences. Isn't Jeremiah in that story? It wouldn't hurt us both to hear that again."

"Sure, my friend, I would love to."

19

XIT Ranch
The Texas Panhandle

The old-timers were spinning yarns about the weather, the scourge of the XITs, and Charlie Goodnight's barbwire fences doing away with the "real cowboys," a cattle disease called Texas Fever, and many a "she did me wrong yarn."

"Their laughter filled the room, and everybody was smiling until one ole cowboy who spoke with a gravelly voice, asked, "What was that young cowpoke's name? Ya know, the one that got himself thrown off a green-broke mare on the XIT. That horse was a rank one, ya know."

"I was there. His name was Jimbo. He was a praying boy," the barber said.

"Not sure that pony was green-broke though, although that's what they told young Jimbo. He came strolling out of the bunkhouse one morning when some cowboys started poking fun at him. He didn't have much experience, but he wanted to show them he could rope and ride."

"I took it all in Charles and spoke not a word. I was spellbound."

The barber continued, "They were daring Jimbo to ride that crazy horse brought over from an XIT line camp. They couldn't handle the pony there.

"Those cowboys were mean to him. At first, Jimbo did a good job of ignoring them, but they just kept making fun of him. 'Come on, ya got religion we hear tell. You can do anything with that Jewish carpenter's help, can't ya, boy? Why don't ya wanna ride that horse? Ya scared? Maybe you're too green like that yearling cow pony. Maybe even yellow?'"

"Everybody gathered 'round to see what was gonna happen. Every eye was on Jimbo. His face was beet red. He just stood there looking at that horse and didn't move. The men laughed at him, threw up their hands, and started walking away. He couldn't have been more than eighteen. The barber watched him throw his shoulders back and begin to walk toward the corral.

"He grabbed a bridle and opened the gate. You could hear the whispers as most of the men came back to watch.

"He bridled her and proceeded to rub the mare all over with a saddle blanket while he whispered to her. One old cowboy yelled, 'Bite her ear.' Another, 'Snub her to a post.' Another, 'She's got crazy eyes.'

"Jimbo ignored them all, except to say, 'She's not crazy, just afraid.'

"Didn't take long for him to get a saddle on her. He climbed on her real slow like and rode with a new found confidence. She seemed to trust him.

"Suddenly, someone cracked a bullwhip and yelled, 'Ride 'em, cowboy.'

"She must have jumped ten feet. And, as everyone hooped and hollered, she reared up, falling over backward on top of Jimbo. The horse got up but not the boy. He just lay there in the dry, dusty dirt. The barber was the first one who got to him, and Jimbo sure didn't look good. He tried to talk, so he bent down close to his mouth to hear his words.

"'Please get my Book, the one that boss Jake gave me.'

"The barber thought he hadn't heard him right, but he said it real clear again.

"'Please get me my Bible.'

"He sent one of the others to fetch it from his saddlebags. He tried to make him comfortable, but there wasn't much he could do. He wondered how he'd explain all this to boss man Jake. When the Book arrived, the barber showed it to him.

'Here, Jimbo, here's your Bible.'"

"'Lay it on my chest and open it to John 3:16, please. Put my finger on those words.'

"He spoke all raspy like. "'Please, do it, please!'

"The barber found that verse and lifted his hand.

Jimbo cried in pain cause his arm was broken. The barber placed his finger on the verse.

"'Tell boss Jake that I made that decision just like he told me I should.'

"With that, he closed his eyes and was gone." The barber had tears in his eyes as he ended the story.

I made three decisions after I heard the barber's story. The first was to name the creek we now live on Barber Creek. The second was to have my boys bury me one day with my Bible opened on my chest with my finger placed on John 3:16. And the third was to give every cowboy who works with us a copy of the good Lord's Word.

Jeremiah and Jacob seemed to be moved the most.

Jeremiah spoke first. "Mr. Willis, our sister Mary told us about that Carpenter. Is He for real?"

"Boys, He's as real as the skin on my bones," I said.

"What does that verse say, Mr. Willis?"

"It says that whosoever puts his trust in Jesus will have everlasting life."

"What does whosoever mean? Who's that?"

"I reckon, Jeremiah, that's you and me and every cowboy and cowgirl. Even the mavericks, the culls, and the undesirables. God swings a mighty big loop. But, there's many a cowboy who doesn't want His brand."

There was a peace in the camp as an unseasonably cool breeze blew in.

Then Jeremiah said, "I want His brand."

Jacob added, "Me, too."

{20}

March 20, 1904
Armstrong County
Goodnight, Texas

The next day Jeremiah and I packed our bags and headed to the railroad depot. We stopped to spend the night in Ft. Worth. I decided to set the *Fort Worth Star-Telegram* straight about Jeremiah's gunfight with Jim Miller. But I did not tell them that Jeremiah still vowed to kill Jim Miller.

Other newspapers began to carry the story. The newspapers quoted Jeremiah stating he did not want ever to see a cow again. And he did not want to return home until he faced Jim Miller one last time. He would aim for his head this time.

After reading that Jeremiah was a man of faith, a man named

J.M. Guffey sent him a telegraph offering him an opportunity.

The J. M. Guffey Petroleum Company had been organized four years before, in 1901. Mr. Gulley requested that Jeremiah meet him at the railroad station in West Columbia, Texas, in Brazoria County. From there, they would travel to Damon Mound, located 12 miles north of West Columbia. Mr. Guffey believed the salt dome had oil beneath it.

Jeremiah answered the telegram and agreed to meet in West Columbia, but once again, luck did not favor Jeremiah. He decided to make the trip in a horseless carriage introduced in Ft. Worth two years before, instead of the train. He was assured he would be there in plenty of time since the vehicle traveled at twelve miles per hour. Within two days, the automobile began to make sounds like a railway locomotive. It was out of gas.

Jeremiah could not have been more dejected. Mr. Guffey had changed his plans in Houston to make a special trip to meet him. Surely God was against him. Jeremiah walked the entire way to the First Baptist Church in Fort Worth. He got on his knees and asked the Lord, "Why, Lord? Why me? What do you have against me?"

Jeremiah looked up, shook his finger at heaven. "I give up— You win. But, I'm still going to kill Jim Miller."

He walked to a nearby hotel, and as he went to sleep, he prayed he would not wake up. But wake up he did the next morning when a porter slipped the *Star-Telegram* newspaper under his door. The vast headline caught his eye from his bed: "Train Derailment! No Survivors." It was his train.

Once again, he walked into the church, but this time he read Psalm 91. Before, he did not believe that God had his back, but now he did, and surely God would help him kill Miller.

Mr. Guffey read the news, too, and was vexed in his soul. However, his anxiety was relieved after Jeremiah sent him a telegram to let him know he had not been on that fateful train. Mr. Guffey set the meeting again.

Once they met, Jeremiah discovered that the J. M. Guffey Petroleum Company was almost bankrupt. Jeremiah did not fret and told the Lord, "I can't wait to see what you do by noon today."

Well, nothing of much of value happened by noon, except Mr. Guffey gave him 160 acres on that salt dome and some worthless stock for his trouble.

Jeremiah's desire to kill Jim Miller faded away. He realized being spared from the train wreck was not for the purpose of killing Miller, even though Miller was still executing people.

Soon after that decision, Jeremiah read Miller had assassinated a man with a scattergun. The law arrested Miller in Ada, Oklahoma. Miller shrewdly retained the best lawyer around—Moman Pruitt. Pruitt was a legend, a dynamic litigator who had never had a client executed, winning acquittals in 304 of his 342 murder cases.

The good citizens of Ada knew Miller would once again go free. Therefore, forty of them broke into the jail, overpowered two lawmen, and pulled Miller out of his cell. Down an alley, they dragged him into an abandoned livery stable behind the jail. The mob wasted no time. They bound Miller with barbed wire and stood him on a box. The same type of barbed wire Charles Goodnight used to become the first Texas Panhandle rancher to build fences from it. It eventually ending the open range.

The men urged Miller to confess to his many crimes.

Miller thrust his chest out. "Let the record show I've killed 51 men." He pulled off a diamond ring and asked for it to be given to his wife. A diamond shirt stud he left to the jailer for some kindness.

As the noose slid around his neck, Deacon Jim Miller asked for his trademark, his black broadcloth coat. "I'd like to have my coat. I don't want to die naked."

Miller shouted, "Let 'er rip!" and stepped off his box to hang. They left him overnight.

Houston's *Daily Post* interviewed Jeremiah for his reaction. "Now, I know what you're thinking. That I believe the Lord orchestrated all this. I'm not saying that. That's between the Lord and Deacon Jim.

"Then again, you might want to ask Charles Goodnight. Better yet, ask Billy Sunday.

"I'm too busy to think about it since the J. M. Guffey Petroleum Company became part of the Gulf Oil Corporation." Jeremiah began producing oil from his salt dome oil field.

A train wreck had caused his life not to be a train wreck.

1916
Hotel Leesville
Leesville, Louisiana

My dear wife, Julia Ann Willis, and I grew more in love on Barber Creek's banks. We decided to visit our son, Dr. Daniel Oscar Willis, in Leesville for a checkup. Julia Ann sensed something was not right with me.

Our son's medical clinic and office adjoined the Hotel Leesville that he built in 1907. He bought the first automobile in the parish in 1909 for $825.00. Although most of his patients did not make that much money in two years, it allowed him to make house calls faster than his horse-drawn doctor's buggy. The Model T could go 40 miles per hour.

Unfortunately, my condition worsened no matter what our son did.

FROM THE JOURNAL OF JULIA ANN WILLIS:

Here, I take up the record my late husband could not finish, for he died of Bright's disease at our son's home. The kidney disease was named after English physician Richard Bright in 1827 after he described 25 cases. They had the same symptoms as my beloved Daniel.

Still mourning his father's death, our son was asked to attend to a 16-year-old girl named Anna Mae Granstaff, who was brought to his office next to the Hotel Leesville. She had lost a lot of blood but could still speak to our son and the sheriff.

"He violated me in every way!" she said hoarsely.

"What do you mean in every way?" the sheriff asked.

Dr. Willis looked him in the eyes. "I'll explain later."

"At least tell me his name."

"Billy Blanchard. Billy Ray Blanchard."

"From over Tenmile Creek way?"

"Yes." She passed out and never regained consciousness.

"Now, Doc, I understand that he had his way with her. But that doesn't normally kill someone, does it?"

"Gangrene does, though."

"I'll get a deputy and head to Tenmile Creek. I know of him.

He's a fifty-year-old man with a family."

Billy Blanchard denied it all. His attorney from Shreveport arrived at the jail. The brash young lawyer had already made a name for himself as a defender of the friendless.

"I'm Huey P. Long. I represent the falsely accused Mr. Billy Blanchard. May I see him, sir?" A deputy led him back to the jail cells.

"Mr. Blanchard. I'm your attorney. We will speak of these fraudulent charges later. What is the best hotel in Leesville?"

"The Hotel Leesville is the only hotel in town," a deputy informed him.

As he walked to the hotel, he spied a man getting out of an automobile. "Mister, you have an automobile, I see. My name is Long. Huey P. Long. I'll be your Governor someday. You will be famous if you drive me."

"No, thank you."

"Aren't you interested in being a friend of the next governor of the great state of Louisiana?"

"Not hardly."

The trial lasted only two weeks. Long made his final argument. "It's this loose woman's word against one of the most outstanding citizens of Vernon Parish. My client has a good job. Works hard. He belongs to the Baptist Church. Although he has stated, he's unable to attend because of his work with less fortunate girls at a home for unwed mothers.

Do you think a man with three daughters and a Christian wife would ever do such a thing? Anna Mae Granstaff was white trash—God rest her soul—and forgive her."

Several in the jury nodded yes.

The jury came to its decision. The court convened at 10:00 a.m. the next day. Huey assured his client that he would be home soon.

Dr. Willis opened his office at 7:00 a.m. A patient had been waiting outside for two hours.

"Come on in, Sir. What's ailing you?"

"Justice!"

"I beg your pardon."

"Doc, how did my sister die?"

"Who are you?"

"Charles Granstaff. I got the news while working cows in East Texas. Rode as hard as my saddle horse could go. How did she die?"

"Loss of blood and gangrene."

"What caused that?"

"Sexual assault."

"Thank you for being honest. I rode once with your father and the Stark brothers on a cattle drive from East Texas to Lecompte. Like them, you do not mince words." Charles Granstaff led his horse to the jail.

"Howdy. I'm here to congratulate my old friend Billy Blanchard."

"He will be out in a couple of hours," the jailer said.

"Cannot wait. I have business elsewhere."

"I'm sure the sheriff will not mind, you being a friend and all. Come with me.

"Mr. Blanchard, I have an old friend of yours who wants to congratulate you."

"Do I know you? What's your name, mister?"

"Justice." Charles Granstaff emptied both of his six-shooters into Blanchard's groin area.

The Leesville newspaper interviewed Long before Blanchard's funeral. "Dr. Willis acted as judge and jury when he incited Granstaff with his erroneous conjecture. He should be convicted of manslaughter. I gave the doctor guidance once by offering him an opportunity of a lifetime. When he rejected my kindness, I should have known he was a man prone to bad choices."

"Will you assist in the prosecution of Willis?"

"I wish I had the time. I must pack in the morning. I'm off to represent a small group that's suing the giant Standard Oil."

The newspaper was on Dr. Willis's desk early the next morning. He tossed the paper aside and made his way next door to the Hotel Leesville.

"I need the keys to Huey Long's room," Dr. Willis said to the desk clerk.

"He's not checked out yet, Sir."

"I figured as much. Give me the keys. I want to give him a special send-off."

Dr. Willis turned the keys and opened his door. "You're past my check out time."

"It's not but 7 a.m."

Dr. Willis grabbed Long by his collar and dragged him down the stairs and into the street.

"I'll sue you," Long screamed as he fell into horse manure in the street.

"What is your check-out time?"

"6:59."

Dr. Willis knew the importance of available medical care to Louisiana. He was not the only descendant of Joseph Willis to understand the need for education. Poverty gripped Louisiana.

☆　　　☆　　　☆

1924
Louisiana College
Pineville, Louisiana

Huey P. Long began his campaign for governor in 1924. On a sunny day, he preached his gospel of prosperity at the Boy Scout Camp on Spring Creek's banks near Longleaf, Louisiana.

Dr. Willis had no desire to hear him, but his brother Ran Willis did. Ran and his wife Lillie's home, the Ole Willis Place, on Barber Creek, was walking distance to the Boy Scout Camp. Barber Creek flowed into Spring Creek, not far from their homeplace. As Ran approached with his three sons, Howard, Herman, and Julian, they could hear Long's reassuring voice.

"I'm for the poor man—all poor men, black and white, they all gotta have a chance. They gotta have a home, a job, and a decent education for their children. The rich man must share his wealth. 'Every man a king'—that's my slogan."

Long looked straight at us. "I don't care about what the big shots say. All I care is what the boys at the forks of creeks like Barber and Spring Creek think of me."

"Is he speaking to us?" Ran asked.

"I don't know, Daddy, but don't you like what he said about free textbooks for all of us?" Howard asked.

"Free! There is nothing free. We will pay for them with increased taxes. Well, I take that back. Your Uncle Doc gave Huey Long a free education four years ago at the Hotel Leesville.

"That's the same year I met a young man at Louisiana College who started his education, but with fewer advantages than we have and a lot less than Huey claims.

"We became friends. He was the son of a poor sharecropper from Beech Springs in north Louisiana. He wanted to get an education like your Uncle Doc and me. He told me his family was so poor that he did not have a bed to sleep in until he was nine.

"Upon graduation from high school, he began the task of choosing a college. One of his neighbors had a college catalog. He told me all about it."

"I was amazed and believed you could order a college just as you ordered something from Sears and Roebuck. I'd never seen a college, had never been on a college campus, but I read it, and it told all about Louisiana College at Pineville. I decided that's where I would try to go."

"But how could he pay for tuition, books, housing, and food?"

"He didn't have any money or know anyone who did. He decided to try to get a job at the college. On his second day on campus, he went to the college employment office and found employment in the dining hall."

"How did you meet him, Daddy?" Howard asked.

"Through our cousin, Willie Strother.

"Willie's a history professor at Louisiana College. The young sharecropper's son attended his classes. He wished to get his degree in history.

"After acquiring the job in the cafeteria, he joined the glee club. Professor Dunwoody assigned him to the college quartet. He sang lead and received a gift, a used guitar. As winter approached, the young man became desperate for money. With his guitar, he began to sing on the street corners in Alexandria. When an officer told him to move on, he moved to another street corner."

"What was his name, Father?" Herman asked.

"Jimmie Davis. He graduated this year from Louisiana College without free textbooks.

"None of this would have happened had it not been for two encounters on the campus of Louisiana College. In his last year of college, Jimmie did not have the money to continue his education. He tried banks for a loan. They all turned him down."

"Everyone ought to be hungry and try to borrow money at least once in their life. To be broke and turned down, well, it's something," Jimmie said.

"With his dreams put on hold, Jimmie found himself in the back of a mule again, plowing and picking cotton from sunup to sundown. After one year in the cotton fields, he was able to return to Louisiana College. He obtained his degree in history after Willie Strother loaned him $120.

"But, there was another encounter on the campus of Louisiana College. It had an even greater impact on Jimmie's life. While walking across campus, a man introduced himself to Jimmie."

"The stranger was striking looking, well dressed, and friendly," Jimmie said. "At first, we talked about football and baseball. The man was the son of a sharecropper, too."

He began to ask Jimmie questions and explained who he was. "I'm Robert G. Lee, and I'm holding a revival in Pineville at First Baptist tonight. Please be my guest. Jimmie, may I ask you something? If the Lord would call you today, would you be ready to go?"

"Dr. Lee, I hope He doesn't call me today because I don't think I could make it," Jimmie said.

"The Lord's been good to you, and it's something you ought to think about. I hope you'll come to church tonight."

"I realized that everything I had, everything I had ever had, and everything I would ever hope to have on this earth had come and would come through the grace of God," Jimmie said.

That night Jimmie went to church. Dr. Lee gave his most famous and beloved sermon, "Pay Day, Some Day."

"There's no doubt of it; the man had the finest command of the English language I've ever heard. Before he had finished, I was ready to go down the aisle. And when he gave the invitation, I was the first one down and made public my profession of faith and united with that church," Jimmie said.

Willie Strother was there. He was a deacon in the church.

Epilogue

December 25, 1941
The Ole Willis Place On Barber Creek
Longleaf, Louisiana

There is nothing quite as serene as the piney woods covered in a white sheet of snow. As the sun sets and the moon rises over the snow, memories can be precious and troubling too. The death of Robert Willis on the *USS Arizona* at Pearl Harbor causes both.

"Should we have had a Christmas tree and gifts this year?" Ran asks Lillie. He turns their Philco radio on for the news. WSM is playing "You Are My Sunshine" by Jimmie Davis, followed by a news broadcast.

President Roosevelt's fireside chat addresses the criticism about the White House's Christmas tree.

"There are many men and women in America—sincere and faithful men and women—who are asking themselves this Christmas: How can we light our trees? How can we give our gifts?

"How can we meet and worship with love and with uplifted spirit and heart in a world at war, a world of fighting and suffering and death?

"How can we pause, even for a day, even for Christmas Day, in our urgent labor of arming decent humanity against the enemies which beset it?

"How can we put the world aside, as men and women set the world aside in peaceful years, to rejoice in the birth of Christ?

"And when we make ready our hearts for the labor and the suffering and the ultimate victory which lie ahead, then we observe Christmas Day—with all of its memories and all of its meanings— as we should.

"It is in that spirit, and with particular thoughtfulness of those, our sons and brothers, who serve in our armed forces on land and sea, near and far—those who serve for us and endure for us that we light our Christmas candles now across the continent from one coast to the other on this Christmas Eve."

Ran and Lillie Willis lights their Christmas candle. The beckoning candle of hope illuminates their hearts!

Ran continues to leaf through his great-grandfather Joseph Willis's leather-bound journal written a century ago.

"Why did the Lord allow Robert's death? He was a good man—better than me. Did Grandpa Joseph ever write anything about that?" Howard asks.

"Not in his journal, but a letter to my father."

Howard shifts in his chair. "Could you read that letter—please, Father? On a day like this, I need direction—advice on what path to take."

Herman runs his hands through his hair. "One minute, all is good. The next all is gone. What's the Lord's purpose in that?"

Ran adjusts his spectacles. He takes a big sip of coffee and places Joseph's journal in his lap. Father must have put the letter in the journal. "Please hand me that kerosene oil lamp."

December 28, 1853

"My Dearest Grandson Dan,

"I received your letter. Concerning your question, "How can a loving God allow deadly diseases like cholera, smallpox, malaria, and yellow fever in Louisiana? Yellow fever killed my best friend."

"Let me begin by apologizing in sackcloth and ashes for asking you a question first. If you had a cure for yellow fever, would you have given it to your friend? Of course, you would have!

"I read in the *Alexandria Town Talk*, 1 in 15 have died in New Orleans this summer. Over 12,000 people dead from yellow fever in New Orleans alone since January, with still more deaths in rural areas like ours.

"People are dying faster than graves can be dug. 'Pretty soon, people will have to dig their graves,' the paper said.

"Would you have given a cure to them? There is no need to answer, for I know your hcart. You would have given the treatment to every man, woman, and child in Louisiana and in fact, the entire world.

"You would have given your life for such a great cause. How glorious it would be to provide forty additional years to a middle-aged man, perhaps a hundred years to a child. What a great cause this would be. More significant than any political cause, for what can be more wonderful than the gift of life?

"Yet, there is a greater cause—an even more excellent gift than a cure for yellow fever. It does not give only an additional hundred years but eternal life. You and I have this good news. How can we not share the gift of eternal life?

"Over the last eight decades, I have received many prayer requests for physical healing, and I have never refused. My twin daughters died of honey poisoning after I prayed for days. My beloved wife died in childbirth. Do not misunderstand me; there is nothing wrong with praying for the sick. But, after their deaths, I realized I was spending more time keeping the saints out of Heaven than saving the lost from hell.

"God did not answer my prayer in the way I requested, but I will be with Him and my daughters and my bride forever in Heaven. The greatest tragedy is being eternally separated from Christ, not to mention my daughters and wife.

"Nothing lies beyond the reach of prayer. I believe that God heals miraculously.

"Sometimes God heals naturally. Sometimes He heals instantaneously. Sometimes He heals in time. God uses doctors and beyond the doctor's skills.

"But the ultimate healing is in Heaven where no disease can touch our new and perfect body. The greater miracle is not a hundred years of life free from illness, but everlasting life paid for with Christ's blood—God's lifeblood—given freely on a tree at Calvary.

"Let us tell our neighbors on our beloved Barber Creek. Let us declare this Good News in the piney woods of Rapides Parish. Let us travel our red-dirt roads to the Calcasieu and Red Rivers. And from the mighty Mississippi and Sabine Rivers to our enormous deltas and vast swamps. Let the Gospel of Jesus Christ ring forth from Driskill Mountain to the Gulf of Mexico. And let that only be the beginning!

"Always, your loving Grandpa"

Beckoning Candle's Characters

Randall Lee "Ran" Willis–Youngest child of Daniel Hubbard Willis Jr. and Julia Ann Graham Willis. He was named after General Randall Lee Gibson. He married Lillie Gertrude Hanks. He learned to play the fiddle, by ear, after his father bought him one in East Texas on a cattle drive. He was known to be the best musician in the area.

He was my grandfather and namesake.

Lillie Hanks Willis–Wife of Randall Lee "Ran" Willis. They married on January 11, 1914. She was sixteen, and he was twenty- seven. They had three sons: Howard, Herman, and Julian Willis (my father).

She moved to Forest Hill, Louisiana, from Branch, Louisiana, at age eleven. She was a firm believer in Christ and was a staunch Southern Baptist.

I remember her deep reverence for the Lord and knowledge of the Word of God. As a boy, I remember walking into the Wardville Baptist Church sanctuary with her early on a Sunday morning in Wardville, Louisiana. The pastor, Bob Galloway, was teaching a Sunday school class. He looked up from his notes and asked, "Mrs. Willis, what does Christ do with our sins?" Without hesitation, she answered, "He throws them as far as the east is from the west." I have never forgotten her words.

She was my sainted grandmother and the wellspring of many of the stories in my books.

Robert Kenneth "Bobby" Willis, Jr.–Entombed in the *USS Arizona*, at the bottom of Pearl Harbor. He was the first casualty from Rapides Parish, Louisiana, in World War II.

Robert was born on February 2, 1923, in Chopin, Louisiana. He graduated in 1939 from Natchitoches High School. His half-sister, Ilie Jewel Willis Close, told me that their father encouraged Bobby to join the military and "make something of himself." Bobby's mother died when he was barely eleven. Only 18, Bobby enlisted in the Navy (as Seaman First Class, S1/C), on July 31, 1940, in New Orleans. He reported aboard the *USS Arizona*, on October 8, 1940, in San Diego as Apprentice Seaman.

He served for 14 months on the *USS Arizona* before the Japanese destroyed it on December 7, 1941. The American Legion Post in Pineville, Louisiana, was named the Robert K. Willis Jr. Post. This American Legion post no longer exists.

Two weeks after the attack on Pearl Harbor, Bobby's father, Robert Kenneth Willis, Sr. received a message from the Rapides Parish sheriff that he was trying to reach him. He rushed to the sheriff's office. Bobby's half-sister, Ilie Willis Close, told me that when their father returned, she knew the moment he walked in the front door that Bobby was dead just from the expression on their father's face.

His cousins rushed to enlist, and America's finest hour began.

He was my father's (Julian Willis) first-cousin.

Robert Kenneth Willis, Sr.–Son of Daniel Hubbard Willis, Jr. and Julia Ann Graham Willis. He was the father of Robert Kenneth "Bobby" Willis, Jr.

Robert Kenneth Willis, Sr. married his first wife, Eulah "Eula" Rosalie Hilburn, in 1903. On February 6, 1919, she died at age 34 in the influenza pandemic of 1918-1919. More people died in the plague than did in World War I.

Robert Kenneth Willis, Sr. married his second wife, Julia Mae Johnson, in 1922. Their son Robert Kenneth "Bobby" Willis, Jr. was born the next year. Julia Mae died February 17, 1934, at age 34, the same age his first wife died. Robert Kenneth "Bobby" Willis, Jr. was only eleven when his mother died.

He was my great-uncle.

Ruth Duke [Willis]–Her life's motto was, "I'd rather have Jesus." She was the best woman I have ever known. She reared five children with a spirit as pure as gold and a servant's heart. She had the rare gift of encouragement and always saw the best in people. She was a Proverbs 31 woman.

She always advised me that the answer to my problems and life's purpose was found in Christ and the Bible. Even today, I often ask myself, "What would her advice be in this or that matter?"

I always know what her answer would be, "Ran, what would Jesus do?"

She married her first husband, John Alex Duke, on December 23, 1933. He was 54, and she was 20. He died on September 24, 1946.

John Alex Duke and my mother had four children, and thus my half-brothers and half-sisters are Johnnie Ruth (Duke) Guillory McDearmont, Gerald "Jerry" Duke, John "Buddy" Duke, and Marjorie Duke Eernisse.

My mother then married my father, Julian Willis, on June 26, 1948. I'm their only child.

Mother's great-grandfather was Rev. Adolphe Stagg (1834-1914). He was a pioneer Baptist preacher to the French-speaking people of Louisiana.

She was my sainted mother.

Julian "Jake" Willis–He was Boss Man Jake and Julian Willis, in my novels *Louisiana Wind* and *Destiny*. He was my father.

See the appendix at the end of this book entitled My Father and Me for a mini-bio.

Howard and Zora Willis–Uncle Howard was our family's master storyteller, and Aunt Zora was the best cook I knew when I was growing up. I sat for many hours, mesmerized by Uncle Howard's stories. As a teenager, he worked for his uncle, Dr. Daniel Oscar Willis, at the Hotel Leesville's front desk. At age 15, he rode freight trains with hobos during the Great Depression.

Uncle Howard shared with me the story of Huey P. Long and Dr. Willis.

He once made a house call with Dr. Willis in his Ford. As they approached the home on a long red dirt road, they could see their lights from the kerosene oil lamps through the cracks in the walls. Their home's wallpaper was newspapers. It was during the Great Depression in the early 1930s. The next day Uncle Howard overheard Dr. Willis's wife complain, "They will never pay us." Dr. Willis replied, "That doesn't matter. If they ever get any money, they will."

Uncle Howard was full of words of wisdom. "Don't get above your raising." And, "A person ought not to be mad at a family member for long."

I once asked Aunt Zora why her tea and coffee tasted better than anyone else's. "The well water from Hurricane Creek," she replied. She was locally famous for her old-fashioned buttermilk pies. Her vegetables from her garden seemed to taste better too. But, above all, what I remember most was her kindness.

Their granddaughter (and my cousin), Kimberly Willis Holt, was inspired by them too. She is a National Book Award Winner, author of *When Zachary Beaver Came to Town*, *My Louisiana Sky*, and the *Piper Reed* series. *When Zachary Beaver Came to Town* and *My Louisiana Sky* were adapted as films of the same names.

They were my aunt and uncle.

Donnie Willis–He planted the first seed in my mind to write about our 4th Great-Grandfather, Joseph Willis. Our sainted grandmother, Lillie Hanks Willis, had a treasure chest of stories about Joseph and insisted I write them down. Donnie has been pastor of Fenton Baptist Church in Fenton, Louisiana, for over fifty years. He is my first cousin.

Daniel Hubbard Willis, Jr.–Great-Grandson of Reverend Joseph Willis. Cowman, Spring Hill area in Rapides Parish Constable, and Confederate veteran. He fought in many of the Civil War's great battles, including Shiloh, Bull Run, Perryville, Murfreesboro, Missionary Ridge, and Chickamauga.

An excerpt from his obituary in the *Alexandria Town Talk*, on June 23, 1900, stated:

"He participated in all the hard battles of that army, and for bravery, soldierly bearing, discipline, and devotion to duty, he was unexcelled in his entire Brigade. He was made Orderly Sergeant of his Company at an early period of the war. It has always been said by his surviving comrades that when any particularly dangerous service was required, such as scouting parties to ascertain the position and movements of the enemy, he was always selected for the place, and never hesitated to go, let the danger be what it may.

"He was for a long time connected with the famous Washington Artillery, and at the battle of Chickamauga so many horses of the battery to which he was attached were killed that they had to pull the guns off the field by hand to keep them from falling in the hands of the enemy.

"He was paroled at Meridian, Miss., in May of 1865, and brought home with him a copy of General Gibson's farewell address to his soldiers and of him it can be truly said that through the remaining years of his life he followed the advice then given by his beloved commander. His love for the Southern cause, and for the men who wore the gray, was not dimmed by years, but he lived and died firmly convinced of the justice of the cause for which the South poured out so much of her best blood and treasure.

"Before death he expressed a wish that he might see his children who were at home, especially Randall L., his baby boy, whom he had named in honor of his beloved Brigadier General, Randall Lee Gibson. He also requested that his Confederate badge be pinned on his breast and buried with him.

"During an intimate acquaintance, covering a period of twenty- five years, the writer never heard a vulgar or profane word pass his lips."

He was the first of four Willis brothers to marry four Graham sisters. He married Julia Ann Graham on January 5, 1867. He affectingly called her Julieann.

When he asked her father, Robert Graham, for her hand in marriage, Robert responded, "Can you feed her, son?" Daniel replied, "I have a horse, a milk cow, a barrel of corn, and a barrel of molasses." Robert exclaimed, "My goodness, you have enough to marry several of my daughters." They were married at Robert Graham's home, near Forest Hill on Barber Creek.

When Daniel died in 1900, he left his wife, Julia Ann, $35,000.00 in gold (the equivalent of $980,000.00 today), a home, land, and the woods full of cows, hogs, and horses on Barber Creek. She lived thirty-six years after his death. She never remarried and provided for her family, even during the Great Depression. Daniel made good his promise to "feed" Julia Ann—and then some.

After Daniel was made Constable of the Spring Hill area, in Rapides Parish, Julia Ann often spoke of the time he captured an outlaw from Texas hiding in Louisiana's piney woods. She said it was too late to make the trip on horseback to the jail in Alexandria. Therefore Daniel handcuffed the outlaw to the foot of their bed for the overnight stay. He then told the outlaw, "You better not make a sound." She added, "Daniel slept soundly, but I didn't sleep a wink all night."

He was a successful rancher. He and his sons would buy cattle in East Texas for $4 per head and then drive them to the railroad's beef pens at Lecompte, Louisiana. They were then shipped to the northern railheads where they would fetch $40 and more per head.

Once, on a cattle drive from Texas, in 1898, the cattle stampeded in the woods. His youngest son and my grandfather, Randall Lee Willis, who was only twelve and riding drag, thought his father had been killed. But, then, he saw his father's huge white hat waving high in the air, in front of the cattle.

He was my great-grandfather.

Julia Ann Graham Willis–Wife of Daniel Hubbard Willis, Jr. and daughter of Robert and Ruth Graham. She would often read her red-lettered Bible, eat an orange, including the peel. When she looked at Daniel's Civil War photo, tears would come to her eyes.

When asked by her grandchildren about eating orange peels, she replied, "I don't know for sure, but I think they're good for you." She was bitten by a ground rattler, at age seventy-five, and survived with home remedies. She swam in Barber Creek twice a day until age ninety. She said it prolonged her life. All her children and grandchildren loved to go swimming with her.

According to her granddaughter Ilie Close, in a letter to me, "She always had food cooked for family and friends. There were lots of blackberries, huckleberries, and fruit of all kinds for good pies. She was reared a Methodist but later joined Amiable Baptist Church and was a devoted Christian. We use to joke, she didn't think there would be anyone but Baptists in Heaven. Her hobby was making quilts, and she kept the family supplied with her handiwork."

She was my great-grandmother.

Nathaniel Willis—Born in Chettle, Dorsetshire, a county in South West England, on the English Channel coast. The county borders a county to the west that also contains my Willis roots, Devonshire. Nathaniel later moved to London, where his son John Willis was born in 1606, only fourteen years before the historic *Mayflower* voyage.

John Willis—Born in 1606 in London. John sailed for St. Christopher (a.k.a. St. Kitts) in the West Indies on April 3, 1635, on the ship *Paul* from Gravesend. Gravesend was an ancient town in northwest Kent situated on the Thames River's south bank near London. John sailed on the *Paul* en route to the New World— America, carrying dreams that would be passed on to subsequent generations, including me.

John Willis first appears in America in Plymouth Colony, Massachusetts, in 1635, when his son John Willis, Jr. was born and again in Duxbury, in 1637, when he married Elizabeth Hodgkins Palmer, on January 2, 1637.

John Willis, a.k.a. Deacon John Willis, was the first deacon in Plymouth Church. John's brothers were also immigrants to the Plymouth Colony area. They were: Nathaniel Willis, Lawrence Willis, Jonathan Willis, and Francis Willis.

The population was about 400 in the 1630s. William Bradford was governor of Plymouth Colony when John arrived in 1635. John Willis held offices in Duxbury in 1637 and at Bridgewater in the 1650s. In 1648, John Willis was a juror at the murder trial of Alice Bishope, hanged for killing her daughter, Martha Clarke.

More than a century later, John Willis's direct descendant, Joseph Willis, would marry a direct descendant of William Bradford, Rachel Bradford.

I am the 4th great-grandson of Joseph Willis and Rachel Bradford Willis.

Elizabeth I—Queen of England and Ireland from 1558 until she died in 1603. Elizabeth took the reins of her country after her sister Queen Mary died. Queen Elizabeth's reign was referred to as the Golden Age or Elizabethan England. Elizabeth's reign supported the creation of works by such greats as William Shakespeare and Christopher Marlowe.

This novel begins in England during the same period, in 1575. That year Nathaniel Willis was born in Chettle, Dorsetshire, a county in South West England on the English Channel coast. The county borders another county to the west that contains my ancestors, too: Devonshire.

Sir Walter Raleigh and Francis Drake were both born in Devonshire. In 1588, Drake served as second-in-command during the English victory over the Spanish Armada.

Raleigh was a favorite of Queen Elizabeth and helped defend England against the Spanish Armada too. She was called the Virgin Queen since she never married and had no children. Raleigh named Virginia in the New World—America—in honor of the Virgin Queen. North Carolina's state capital was named after him.

William Bradford—English Separatist leader and signatory to the *Mayflower Compact*. The Mayflower Compact was an early, successful attempt at democracy and undoubtedly played a role in future colonists seeking permanent independence from British rule and shaping the nation that eventually became the United States of America.

William Bradford is believed to have written the Mayflower Compact by many historians. Separatists are commonly referred to as Pilgrims. The first use of the word pilgrims for the Mayflower passengers appeared in William Bradford's journal "Of Plymouth Plantation."

The *Mayflower* arrived in Plymouth Bay on December 20, 1620. During their first winter, more than half of the 102 passengers died. As a result of hard work and assistance from local Native Americans, the Pilgrims reaped an abundant harvest after the summer of 1621. Bradford served as Plymouth Colony's Governor, intermittently, for 30 years between 1621 and 1657.

In 1623, Governor William Bradford proclaimed November 29 as a time for pilgrims, along with their Native American friends, to gather and give thanks. His proclamation contained these words: "Thanksgiving to ye Almighty God for all His blessings."

It would later be known as Thanksgiving.

Agerton Willis—Father of Joseph. Husband of Ahyoka Willis. Wealthy Bladen County, North Carolina plantation owner.

He was my 5th great-grandfather.

Ahyoka Willis—The mother of Joseph Willis. Her real name was Mary Willis. Joseph told his children and grandchildren that his mother was a Cherokee slave.

She was my 5th great-grandmother.

Rachel Bradford Willis—First wife of Joseph Willis and daughter of William Bradford of Bladen County, North Carolina. Rachel was a direct descendant of the English Separatist leader William Bradford. Therefore I too descend from him.

Joseph Willis married Rachel Bradford in 1784. Their first child, Agerton Willis, was born in 1785. He was named

106

after Joseph's father, Agerton Willis. Their second child, Mary Willis, was born in 1787. She was named after Joseph's Cherokee mother, Mary.

To honor Joseph Willis's parents, Joseph Willis and Rachel Bradford Willis waited for the birth of their third and fourth children to name an offspring after themselves. Their third child, Joseph Willis, Jr., was born in South Carolina in 1792, and their fourth child, Rachel Willis, was born in 1794.

She was my 4th great-grandmother.

Joseph Willis—Preached the first sermon by an evangelical west of the Mississippi River in 1798.

He was born into slavery. His mother was Cherokee, and his father a wealthy English plantation owner. His family took him to court to deprive him of his inheritance, which would have made him the most affluent plantation owner in Bladen County, North Carolina, in 1776.

He fought as a patriot in the Revolutionary War under the most colorful American general, Francis Marion, The Swamp Fox.

His first wife, Rachel Bradford Willis, died in childbirth, and his second wife died only six years later, leaving him with five young children.

He crossed the mighty Mississippi River at Natchez at the peril of his own life, riding a mule! He entered hostile Spanish- controlled Louisiana Territory when the dreaded Code Noir (Black Code) was in effect. It forbade any Protestant ministers who came into the territory from preaching. His life was threatened because of the message he preached in the Louisiana Territory.

His denomination refused to ordain him until 1812 because of his race. On November 13, 1812, Joseph Willis constituted Calvary Baptist Church at Bayou Chicot, Louisiana. He went on to plant more than twenty churches in Louisiana.

On October 31, 1818, Joseph Willis founded the Louisiana Baptist Association at Beulah Baptist in Cheneyville, Louisiana. Joseph Willis founded all five charter member churches.

After overcoming insurmountable obstacles, he blazed a trail for others for another half-century that changed American history.

He was my 4th great-grandfather.

Dragging Canoe–Cherokee warrior and leader of the Chickamauga. He was the greatest Cherokee military leader. He once asked his father to include him in a war party against the Shawnees, but his father, Attakullakulla, refused unless he could carry a canoe. The vessel was too heavy, so the boy dragged the canoe. From that time forward, he was known as Dragging Canoe.

Daniel Oscar Willis, M.D.–Son of Daniel Hubbard Willis, Jr. and Julia Ann Graham Willis. His father died at his home in Leesville while being treated for Bright's Disease, known as Kidney Disease today. He began his medical practice in 1904 and was the first medical doctor in Vernon Parish.

He owned the first automobile in the Parish. He served in United States Army Medical Corps in World War I.

He owned the Hotel Leesville. After being slandered by a young lawyer in a trial, he bodily removed the lawyer from his room at the Hotel Leesville and then threw him into the street. The young lawyer's name was Huey P. Long, later governor of Louisiana and Senator. Long was assassinated in 1935. Daniel Oscar Willis was my great-uncle.

John Willis–First cousin of Joseph Willis of Bladen County, North Carolina. He donated the land for Robeson County, Lumberton, North Carolina, from his Red Bluff Plantation.

Known as the "father of Lumberton," he represented Robeson County as a state senator in 1787, 1788, 1789, 1791, and 1798. He served in the House in 1794 and 1795 and at the state convention of 1789, where North Carolina ratified the United States Constitution and became the twelfth state. Governor Samuel Ashe commissioned John Willis as a Brigadier General in the 4th Brigade of the Militia, Continental Army.

He gave all of this up to follow Joseph Willis to the Louisiana Territory but died in Natchez, Mississippi, on April 22, 1802.

Henry Elwa Willis–Eldest son of Daniel Hubbard Willis, Jr. and Julia Ann Graham Willis. He is buried at the Paul Cemetery between Lecompte and Forest Hill. He named one of his eight children, Kit Carson Willis, after the famous dime-novel scout.

He was my great-uncle.

Jeremiah and Jacob Stark–Based upon Mary Stark Hank's brothers Rufus and Thomas Stark. Their stories in this book are purely fictional.

Mary Stark Hanks was the mother of Lillie Hanks Willis. She traveled with her parents John and Celina Marie Deroussel Stark, by covered wagon to Branch, Louisiana. After six children's birth and the premature death of her first husband, Charles Oliver, she married Arthur Allen Hanks. They had five children. He later abandoned her and their children.

Mary Stark Hanks was my maternal great-grandmother.

Billy Sunday–The most celebrated American evangelist during the first two decades of the 20th century. He was a strong supporter of Prohibition, and his preaching played a significant role in the adoption of the Eighteenth Amendment.

Jimbo–Inspired by my three sons: Aaron Willis, Joshua Willis, and Adam Willis. Their strength of character has been demonstrated many times in how they treat people who can do nothing for them. They inspired the responses of the character Jimbo in three of my novels.

Charlie Goodnight–He guided the Texas Rangers to the camp leading to Cynthia Ann Parker's recapture. He later became friends with her son, Quanah Parker. He developed one of the nation's finest herds through the introduction of Hereford bulls. Goodnight also invented the chuck wagon.

He was the best-known rancher in Texas history. Historian J. Frank Dobie wrote, "Goodnight approached greatness more nearly than any other cowman of history."

Quanah Parker–The last chief of the Comanche Indians, son of Peta Nocona and Cynthia Ann Parker, an Anglo-American who was kidnapped, at age nine, by the Comanche.

General Randall Lee Gibson–Confederate general in the Civil War. He was a member of the House of Representatives and

U.S. Senator from Louisiana. He was president of the board of administrators of Tulane University.

My grandfather, Randall Lee Willis, was named after him by his father, Daniel Hubbard Willis, Jr., who served with him in the Civil War.

I was named after my grandfather.

Huey P. Long–Served as governor of Louisiana from 1928 to 1932 and as a member of the United States Senate from 1932 until his assassination in 1935.

Jimmie Davis–Singer, songwriter, and governor of Louisiana. Jimmie Davis would change Louisiana's history and impact the lives of thousands through his music and life. In 1999, "You Are My Sunshine" was honored with a Grammy Hall of Fame Award, and the Recording Industry Association of America named it one of the Songs of the Century.

Jimmie Davis wrote of his beloved Louisiana College, "Every man needs God as a partner because you can't make it by yourself. I knew it was my duty to try and contribute something to life, not just take from it, and I determined to try to be a better citizen. I believe that was the most important thing I learned at Louisiana College."

Robert G. Lee–Dr. Robert G. Lee will forever be remembered as the man who warned the world that there would indeed be a "Pay Day Someday!" While he was pastor of Bellevue Baptist Church, Lee served three consecutive terms as president of the Southern Baptist Convention: 1949, 1950, and 1951. Presiding at the 1951 meeting in San Francisco, he introduced a young Billy Graham to the SBC. Evangelist Billy Graham preached on the Louisiana College campus the same year during a 1951 revival.

Hidden Free Book
LOUISIANA WIND
a novel of Louisiana

INTRODUCTION

"The best men I've known have been cowmen.

"There's a code they live by—it's their way of life. It starts with an abiding reverence for the Good Lord.

"They're taught to honor and respect their parents and to share both blanket and bread. Their words are their bond, a handshake their contract.

"They're good stewards of His creation, the land. They believe the words in His Book.

"Learn from these men—from their stories of triumph over tragedy—victory over adversity, for the wisdom of others blows where it wishes—like a *Louisiana Wind*."

—Daniel Hubbard Willis, Jr., 1900

This is the story of such men....

PROLOGUE

March 20, 1900
Barber Creek
Babb's Bridge, Louisiana

I'd give anything to be mounted on a fast saddle horse again. I'd give him his head and point him due West—West to East Texas, that is. There, I'd buy another herd of longhorns, maybe even a Hereford bull or two.

My son, Daniel Oscar, says I might have Bright's Disease and may never be able to ride and rope again. I don't believe it, not for a Yankee minute. He's studying to be a medical doctor. I told him I'm only a half-step slower than I used to be. Well, maybe a full step. But here's my reasoning: there are more ole cowboys than there are ole doctors. We're a stubborn, durable lot. I've lived through drought, flood, blight, range wars, blizzards, dust storms, bank failures, lightning bolts, snake bites, stampeding cows, and some of the worst trail driving cooking imaginable.

And I'm still upright and breathing. But even if this doctor-boy of mine is right, at least my sons will continue our way of life. I've passed on to them the family grit, love of nature, codes of honor, Christian morals, and my mama's manners. Tradition is big where I hail from. We uphold it.

My name is Daniel Hubbard Willis, Jr. I remember well back in '61 when a mighty Louisiana Wind threatened our way of life, even our very existence. But first, let me tell ya of a happier time. Oh, yeah, it was the happiest of times! Come to think of it; it was two years ago—today.

NARRATIVE

DAY 1

March 20, 1898
The Beef Pens
Mayflower, Newton County, Texas

It had taken us five hard days to ride to Mayflower, in Newton County, Texas, to buy 2500 rangy tough Longhorn steers, cows, and heifers. I preferred those crossbred with Durham and Hereford bulls. I'd made the trip every spring since the end of the War of Northern Aggression in '65. (Weren't nothing "civil" about it.)

This day, I needed to fulfill a promise to our Cookie, Rooster, the best cook this side of the Brazos. I agreed to buy him a chuck wagon like my friend Charlie Goodnight had rebuilt from an army surplus wagon. Now, admittedly, I was slow to change, but it was time to move forward with this modern advancement.

I would no longer need my hoodlum wagon I'd used for years to carry our food, gear, and bedrolls. Rooster wanted one with a water barrel and coffee mill attached. He also wanted me to buy enough soap, salt pork, boxes of bacon, dried fruit, flour, coffee, black-eyed peas, corn, beans, sugar, pepper, salt, onion, potatoes, lard, and sourdough starter to feed Robert E. Lee's Army of Northern Virginia.

After revising and reducing his list, I also bought assorted supplies from the general store to stock the wagon: eating irons, tin plates, bedrolls, tents, and, of course, a Dutch oven. Rooster also requested two bottles of rye whiskey for medicinal purposes, which I declined, knowing liniment and quinine would do. I did buy a white hat, though, so everyone could locate me under the heavy longleaf pine canopy along the trail.

There was this fiddle and leather case just sitting on the store's shelf. Knowing how my youngest son Ran loved music, I bought it for him for his birthday. I also bought him three Big Chief writing tablets to have a record of this cattle drive. Then I hired twelve more trailers and a horse wrangler. We would need every one of them to trail the Longhorns through the thick piney woods of Louisiana.

If the weather held in our favor and we were blessed with no injuries or accidents, the return trip to the beef pens at the railroad in Lecompte would take nine days.

My four sons rode with me: Henry Elwa, the eldest, was thirty-one; Daniel Oscar was twenty-three; Robert Kenneth was twenty-one; and Randall Lee, whom we call him Ran, was only twelve. It was Ran's first cattle drive and his birthday to boot. He had read everything he could about cattle trailing and cowmen. Like me, when I was his age, his dream was to be a cowboy. I'd told him he couldn't believe all that stuff about Wild Bill and Elwa's favorite, Kit Carson. Now, Wyatt Earp, well, that was a different matter, every word of that being true. I oughta know 'cause I'm a lawman too. Ran would soon discover the vast difference between a dime novel cowboy and the real deal.

It also afforded me the opportunity to share round the campfires each night the story of our family in a land of red dirt and tall pines. For, you see, Louisiana is our home.

And if that wasn't enough, it was the 100th anniversary of my great-grandfather's swim across the mighty Mississippi, riding only a mule to settle our family in what was then known as the Louisiana Territory. Oh, no, the Cherokees and Choctaws did him no harm, not even the outlaws.

The same couldn't be said of a couple of plantation owners and a few religious folks. I thought surely we wouldn't encounter as many dangers as he had. But, alas, I thought wrong. One of the things we say in Louisiana is, pray for blessings but keep your powder dry. I was an optimist, but nobody's fool.

DAY 2

March 21, 1898
The Beef Pens
Mayflower, Newton County, Texas

After bedding down along the way in the home and barn of my old but now deceased friend Wade Mattox, who had died during the war, we arose at 3:30. Rooster had prepared biscuits in a big dough pan and coffee that would wake the dead. I preferred Arbuckle's coffee. Some called it six-shooter coffee, as it was said to float a cowboy's pistol. But then, if you expect to be operational in the middle of the night, you need a jolt of liquid that can open your eyes, quicken your nerves, and put a spring in your step. Rooster's brew filled the bill in those regards.

I reminded everyone that I had an unwritten rule prohibiting any man from complaining about another's cooking. Only a fool argues with a skunk, a mule—or a cook. But woe is the cook who didn't get our meals ready on time.

"We need to move the herd at a steady pace," I told Rooster. "I want the beef to still be on them when we get to our destination. We'll pause to let them graze now and then. Meanwhile, you drive on ahead, find a spot for us to bed down for the night at Burr's Ferry, there on the banks of the Sabine River. I'll send Robert Kenneth with you to help get things set up and arranged."

"You fellers will be hungry by the time you catch up to me," said Rooster. "You'll be plenty glad you got me this new wagon. I'll have hot grub waitin' fer all of you."

"Break out molasses," I suggested. "Something a little sweet will take out the dryness of this dusty trail."

"Got enough hand-to-mouth vittles to get you boys through the daylight hours?" asked Rooster.

"Sure enough," I said. "Canteens are full, and we've got hardtack, pemmican, parched corn, and beef jerky in our saddlebags to tide us over until we see you this evening."

"You watch out for your cowhands; I'll give you that," said Rooster. "Fair enough. I'll pack up and be on my way." He pushed back his sweat worn hat, pulled his faded bandanna to the right, and ran his fingers through his grey beard. He was as raw and feisty as a cockfighting champion, thus justifying his nickname.

I told the others we'd bring them up and spread them out along the bank, with the lead cattle headed downstream. The leads would get to drink clear water that way, and as the drags kept coming, they'd get clear water, too, because they would be upstream.

We would attempt to make the first ten miles to the Sabine River by sunset. I'd brought a dozen Catahoula leopard dogs, my Jersey bell-cow Ethel, a remuda of horses, and six big rawboned mules for the chuck wagon from our home in Babb's Bridge. I'd also brought my most oversized covered wagon to hold the calves born on the trail. I wasn't about to leave them behind for the red wolves and coyotes, as some did. At first light, we headed the herd up, took a deep seat, a faraway look, and kept our minds in the middle—the middle of that herd, that is.

We hadn't ridden but a mile or so when two young cowpokes rode up in a trail of dust. Eyeing them told me they might be brothers, but they were also toting guns. I sure wasn't looking for trouble.

The older one asked, "Who's the trail boss?"

"You got him. Name's Daniel Willis, and this is my son, Elwa, our foreman."

"I'm Jeremiah Stark, and this here's my brother, Jacob. Heard you were hiring back in Mayflower. We just missed ya. Sure could use the work. We've worked the drives out of the beef pens from Weeks Chapel to Toledo. We can rope, ride, and help ya with any outlaw or rustler problem.

"We get a tad bit more than other drovers cause we're known to be the best in these here parts with a gun."

"Is that so? How'd ya get those biblical names?"

"I reckon it was our mother, Celina Marie Stark, who named us," Jeremiah answered. "She died shortly after Jacob was born. Our sister Mary said she was one of those Bible thumpers. She should know, since she's one too."

"Boys, I've got enough help. You both look healthy, but I live by a rule—no gunslingers. Don't get me wrong; we have guns cause I'm the constable back home in Rapides Parish, and my boys carry squirrel guns and the lot, but not like those .45s on your hips."

Jacob had a look I couldn't read.

"But, Mr. Willis, you have a Colt .45 Peacemaker on your hip too," Jeremiah replied.

"The difference is, mine doesn't have a dozen notches carved into its handle."

"To each his own. We're bunking over in Burkeville. Mind if we ride along until the trail veers off?"

"It's a free country."

I decided to let them join us for those few miles. Figured they wouldn't have time to become a problem. We were doing right well. I was riding point with Ethel. She was our "lead steer." Jeremiah and Jacob rode with us. Ran was riding drag with two trailers. Elwa and the other drovers were spread out in pairs in the flank and swing positions as the cattle stretched out in a thin line for some two miles.

The brothers rode tall in the saddle, but those notches still bothered me. My years as a lawman had made me a keen judge of character and a shrewd observer of strangers.

We had ridden almost to where the trail forked to Burr's Ferry and Burkeville when clouds suddenly moved in. It was an East Texas thunderstorm moving faster than a ring-tailed cat with its tail on fire. I sensed the cattle were getting restless. All of a sudden, a sky fire exploded nearby.

The spotted Appaloosa gelding I was riding, Augustus, almost jumped out from under me. He was barely three years old and was still a little skittish. That would be putting it mildly. I once saw him sidestep his own shadow.

Lightning shot down on the forest. The cattle spooked and started running through the tall pines at a breakneck pace. I yelled, "Stampede!" The other drovers echoed my warning. I also heard them yelling words they hadn't learned in Sunday school. My thoughts turned to my youngest son's safety. But then again, that's why I had him riding drag—to appease his mama.

Jeremiah yelled to his brother, "Take cover behind those rocks and take Mr. Willis's bell cow with ya."

Jacob was headed toward a rock embankment when he called back, "Will do."

I watched him do some fancy riding on his cow horse as she dodged four-legged death. He needn't have worried about Ethel; she was already there.

The sound of those vast horns scraping the pines and knocking against each other gave me chills. The wood chips were flying faster than a hundred lumberjacks with axes.

My Catahoula hounds were trying to turn them. One had a steer by its ear and another by its tail, but they were way too outnumbered to make much difference. Jeremiah spurred his horse and was at full gallop. He was able to slow them enough to let me move ahead while I tried to circle them to the right to get them to mill by waving my hat. Milling cattle soon become exhausted, but these were hell-bent for leather. My plan did not work.

There were moments when I was sure I'd get crushed against the trees as the ground shook with thundering hoofbeats. If Augustus stumbled, it would be all over except the obligatory, "He died doing what he loved most." I asked the Lord to protect my boys cause it was now a matter of life or death.

The prayer for our safety by my sweet wife before we left home echoed in my ears as loud as Ethel's copper cowbell.

The cattle stampeded through the woods and tore up the dirt like a turning plow. There was an earthy smell of pine that might have been enjoyable under other circumstances. I finally concluded that turning the herd was impossible. I assumed they'd wear themselves out. I figured wrong. Thank the Lord; my Indian cow pony could run like a deer and was as sure-footed as a mule!

Then suddenly, they stopped. No, it wasn't our cowboy skills. It was the Sabine River.

We'd passed Rooster with his chuck wagon. He was now about three miles back, but still intact. His six-up mule team was dilapidated looking, though. Jacob had saved my bell cow, or at least that's what he told everyone. Ethel would never sleep with the herd again.

From that day forward, she bedded down with the horses and mules. I thought for sure my dogs had been trampled. But, nope, they were all now cooling down in the Sabine. The drovers had all made it too. But what about my sons? All were accounted for, but were pretty scratched up, bruised, and a worn-out bunch.

Ran came hobbling up to me and said, "This ain't how they tell it in the dime novels. No one said anything about getting hit with cow manure, rocks, dirt, and flying pine tree limbs. Talk about being baptized by fire as a new cowpoke. I, sure enough, got mine. Daddy, didn't you say something about me having the safest job?"

I laughed, hugged him despite his wretched appearance, and said, "I'll give you a break from riding drag after all that. Ya smell bad, but I don't detect any broken bones. Hope you've got those Big Chief writing tablets handy, because now you'll have one whopper of a story to put down on paper."

"Assuming my poor raw hands can hold a pencil and I can stay awake long enough tonight to make some notes," said Ran.

What a reunion we had that night as we all sat round the campfire, except for a few of the drovers who were night herding in two-hour shifts. We ate plenty of Rooster's sourdough bullets and Pecos strawberries from his Dutch oven over an open fire.

Those biscuits and beans, along with his beef steaks, hit the spot. And, yes, he even measured out a portion of molasses for each of us.

All that was lacking was my dear wife Julia Ann's apple pie, and, oh, yes, her Louisiana coffee made with the sweet waters of Barber Creek. I sure missed her. Everything tasted as good as a king's banquet and reminded me of our annual Willis Feast of Thanksgiving, for it was a day to be thankful—very thankful.

What prompted me to share the most memorable Willis celebration I'd ever seen was Ran's comment, "Father, I thought you were a goner until I saw your white hat waving above the Longhorns."

"Not hardly, son—but almost."

NIGHT 2

March 21, 1898
Burr's Ferry
Texas side of the Sabine River
On the Middle Fork of the Beef Trail

As we sat round the campfire in the cold night breeze, on the banks of the Sabine, I shared a story that has been etched into my mind with the healing hands of time.

I recalled events in September of 1854. The colorful leaves had begun to fade in the mist of the chilly autumn air. I was only knee-high to a grasshopper, all of fifteen, but I remembered it as if it were yesterday. The celebration was the most glorious in our family's history.

There were songs sung and stories told. Family and friends had gathered as far as the eye could see. Some came by wagon, some by buggy, still others by way of steamboats on the Red River. Many rode horses and mules. And some even walked long distances.

I'd never seen so much love, nor had I ever gotten so many hugs. It was the most massive supper on the grounds that ever had been—at least in our neck of the piney woods.

Fried chicken, roasted potatoes, green beans with pork, biscuits, gravy, cornbread stuffing, fresh watermelon, fried green tomatoes, okra and cabbage, and corn on the cob were all added to the apparent main platter favorite of beef steak. When the best cooks connect with the best available fixin's, you can bet it was a feast to remember.

The dewberry pie had a special meaning that day. Although, I decided not to taste it in this particular instance, for you see, it was my Great-Grandfather, Joseph Willis's favorite.

Just five days before, on his deathbed, he had looked me straight in the eyes and said, "I've preached on Heaven many times, but I've never done it justice.

"There's Jim Bowie, but with no knife. I see Ruth and Naomi. Oh, my, oh, my, it's Him!"

With that, Great-Grandfather smiled, closed his eyes in peace, and was with the One he had so longed to see. Oh, yes, there were tears of sorrow because we would miss him. But, there were more tears of joy, for you see, he was home— *home at last.*

His legacy was one that proved one man could make a considerable difference in this world. He had preached and traveled and witnessed. He fulfilled the calling he felt God had put upon him, and he did so with determination, fearlessness, and overflowing love for those who would allow him to share the gospel message.

To that end, he left me and all others in our family with a standard to live up to. I was thoroughly convinced I would see him again one day with I joined him in Glory. That thought was comforting.

DAY 3

March 22, 1898
Burr's Ferry
Texas side of the Sabine River
On the Middle Fork of the Beef Trail

Daylight was burning in my mind cause I'd slept to 5:30. Rooster had been up since 3:30, as always. We needed to make at least ten miles today, and twelve would be better. The cattle were calm, and that was a blessing considering the stampede we had endured. Even their bellowing was music to my ears. We kept a keen eye out for injuries.

But first, we had one not-so-small task to perform— swim the Sabine River. It wasn't precisely the swift Neches or even the muddy Red in Alexandria, but it was dangerous enough. The river was up two feet from the storm, maybe even three.

We loosen up the cinches on our saddles so the horses will have plenty of room to breathe and have more freedom in swimming.

Our bell-cow Ethel took the lead to the water; the others followed. I'd been taught to expect the unexpected on these cattle drives.

I'd expected the two-dollar ferry fee for my wagons and even the twenty-five cents for Ran and his saddle horse. The six cents a head for my cattle was reasonable enough, but there were too many, so that's why I felt the need to risk swimming them to the other side. Praise the Lord. We didn't lose a single head. But we almost did.

What I wasn't expecting is what the Stark brothers did. When I wasn't looking, one of my thousand-pound steers turned and started to make his way downstream. Even worse, more than a dozen head started following after him. If others followed suit, we could have a split herd on our hands and possibly lose dozens of our livestock.

That's when something crazy happened. Those wild and fearless Stark brothers raced into the Sabine River, pulling off their outer clothes as they rode. They jumped that mammoth steer, grabbed him by his thick, sharp horns, and turned his head in the directions of the opposite bank.

Still holding on to the horns, the Starks swam with that steer until it walked up the bank, leading the other cattle right behind it. It was the dang'est feat I'd ever witnessed. In fact, I'd never even heard of such a stunt like that before, with the possible exception of the story of how my great-grandfather swam the mighty Mississippi clinging to his mule.

I rode up to the Starks and said, "I've worked and driven cows many times, but I have never seen anything that can beat that, boys. If your offer is still open, consider yourselves working for me for the rest of this drive." They nodded and smiled.

We then drove the herd some twelve more miles without incident. Those Stark brothers, notched guns or not, had proved their merit.

NIGHT 3

March 22, 1898
The Middle Fork of the Beef Trail
Caney Creek
Vernon Parish, Louisiana

After what I witnessed with that steer earlier in the day, I wanted to learn more about the Starks.

"Now, Jeremiah and Jacob, tell me where you boys were fetched up? I'd like to know more about ya."

Jeremiah jumped right in. "Mr. Willis, we never got to tell ya why we wanted to be on this cattle drive in the first place. We're from Louisiana."

"Whereabouts?"

"Branch, sir, but our sister Mary now lives in Lecompte. When we heard that's where you were trailing your herd, we figured if you hired us, we could visit her. Her first husband, Charles Oliver, died in '87, leaving her with six younguns.

"Three years ago, she married a young fellow seventeen years her junior named Arthur Allen Hanks. The age difference is a concern to us. We've heard stories about him, too, down in Branch. I told Mary don't be surprised if he runs off, but he better run far—real far if he does.

"They've moved to Lecompte to start a meat market. They now have a three-month-old baby girl named Lillie Gertrude Hanks. We do want to see and hold our little niece. We're hoping to live there if we can find employment."

"About finding livelihood, talk to Elwa. He's moving to Lecompte, too, to handle our cattle business. We need him there to make sure the Texas and Pacific Railway does what it promised. That's a story for another day. I'm sure we can work out something, and you boys can spoil baby Lillie all you want. And, God forbid if Hanks should ever take flight with, let's say a younger filly. He'll flee Louisiana for good once he sees those notched .45's on Jeremiah's hips."

"We don't seek any trouble, Mr. Willis, but we don't back down either. We've found that being two of us, always together, sometimes puts things to rest without the need to clear leather. Still, any advice or help Elwa could provide us; we'd take it kindly."

"Not to worry on that account," I assured them. "Our family will always be there for you fellows. For Mary, too, and baby Lillie. Every single one of us will be, from me to my sons, even young Ran. That's the cowman way. That's the Willis way."

The brothers nodded their understanding and appreciation. "Now, one last question. Who are your father and mother?"

"John and Celina Marie Deroussel Stark."

I pushed back my hat and threw another log on the evening campfire. "Yep, I had surmised you boys were Cajun French. I love your people. Without them, what would Louisiana be? The food alone was worth trailing cows through the swamps of South Louisiana after we lost the cause."

Thinking back to earlier that day, I said, "For Cajuns, you sure can ride those Spanish cow ponies."

Jeremiah smiled. "Mr. Willis, we call them quarter horses. They can run like a deer, at least for a quarter of a mile."

"It would appear they saved your lives today."

Jacob agreed. "Yes, sir, all our family seems to stay healthy. We had to shoot one of our kin to start a cemetery."

Everyone laughed, but I looked at their guns again.

As we gathered round the campfire, Ran asked me to share one of Great-Grandfather Joseph Willis's stories from days long since past. I thought of one he'd shared with father and me on a three-day wagon trip in 1852.

Great-Grandfather and his wife Miss Elvy Willis had taken a little trip to N'Orleans on the Riverboat *Natchez* in 1828. On the voyage back home, they stopped in Baton Rouge. The French explorer Sieur d'Iberville had named the city after seeing a red pole that marked the Bayougoula and Houmas Indians' hunting boundary.

It was there that Great-Grandfather met a young man who was headed home on a flatboat from N'Orleans. He caught his eye, being so tall. His face had a determination far beyond his years. He was mighty upset after watching slaves being mistreated at a N'Orleans' slave market.

After a spell, the young man asked his traveling companion, a Mr. Gentry, "Why doesn't someone do something?"

He then turned to Great-Grandfather. "You're from Louisiana, sir, and your wife says you're a Baptist preacher. Why doesn't the church do something?"

The young man continued to pour out his heart, "There are more slaves in N'Orleans than any other city in this country, and I read that Louisiana has become very wealthy off their labors. I've seen men and women shackled, collared, and treated like animals this week.

"I'm only nineteen, sir, and I know you cannot help the poor by destroying the rich. But something must be done to stop this. I wish I could make a difference. I'm as poor as a church mouse with little education.

"My heart has been crushed by my sister Sarah's death this past January while giving birth. We've had to fight off seven men who tried to rob us of our cargo during this trip.

"We were just trying to make a living, and then we stumbled upon a slave auction. Who am I to think that I can turn the tide in my own life, much less this scourge of human bondage? Have you ever seen a man with so many odds against him?"

The young man hung his head in an expression of self-defeat. His feelings were genuine, but he saw little chance for him to correct a situation that seemed far greater than he could impact or alter.

Great-Grandfather replied, "Yes, I have, and I know it seems impossible, but with God, all things are possible. I believe and trust that God will choose such a man to address this evil when the time is right.

"Joseph, in the Bible, was seven years in prison, but then he became the second most powerful man in Egypt and was able to help his family and the other Jews in his homeland.

"Moses wandered the wilderness for forty years before God told him the time was right for him to step forward and become the leader of God's chosen people.

"The Bible tells us that God's hand is not short, and his ear is not deaf. He sees and hears and knows the evil ways of mankind. And he knows the ways to remedy it. Keep praying, young man, and never lose your sympathy for what you have observed."

He bade him farewell, but then paused and said to the young man, "I'm sorry, but I did not catch your name?"

"Abraham, sir, but most folks just call me Abe."

DAY 4

March 23, 1898
The Middle Fork of the Beef Trail
Vernon Parish, Louisiana

I'd figured we had had enough excitement for one cattle drive. What I didn't know was it had only begun. One old man and two younger ones rode up to me at the break of day. The older man had a worn leather look. The cocky younger ones rode as if they were on ten-dollar horses with forty dollar saddles. I wasn't in the mood for either.

"We're interested in your cattle," the elder spoke with a wicked glee.

"They're not for sale."

"We're not here to buy."

It has never taken me long to examine a horseshoe. Especially when all three had Winchesters out of their scabbards. Nevertheless, it would appear it was hog-killing time, and I was the hog.

"We only need a couple hundred. You'll hardly miss them. They're not worth dying for, mister," the old man said with a smirk.

I told them there were three things I couldn't abide: cold coffee, wet toilet paper, and cattle rustlers. Just when I figured it was the end of the trail for me, Jeremiah rode up and took over the conversation.

"You try to take those cows, and the only thing that's going to be missed is you."

"Don't I know you?" the old man asked.

"Yep. I know you, too, Scar Bartholomew."

"Jeremiah Stark! I thought you were dead. Do you think two on three is a dogfall?"

"My friend Sam makes it even."

"Sam? Where's he?" the old man snickered.

"Samuel Colt, right here—on my hip! I heard you were a lying, thieving Jayhawker in the war. Abe Lincoln may have freed all men, but Sam Colt made them equal."

About that time, Jacob rode up. Just as Scar smiled again, one of his cohorts pulled his gun, and Scar followed suit. Neither had cleared leather when .45 caliber bullets ripped through both their hearts. The third bandit was just a trail of dust by the time their handguns had ceased smoking.

This would be eighteen-year-old Jacob's first notch on his gun. I'd hoped it would be his last. My plan was to cut them loose when I first met them, but now, as my great-grandfather always said, "You've got to dance with the one that brung ya." I reckoned I would have had my last dance without them.

We stopped the herd long enough to bury the scoundrels. I didn't feel like a cross was fitting, so we stacked a few rocks on them. Maybe if the coyotes got hungry enough, they might pore through the rocks and dig out the carcasses. Nature had its ways, and so did man. I had no words to say over their graves. Not any that would have mattered.

The Stark boys spoke not a word until Jacob asked me, "How do you feel about all this, Mr. Willis?"

I squared my white hat on my head, and got back on my mount. "There's a few men in Louisiana that need killing, but no cows that need stealing."

"A woman's heart should be so hidden in God that a
man has to seek Him just to find her."
—*Joseph Willis* 1785

NIGHT 4

March 23, 1898, at dusk
The Middle Fork of the Beef Trail
Castor Bayou
Leesville, Louisiana

Now Daniel Oscar was from Leesville, so as we
approached the town he decided to spend the night there with
his wife Ella. None of us knew that when he invited his
younger brother Ken to share some of Ella's fine Louisiana
cooking a plan had already been hatched. It involved Ella's
friend Eulah Rosalie Hilburn. When Ken first laid eyes on
Eulah the welfare of our cattle seemed to become a faded
memory.

Eulah was a frontierswoman in that she had no flab on
her arms or neck. She was as hard as nails. Although she had
a rather aristocratic heritage, she was a product of life on a
farm. Her dark brown hair could fall half-way down her back,
except that she kept it braided. Her teeth were straight, her
eyes were a deep blue, and her smile was engaging.

She wasn't perfect, however. Due to an early bout with
chickenpox, she had a few small scars on her forehead and
left cheek, and her right foot had a minor limp caused by a
horse kick when she was a child. All things considered,
however, she was an impressive specimen of womanhood,
especially in parts of the country where men valued a gal's
ability to cook, garden, sew, and read as much as they did
their appearance.

After supper, Eulah invited Ken to her father's farm just down the road to see a horse she needed advice on. Early the next morning, Elwa rode back to camp and informed us Ken's saddle horse seemed to have suddenly developed a slight limp. He would catch up with us in a day or two.

Eulah's horse had a pedigree as long as her arm that was meant to impress. Ken was impressed. Not with the horse, but with Eulah. In his opinion, she was stunning, so he asked her if they could discuss the horse in more detail the next morning at the Hotel Leesville. They had an excellent café, with dark roast coffee, to start the day. He couldn't have cared less about that horse by then.

I later asked Ken, "I thought I'd taught you always to tell the truth?"

He replied, "I did, Father. I told her over coffee I would love to court her."

Ken added, "She seemed unimpressed and certainly not amused. She said she was only there for advice and was a lady that adhered to Southern traditions. Eulah made it clear she did not wish to mislead me. I didn't have a clue what she was talking about, especially the Southern tradition part. The only Southern tradition I knew was on a horse with a rope or in a field behind a plow.

"Then she said, since she'd just met me, unfortunately, she would have to decline any overtures of friendship, especially courting. That is, until I met her mother. Lo and behold, she then invited me to join her and her mother for breakfast the next morning so she could learn more about horses, and I'm sure her mother more about me."

Well, according to Ken, her mother started asking him more questions than a Baton Rouge lawyer.

"Tell me about your education, young man. I understand you know a lot about horses, but can you read and write? Do you know Latin or any other language?"

134

"I trailed cattle and horses from Texas, ma'am, so I've had to learn enough Spanish to do horse tradin' and cattle swappin'. And, yes, I enjoy reading and have been blessed with a sizeable library put together by my mother. My favourites are Robert Louis Stevenson, Mark Twain, Ambrose Bierce, and Edgar Allan Poe."

Eulah was as sharp as a tack, and her English blood gave her a charm and grace such as Ken had never seen before, except when she exclaimed, "Don't ask any more questions, Mother. Cowboys love to brag about everything. How everything they do is bigger and better."

Her mother was not dissuaded and asked Ken, "Mr. Willis, just how many cows do you own?"

He told her 200. That wasn't near as many as she'd been led to believe by her Eulah Rosalie.

Ken began to sweat like General William Tecumseh Sherman in church.

"That's in my smokehouse," he explained. They both smiled, and her mother seemed to ease up on him, at least for the moment.

Eulah finally told Ken, "I'd like to see those 200 cows. Maybe even the live ones, too."

"They await your inspection, Miss," said Ken, with a modest bow of the head. "And your mother is welcome to join us."

So, indeed, the proper courtship began and flourished. Before long I had another beautiful daughter-in-law. Albeit, with a lot fewer cows than Ken remembered that day.

But, then again, I later learned that Eulah Rosalie knew more about horses than all of us put together.

Ran knew his brothers had heard my war stories on these cattle drives many times, but he hadn't, so he asked, "Father, can you tell me a story of the War of Northern Aggression?"

"Sure I will, son. I'll tell ya my favorite!" I began to unwind a story of despair, hope, redemption, and promise.

"It starts, Ran, in the winter of 1863 when a beautiful young southern belle got the news that her handsome beau, a Confederate soldier for the cause, had been killed at Chickamauga. Her grief could not be abated.

"Each day she would read her *Red Letter Bible* and ask the Lord, 'Why?' She got no answer. Each day she would reach into her trunk and take out a photograph of him dressed in his uniform. Tears would come streaming down her cheeks. As the months went by, she had resigned herself to living out the rest of her life as an old maid."

I paused a moment to stir the embers before us and to adjust my bedroll against my back.

"At the end of the great War Between the States, she would feed the men from the Army of the Confederacy who traveled down the red dirt road in front of her father's home. Many were barefooted; all were hungry. She did this to honor her sweetheart's memory.

"Finally, one day, her father told her, 'Darling, we have no more to give.'

"She then would take her own supper and give it to those who traveled by on their way home to their loved ones. When her father discovered her sacrificial act of kindness, he insisted she stop for the sake of her health. He added, 'See, it's never-ending. There's yet another straggling, hungry soul.'

"As that soldier got closer, the young girl looked up, and suddenly stood, dropped her plate of food, and ran down the red dirt road to the tattered soldier. She hugged him, kissed him, and practically carried him to the front porch.

"Now, Ran, that was the greatest day of the war for the beautiful young southern belle and for me, too. You see, that soldier was me, and the young girl was your mother.

"Rumors of my death had been somewhat exaggerated, as Mr. Twain once put it. Indeed, several of the men in my unit had been waylaid, scattered, and assumed to be dead. Communication was very poor in those outreach areas, so incorrect reports very often were not corrected.

"Once three of my companions and I finally were able to link up with another regiment, word had already been relayed that I was presumed dead. I never was told that such a report had been sent to my wife.

"I eventually rejoined my company and suffered greatly. We were low on ammunition, food, clothes, and even water. I was then captured and made a prisoner of war.

"Once we got word the fighting was over, I was paroled at Meridian, Mississippi, on May 14, 1865.

"I had to walk back home. I was dirty, exhausted, bearded, and starved. But the image of my sweet wife kept me putting one foot in front of the other. It was tortuous, but well worth it all."

"Father, Mother told me that story, too. I so loved it, but she didn't mention the part of her remaining an old maid forever—I don't recall the handsome beau part either."

DAY 5

March 24, 1898
The Middle Fork of the Beef Trail
Castor Bayou
Leesville, Louisiana

We saddled up while wolfing down Rooster's coffee and biscuits. The Louisiana sky was ablaze with colors. A cool wind blew across our faces as we set out for hopefully an uneventful day. And it appeared it would be until young Ran followed his favorite Catahoula cow dog, one-eyed Jack, into the thick post oak.

The chattering noise from the underbrush was unfamiliar to him, but not to Jack. Suddenly there was a loud growl as a wild boar began to charge Jack like a runaway train. Jack attacked him as if he was nothing more than a rabbit. The hog's tusk caught his belly and slit him from end to end, as he jumped.

Jack's piercing squeal echoed through the woods as Ran arrived on his mare. Rearing up, his horse fell over backward, throwing him just yards from where the boar was pawing the ground like an angry bull. He now took aim at Ran just as I rode up.

Jack, bleeding profusely, got up, and this time went for the boar's hindquarters, clamping his jaws on his tail—refusing to let go and allowing me time for one shot. I knew my handgun would not even slow him down. I took aim with my lever-action Winchester 73 and fired, hitting him in his thick skull, right between his eyes. The .44 caliber cartridge killed him, just a few feet from Ran.

Thankfully, the boar's tusk did not go deep enough to cut Jack's intestines or any vital organs. I'll tell ya, Jack has nine lives. He'd already lost an eye when he grabbed a mule by the tail. After that particular time, I had wished he would not behave with such reckless abandonment.

Thank the Lord, that wish did not come true.

Daniel Oscar cleaned the wound and coated it with coal oil and Pond's Extract and then wrapped him in silver-coated bandages from Rooster's wagon. He had packed gauze with carbolic acid and wound dressings treated with iodine in his saddlebags.

My future people doctor proved to be quite the veterinarian that day. He believed in Louis Pasteur's theory of germs. Others thought it was ridiculous fiction.

Ran laid Jack in the big wagon with the newborn calves with strict instructions for him to stay still. He loved that dog more than most of the people he knew. Today, he was not the only one. He then rode with the wagon and kept an ever protective eye on Jack until we camped. Fortunately, the dog would soon heal.

All I could think of was, *Thank you, Lord, and thank you, Jack.* Also, I wondered what I was going to say to Julia Ann. It crossed my mind once, or maybe twice, perhaps even more....

That night, Rooster prepared a rare supper of roasted pork over a fire he had kindled with pine cones. For some reason, Ran had no appetite for pork, but he did take a slice to Jack. He refused it, too.

"I wish I could find words to express the trueness, the
bravery, the hardihood, the sense of honor, the loyalty to
their trust and to each other of the old trail hands."
—*Charles Goodnight*

NIGHT 5

March 4, 1898
The Middle Fork of the Beef Trail
Burton Creek
Vernon Parish, Louisiana

Sitting around the campfire at night was an excellent way
to unwind after a long day in the saddle. Sometimes one of
the boys would pull out a harmonica and play a few ballads
or hymns, and quite often, we'd sing a chorus or two.

Ran had his fiddle with him, and he'd serenade us in
three-quarter time occasionally with a new waltz he was
working on. A couple of the fellows would break out a deck
of cards if the campfire and the stars were bright enough to
make out the numbers and face cards. However, most nights
were spent sharing yarns, memories of other cattle drives,
stories of interesting people we'd met, sagas of the years of
the war, and recollections of our family members, close
friends, teachers, pastors, and neighbors.

For my own part, I was often prompted by Ran, who had
a hankering for stories about the West. I never got very
detailed or graphic regarding battles I'd been in during the
war, nor some of the face-offs I'd had in my role as a lawman.
But one night, Ran asked me to think back to my early days
as a cowman and share some events and episodes from that
period of my life. On that topic, I was open and agreeable.

"What you're about to hear, son, is a story about times not that long ago, and particularly about a circumstance that drastically altered my way of thinking about being a cowboy, and even about how to live life itself."

As I was being fetched up in Louisiana, I dreamed of being a cowman, so that's what I set out to do after the War of Northern Aggression. Since I had no money, I joined in "making the gather" in Texas. With five of my younger brothers' help, we rounded up wild and unbranded maverick Longhorns that had roamed free during the war. Before the railroads were built, we drove the herds on the Opelousas Trail through the swamps to N'Orleans to be shipped north by steamboats. What we couldn't sell we kept on the open range in Rapides Parish to begin building a herd.

Many of those were later driven to Vidalia's shipping points on the Mississippi, but some were driven to Shreveport. The buffalo flies were so bad on the trail to Shreveport the cattle would run off. They hated the stinging, the buzzing, the annoyance. Who could blame 'em.

Trailing cattle to Louisiana began long before they were trailed to Kansas by those Texas cowpokes. As early as the 1830s, cattle were trailed from Stephen F. Austin's colony to N'Orleans, where they fetched twice as much as they did in Texas. Folks used to say "cotton is king," but for my money, I knew that beef was every bit as desirable to Yanks as it was to us southerners.

As the years passed, I survived well, but I never seemed to be pulling in the rewards for my efforts that I had early-on envisioned would be mine. Turned out, I wasn't bringing to market the high-quality steers and cows that brought in the best money. Being stumped about this, I was eventually blessed to cross paths with someone who realigned my thinking.

Indeed, it was a grand day when I met an enterprising rancher named Charlie Goodnight, who had also joined in "making the gather."

We were at a Confederate Reunion in Houston. He had been a scout for the Southern cause. Before that, he'd trailed cattle to Louisiana. After telling me all about it, he offered me a cigar, which I declined, and gave me advice on improving my herd through cross-breeding with Hereford bulls.

Based on Goodnight's experience and keen observations about cattle, weather, trails, and buyers of cattle, he convinced me that I needed to buy more high-grade bulls to build a top-grade herd. Resistance to heat and insects counted. Disease resistance counted. Forage counted. And yes, crossbreeding counted, too! Herford bulls may weigh up to 1,800 pounds. Their offsprings were surviving rough ranching conditions and with improved beef quality.

In order to raise and market prime beef, there had to be premium breeding, proper grazing, and adequate protection from insects and storms and droughts, predators, and injuries. I drank in every word of advice this gracious man was willing to share with me.

Goodnight invited me to the JA Ranch in Palo Duro Canyon, but then I got word he no longer managed it. He had a stomach ailment that almost proved fatal, too, so I figured if I ever was going to visit him, I'd better do it soon. I purposed in my heart if the opportunity ever arose, I would do just that.

That opportunity came in '87 when the Fort Worth and Denver City Railway was built through the Texas Panhandle. Goodnight was now ranching in Armstrong County near the Fort Worth and Denver City line.

But, first, I wanted to see what the new XIT Ranch offered in the way of Longhorn bulls, maybe even a Durham. So, in 1888, I boarded the Texas and Pacific Railway at Alexandria and made my way to Channing, Texas, to visit the XIT. Surely I could find a few top-grade Longhorn bulls on their three million acres with more than 150,000 head of cattle. I wanted to see to survey all my choices.

If not, perhaps Goodnight would sell me one or two of his Hereford bulls. His rawhide toughness was tempered with a good-humored yet competitive manner. He was a Christian gentleman with an affable nature. I trusted him.

I liked Longhorns because they were tough and rangy, but they were mostly long legs and long horns and not near as beefy as Herefords. Well, at least that's what Goodnight had told me. I would then sell my culls and undesirable bulls. Channing, a new town, was now a central shipping point, so I had a way to ship them—my new prize bulls—back home.

It was a long way from Babb's Bridge, but I finally made it to Channing. I didn't want to look like something the cat had dragged in when I first met their range foreman, so I made my way over to the barbershop. I needed a shave, haircut, and bath. I sat on an old crate, waiting my turn for a nickel haircut and a dime shave. The bathhouse was outback. The quarter for the hot bath would be the most expensive I'd ever had. The soap made me smell like a flower, though. I decided to buy some for Julia Ann, even though I preferred our lye soap back home.

The old-timers were spinning tales about the weather, the scourge of the XIT's and Charlie Goodnight's barbwire fences doing away with the "real cowboys," a cattle disease called Texas Fever, and many a "she done me wrong yarn." Their laughter filled the room, and everybody was smiling until one ole cowboy spoke with a gravelly voice, asking, "What was that young cowpoke's name? Ya know, the one that got himself thrown off a green-broke mare on the XIT. That horse was a rank one, ya know."

"I was there. His name was Jimbo. He was a praying boy," the barber said.

"Not sure that pony was green-broke though, although that's what they told young Jimbo. He came strolling out of the bunkhouse one morning when some cowboys started poking fun at him. He didn't have much experience, but he wanted to show them he could rope and ride."

I took it all in and spoke not a word. I was spellbound. The barber continued, "They were daring Jimbo to ride that crazy horse brought over from a XIT line camp. They couldn't handle the mare there.

"Those cowboys were real mean to the boy. At first Jimbo did a good job of ignoring them, but they just kept making fun of him. 'Come on, ya got religion we hear tell. You can do anything with that Jewish Carpenter's help, can't ya, boy? Why don't ya wanna ride that horse? Ya scared? Maybe you're too green like that yearling cow pony. Maybe even yellow?'

"Everybody gathered 'round to see what was gonna happen.

Every eye was on Jimbo. His face was beet red. He just stood there looking at that horse and didn't move. The men laughed at him, threw up their hands, and started walking away. He couldn't have been more than eighteen. I watched him throw his shoulders back and begin to walk toward the corral. He grabbed a bridle and opened the gate. You could hear the whispers as most of the men came back to watch.

"He bridled her and proceeded to rub the mare all over with a saddle blanket while he whispered to her. One ole cowboy yelled, 'Bite her ear.' Another, 'Snub her to a post.' Another, 'She's got crazy eyes.'

"Jimbo ignored them all, except to say, 'She's not crazy, just afraid.'

"Didn't take long for him to get a saddle on her. He climbed on her real slow like and rode with a newfound confidence. She seemed to trust him. It beat all we'd ever seen. Left alone, Jimbo would have had that horse at his mercy in another minute or two.

"But, suddenly, someone cracked a bullwhip and yelled, 'Ride 'em, cowboy.'

"That scared pony must have jumped ten feet. And, as everyone hooped and hollered, she reared up and toppled over backward on top of Jimbo.

144

"The horse got up but not the boy. He just lay there in the dry, dusty dirt. I was the first one who got to him, and he sure didn't look good. He tried to talk, so I bent close to his mouth to hear his words.

"'Please get my Book, the one that boss Jake gave me.'

"First, I thought I hadn't heard him right, but he said it real clear again.

"'Please get me my Bible.'

"I sent one of the others to fetch it from his saddlebags. I tried to make him comfortable, but there wasn't much I could do. It was obvious his ribs were busted, his collar bone was broken, and his hips were crushed. His life was measured in minutes at that point, and I believe he knew it. I wondered how we'd ever explain all this to boss man Jake. When the Book arrived, I show it to him. 'Here, Jimbo, here's your Bible.'

"'Lay it on my chest and open it to John 3:16, please. Put my finger on those words.'

"He spoke all raspy like. By then, blood was bubbling in his mouth from all the internal bleeding. He coughed hoarsely, but still pressed with his demand.

"'Please, do it. Please!'

"I found that verse and lifted his hand. He cried in pain cause his arm was broken, too, it turned out. I placed his finger on the verse."

"'Tell boss Jake I made that decision just like he told me I should.'

"With that he closed his eyes and was gone. No terror, no anger, no pleading. Just slipped away."

The barber had tears in his eyes as he ended the story.

I paused a minute, then said, "Boys, I made three decisions after I heard the barber's story. The first was to name the creek we now live on Barber Creek.

"The second was to have you boys bury me one day with my Bible opened on my chest with my finger placed on John 3:16. And the third was to give every cowboy who works with us a copy of the good Lord's Word. Your copies are in the chuck wagon. Rooster will show you where."

Jeremiah and Jacob seemed to be moved the most. Jeremiah spoke first, "Mr. Willis, our sister Mary told us about that Carpenter. Is He for real?"

"Boys, He's as real as the skin on my bones."

"What does that verse say, Mr. Willis?"

"It says that whosoever puts his trust in Jesus will have everlasting life."

"What does whosoever mean? Who's that?"

"I reckon, Jeremiah, that's you and me and every cowboy and cowgirl. Even the mavericks, the culls, and the undesirables. God swings a mighty big loop. But, there's many a cowboy who doesn't want His brand."

There was a peace in the camp as an unseasonable cool breeze blew in.

Then Jeremiah said, "I want His brand."

Jacob added, "Me, too."

DAY 6

The Middle Fork of the Beef Trail
Somewhere between Burton and Mill Creek
Vernon Parish, Louisiana

Two of our drovers from the night watch rode into camp before sunrise.

"We got a problem, Boss, and it ain't rustlers. We were doing a wide swing before coming in, and a mile back, we found two steers mauled to death, one with a broken neck. Bear tracks were everywhere. They seem to be a massive male's tracks—hind feet near a foot long. I recon his stride is over four feet, closer to five. I am guessing over 600 pounds.

"We pulled our rifles and tried to follow a trail, but it was too dark. Besides, I know enough about Louisiana black bear to know ya don't go huntin' them alone. You want us to go back there; we will if you need our help."

"Naw, you fellers need some grub and a bit of rest. Let me ponder how to handle this."

I knew that the local black bears had once been sparse, but not anymore. Thanks to open range steer stragglers, these bears had had days of feasting that had allowed them to grow big, produce healthy offspring, and now even to become brazen enough to ignore the stragglers and attack grazing or resting herds. These bears were plentiful, dangerous, and fearless.

As a boy, I learned that Louisiana black bears were agile tree climbers, unpredictable, and bold. I'd heard their charges were pure bluff. I didn't plan on testing that theory, though. I also knew whoever had mauled our steers would be back this night, so I planned a trap. I'd used the leftover hog and a little honey as bait. A bear's sense of smell is exceptionally keen.

I scouted a spot where I thought Elwa and I could hide downwind.

"Stay on your mount, but don't make any noise," I cautioned, "and don't make any sudden moves. We'll need to both be pumping lead into him once he comes out in the open. Be ready."

Sure enough, half an hour later, the biggest black bear in Louisiana came lumbering out for supper. It was apparent our two drovers had underestimated his size—by a lot. But he stopped briefly when the wind suddenly shifted. He got a whiff of human or horseflesh, and in that instant, he wasn't going to settle for a dab of honey and a slice of bacon. No, sir, he bounded forward at full throttle to do to Elwa and me what he'd done to the steers the night before.

My horse Augustus either sensed or saw him first because he must have jumped twenty feet. I had to use both hands on the saddle horn to keep from being thrown head over heels. In the process, my rifle went flying.

Just when I thought it couldn't get worse, it did. Elwa drew a bead on the beast and misfired. Here came Mr. Bear with teeth bared and claws in motion. I had no rifle, and my sidearm wouldn't even scratch a monster that size.

The only thing I had left was my lariat. Now, any man with half his wits knows that you never throw your loop around a fast-moving train or a falling tree or a charging Louisiana black bear. But with no other options, and Elwa seconds away from being barreled over by this juggernaut, I unfurled my rope, gave it three twirls for speed, and landed it absolutely perfectly around that bear's neck. It was a beautiful sight to see—for three seconds.

However, all my rope did was to annoy that brute. He swatted the rope so fiercely, he yanked me and Augustus to the side like we were rag dolls. I grabbed my knife and cut the rope. It recoiled and snapped, forming a tangled web around the bear. Baffled as to what had ensnared him, the bear tripped, rolled, came up bellowing and thrashing.

His claws and teeth severed some of the rope, but it delayed him long enough for both Elwa and me and our horses, birds, and all other forest species to make a getaway. We looked back and saw the bear, finally free of the manmade spider web, amble off toward the hog and honey. Something, apparently, was better than nothing.

All that being said, I assured everyone that my bear roping days were over. In fact, if I ever laid eyes on that beast again, I, personally would cook him a steer and serve it to him on a silver platter—with all the fixings.

At a great distance, that is.

NIGHT 6

March 25, 1898
The Middle Fork of the Beef Trail
Mill Creek
Vernon Parish, Louisiana

As we sat listening to Ran play by ear on his fiddle two tunes called "Green Grow the Lilacs" and the "Yellow Rose of Texas," I was transfixed by the popping sounds and the glow of our campfire. I also marveled at how quickly he'd learned these melodies on his fiddle. When I complimented him, he smiled and said, "Not much else to occupy my time when I'm not in the saddle. This fiddle provides me with a diversion, a challenge, and a way to keep my fingers nimble."

One of our cowpunchers by the name of Gerald Duke had taught him the tunes while they worked their shift as a night herder team. As they circled the herd from the opposite direction of the other nighthawks, Gerald would sing. His melodious voice kept the cattle calm. I suspected it was to keep themselves awake, too. Ran remembered each tune and later would practice it until he got it right on his new fiddle. (As time passed, he eventually could play anything with a string on it.)

When I first saw Gerald on his saddle horse Majestic, I knew he was a real cowboy. Oh, no, not by his clothes or such, but by his open countenance and the way he looked me straight in the eyes.

He was not innocent, of course; but living next to nature was stamped on his face. His vices had left no scars that the open range had not healed. I consider myself a pretty good judge of character, and I liked Gerald from the onset. I nicknamed him Jerry.

As Ran finished his tunes, Ken spoke up. "Father, I have a couple of questions of my own tonight."

"Well, good then, ask them."

"I heard tell that you were part of the group that cleaned out those scoundrels on Jayhawkers Island. Some even say you had a part in Ozeme Carriere's demise?"

Ran couldn't resist chiming in. "My friends say I shouldn't even speak to one kid at school cause his papa was a Jayhawker. Were they that bad?"

"Boys, they were a bad lot, the very worst of lots. It was bad enough they were draft dodgers and deserters, but when they started stealing horses, weapons, cattle, and food from our neighbors, they became my enemies.

"Then, to top it all off, when the Yankee General Nathaniel Banks invaded Alexandria in '64, he enlisted them to seek revenge on us. Banks called them scouts. I called them murderers, thieves, and conscripts.

"They burned our homes and even murdered civilians. They took advantage of our womenfolk while we were defending our homeland. No, I didn't shoot Carriere. I was in Alabama fighting in the Battle of Spanish Fort in May of '65 when Carriere was killed. I didn't kill him, but a friend of mine did. His name was Colonel Louis Bringier. Well, to be more precise, at least his cavalry did. They cleared out the scum down on Cocodrie Lake's Jayhawkers Island."

I paused long enough to toss a few logs onto the campfire and to let my mind drift back to those days. The memories were sharp, but telling them to my boys would take some tact.

"I reckon there are two reasons these rumors of my connection to Carriere will not die a natural death. After the war, another friend, David Paul, was elected Rapides Parish Sheriff and then Mayor of Alexandria. His reputation had grown when he allowed no consideration to the Jayhawker varmints and exacted the most severe retribution. Sheriff Paul later helped me to become Constable.

"Those two friendships branded me as an enemy of the Jayhawkers. Don't get me wrong, I was, but the truth is that I was with General Randall Lee Gibson at places such as Shiloh, Chickamauga, Nashville, and, finally, in a Yankee prisoner-of-war stockade in Meridian courtesy of one William Tecumseh Sherman."

General Gibson is my namesake, I've heard you tell many times, Father," said Ran.

"Indeed, true. We should keep the name Randall Lee always going to honor my great commander and dear friend. You give that some careful consideration as you get older, son."

The fire crackled, and I shifted in my seat. After a brief pause, I resumed my story.

"Now William Tecumseh Sherman was another matter. His own men called him Uncle Billy because they trusted him so much, but he was ruthless, vain, and cold-hearted as ice, in my opinion. Odd thing about him, though, on his so-called 'March to the Sea,' he only burned Protestant churches, including one that my great-grandfather helped organize. Since Sherman himself was a Catholic, he left their places of worship unharmed. It'll be interesting to see how the Good Lord passes judgment on him for that."

There was a sardonic snicker and mild guffaw around the fire at that statement.

"Lincoln freed the slaves, and I think Sherman felt some kind of obligation to help them. So, he told his men to ignore the fields of black-eyed peas while destroying all the other crops and orchards, as the peas were a major food staple of plantation slaves.

"Some say that the peas were all the slaves had to celebrate with on the first day of January, in 1863...the day the *Emancipation Proclamation* went into effect. From that time on, they have always been eaten on January 1. I've never owned a slave, nor have any of my friends, neighbors, or family.

"Nevertheless, I don't eat black-eyed peas cause they remind me of Sherman."

"But getting back to the Jayhawkers, Father...." I nodded, pushed back my hat, scratched my forehead, and said, "Right, yes. So, about Carriere. What connected our family to him was an event your mama will not talk about to this very day. It's a situation that shows God's word does not return void, as the Good Book promises. Don't tell your mother I shared this story with you, but I think it's worth hearing if for no other reason than the validity of your dear mama's testimony."

My sons, and even the fellows who worked for me, all leaned forward a bit, expecting they were about to hear an anecdote worth retaining.

"Boys, your mama was living at the Ole Willis Place down on Barber Creek during the war.

One day a young man attired in the uniform of a Confederate officer came riding up to our home. He had some thirty men with him. Because of his uniform, your mother invited him and his men to come in for supper. She cooked for hours. After one of her famous meals, she provided them quarters in our barn.

"The next morning before breakfast, she said a prayer and read a scripture to them from the Bible. The young officer then gathered his men. As they started to ride away, he turned and looked directly at your mama.

"He asked, 'Do you know who I am? I am Carriere, the notorious Jayhawker. We were going to take your horses and burn you out. Maybe even shoot you since you said your husband was a Reb.'"

Even though the campfire was not as bright as daylight, I could see that the blood had drained from the face of my boys. They had no idea their mother had come that close to getting killed and never giving birth to them.

"Why didn't he, Father? Why didn't he shoot mama?" Ran asked.

"As he and his men rode off, he yelled to your mama, 'The words from your Book changed my mind. Anyhow, it would be a real shame to shoot the cook of the best meal I've ever eaten.'"

"Father, what scripture did mother read to him?"

"I know it by heart," I said. "'For what shall it profit a man, if he shall gain the whole world, and lose his own soul?'"

DAY 7

March 26, 1898
The Middle Fork of the Beef Trail
Mill Creek
Vernon Parish, Louisiana

As the sun rose over the rolling hills and filtered through the longleaf pines, I felt renewed and asked Elwa and Ken to ride point with me. If their intent was one day to own and manage herds of their own, they both knew they'd soon be riding point without me. Now it was time to start talking about how to carry on the business of making a living off a cow. The cattle business had changed since I had first mounted a cow horse. My boys were progressive thinkers, as most young folks are. They wanted to expand with other breeds, maybe even buy some of them muley-headed cows.

We already had crossbred with Shorthorns from England. Those Durham's were all right, but I preferred Hereford bulls to crossbreed with our Longhorn cows.

Elwa spoke first. "Father, we want to buy a couple of Brahman bulls. We've got to do something to fight this Texas Cattle Fever."

"It's a problem, all right," I admitted. "Go on, tell me more of what you're thinkin' about it."

"Well, sir, it's your friend Shanghai Pierce who says they're resistant to ticks. He believes it's the ticks that cause the fever. They also don't get the pinkeye. They can travel long distances on very little water, too."

And here was where the experience of an older man, namely me, came to be challenged by the more modern thinking and speculation of a generation that had garnered its know-how from books and newspapers and more years in school.

I stood at a fork in the road, in that I wasn't about to throw away the knowledge I'd gained by working steers across every form of terrain a man could imagine. However, I'd always been one to hear a man out, glean what I could from his experiences, and weigh the merit of what was being shared with me.

In more than one instance, as I've noted with my good fortune of listening years ago to Charlie Goodnight, I've advanced myself by heeding lessons from others. So it was, then, that I gave credence to what my boys wanted to share with me.

"Father, we know you come from a generation that doesn't know much about these things. We mean no offense, sir, but formal education has come a long way. Since The Texas Agricultural Experiment Station was established in 1887, near a post office called College Station, there's a whole new way of looking at things.

"The emphasis these days is on science. You know, verifiable research. Worthwhile experiments. Progress, advances, discoveries. We understand your love of Hereford bulls, but would you at least consider a change? Ken and I have done a lot of digging into this matter."

I offered a slow grin, evidencing tolerance for their eagerness and appreciation for their respect for my position as head of the family.

"Now, grant it, boys, I'm just a hayseed cowman, but I did manage to pick up a thing or two along the way. I certainly don't know all the fancy lingo used by your generation of educated fellers. But that doesn't mean I'm no judge of beef and bone. Truth of the matter is, I'm a bit ahead of you boys in this matter. I did attempt to do my own feeble research about the breed."

The boys blinked in genuine surprise. Ken asked, "Really, Father? We didn't know. When was this? What did you find out?"

"Back in '85, two years before the college you spoke of opened its doors, I rode a train to San Antone to explore the ideas you boys have today. I stayed at the Menger Hotel because Robert E. Lee had stayed there.

"I was introduced to a fellow there named Richard King. I later learned he passed away in the hotel just days after our meeting. He told me of his 600,000-acre ranch with grasslands along the Santa Gertrudis Creek. I asked him about his Brahman bulls that he'd bought a decade before down in N'Orleans and explained to him that's why I wanted to meet with him.

"Turns out, Mr. King had been a riverboat captain. Darn good one, for a fact. He knew the bends and eddies and channels of the Mississippi with no need of a map or compass. And he wasn't the only one.

"During our visit, he gave me a copy of a book written by another riverboat man that same year. The book was entitled *Adventures of Huckleberry Finn*. The author and King received a lot of their education on rivers, such as the Rio Grande and the Ole Miss. Now, don't get me wrong, I believe in formal schooling, but never forget that much of education is monkey see, monkey do. It should never be a substitute for good ole horse sense and the lessons learned on the rivers of life.

"But here I stray from my narrative. So, where was I? I first explored the possibility of buying a few Brahman bulls more than thirty years ago after Richard Barrow had four shipped by the British government to Louisiana. That was in '54. I didn't press the matter back then, but that's not to say it isn't worth revisiting these days. I appreciate your suggestions, boys, but I want you boys to make this decision. It's your call this time, not mine."

Ken became relaxed, as though something he had been dreading was now over, and it had not turned out poorly.

"Father, we've talked it over, and we think we should buy ten Brahman bulls from Shanghai Pierce," Ken said.

"I hope you'll respect our decision. Certainly, it is why we came to talk to you first about it."

"And I appreciate that. Your thinking is logical, and it's worth a try to see how it pans out. I just wanted to make sure you had the gumption to stick by your beliefs. Your bulls will be at the beef pens in Lecompte when we get there."

Ken wrinkled his brow, squinted his eyes, and said, "But, Father, it will take weeks for us to travel to Texas, make the best deal, and have them reach Lecompte by rail," he replied.

"He's right, sir," said Elwa. "There are details to be worked out."

"Yep, that's true, isn't it? But what I held off telling you was, I bought twenty Brahman bulls two months ago. They should be in Lecompte at the beef pens by now."

The boys' mouths fell open. So, the old man wasn't as far behind the times as they might have feared.

"By the way, Richard King also told me he had an idea that he hoped his descendants would carry out someday. It was to crossbreed Brahman bulls with Beef Shorthorn cows. If they ever do, he wants them to name the breed after the Santa Gertrudis Creek on his ranch."

The boys slapped me on the shoulder, recognizing that I'd been a jump ahead of them. I laughed it off.

I said, "It never ceases to amaze me how us old folks can still have a good idea now and again. Imagine that, even an ole blind hog can find an acorn now and then—if he does some rooting."

Elwa assured me, "Father, we know you have great ideas. We use them every day!"

"That's good. You know, they say Richard King's ghost wanders the halls of the Menger Hotel!

"I promise not to haunt you. Well, then again, I just might if these Brahman bulls don't work out!"

NIGHT 7

March 26, 1898
The Texas Road
Big Creek
Rapides Parish, Louisiana

It had begun to rain mildly as we sat round the fire. The smell of Rooster's stew promised some relief from the chill. We pulled our ponchos over our heads and around our shoulders and leaned closer to the heat.

"Mr. Willis, Ran told me he'd lost two sisters and a brother. How did you deal with that?" Jacob Stark asked.

Jeremiah gave a stern look at his younger brother. "You don't ask questions like that."

I lifted a hand for peace. "Naw, naw, it's all right Jeremiah. I don't mind. I've spent several nights filling your heads with tales of the war and episodes as a lawman and adventures about previous cattle drives. It's only fitting that I share some insights on some of the more serious matters in life."

"I didn't mean to intrude on your privacy, Mr. Willis," Jacob said. "It's just that, like we told you before, we've got a sister named Mary and her family that we care for deeply. And life here on the trail and even on the farms just isn't all that easy. Never know when a family tragedy could befall us. I'd like to hear how you dealt with that. I hope I'll never need it, but better to be prepared than caught off guard."

I nodded my understanding. "Wise thinking, son. And I'll tell you upfront that I don't have all the answers as to how one copes with loss and emotional pain, and severe heartache. But I can share with you what happened in our family and how my dear wife and I came to terms with it."

Rooster distributed the vittles, and we all took a few minutes to eat the stew while it was still hot.

He'd baked some sourdough biscuits that morning, and he passed the leftover ones around to each of us to mix with the beef and carrots and beans. Tasty and filling. Just what a cowboy needed at the end of a long day in the saddle.

I set my bowl aside, wiped my mustache, and pulled back the moist poncho. The rain had let up, but the fire was still very appealing.

"Our story goes back more than a decade," I began. "After Elwa was born, Julia Ann and I had two beautiful girls, Carvelia and Minnie. Then we decided it was time to have another cowboy. Elwa was about four then, and we figured he needed a little brother.

"It was in January of 1872 when this new boy was born. We named him David Eugene after David in the Bible. He was tall and lanky by the time he reached eight years old. He was smart and kindhearted, a lot like his mother. Just a month after his birthday, in 1880, Julia Ann and I decided to visit my father's home. My daddy was a Baptist preacher like his own grandfather and was now pastor at Amiable Baptist Church, which Great-Grandfather Joseph had founded a half-century before.

"On the way to Amiable for church on a beautiful Sunday morning, Julia Ann told me, 'Stop the buggy, Daniel, I feel something is wrong at home.' I turned the buggy round as fast as I could and kept the horse at a trot. When we arrived home, David Eugene was deathly ill. How my wife sensed this, I'll never know, but I've never been one to doubt a mother's intuition. And, sure enough, when we got there, we discovered that little David had a terrible pain around his belly button and he was running a grievous fever.

"Julia Ann was beside herself with anxiety. She knew it was more than a twenty-mile ride to Alexandria, where the nearest doctor could be located. She turned to me and said, 'Ride your horse as fast as you can if need be, but get our boy some help.'

"I mounted my fastest horse and rode him into the ground with my boy crying out in pain with every leap and jump. I made the twenty-mile plus ride to Alexandria in just two hours, but it seemed like a year. I carried David in my arms and burst right through the doors of the doc's office. Thank goodness, he had just returned from delivering a baby on one of the nearby ranches. He had me put David on the examining table, and in five minutes, he determined that David had a ruptured appendix.

"That old doc could mend broken bones, sew up wounds, bring babies into the world, and even pull bad teeth if need be. But, he was not a trained surgeon. No one in those parts was.

"The nearest person with those kinds of skills was a hundred miles away in Shreveport. Little David overheard that old sawbones share that sad news with me, and he looked at me with sheer terror in his face, worrying that I might try to put him back on my horse and bounce him another hundred miles. He pleaded with me, 'No more, Papa, no more.'

"The doc had some laudanum that helped reduce the pain in David's gut. I lifted the little fellow into my arms and held him and kissed him and smoothed his hair until he breathed his last. I then laid him gently back on the examining table, dropped to my knees, and wept with such a deep agony; I wondered if I'd ever recover.

"The old doc had left me alone with my dying boy, and he'd gone to fetch the undertaker. When they both got back and saw that David had died, the doc told me to leave my bone-weary steed and borrow a horse from the livery owner. He told me to ride back, tell my dear wife what had happened, and then return in a day with a buckboard to retrieve the body. It would be wrapped in linen and laid in a coffin by then.

"Over and over, the doc told me that there was nothing Julia Ann or I could have done to have prevented this death.

"We could feel great sorrow, but there was no guilt or shame on us for what was something that just happened to folks with no rhyme or reason. It was what it was, and it was now up to us to give our boy a proper burial and then to turn our attention to rearing our other young'uns.

"That ride back was worse than anything I had ever suffered during the war, even in a prisoner of war camp. If I could have, I would have swapped places with little David, but, alas, that was not an option. As I neared the home, Julia Ann was on the porch. Amazingly, she was already dressed in black, head to toe. Again, her maternal instinct had told her that her son had passed. I dismounted, and she came into my arms, comforting me and allowing me to comfort her. We spoke no words.

"Three days later, we buried our boy in the Graham Cemetery on a hill next to Robert Graham's home, where I'd asked for David's mother's hand in marriage. How could one location have so much joy and so quickly so much sorrow? We now knew the unimaginable pain that Great-Grandfather Joseph Willis experienced when he lost his precious twins, Ruth and Naomi."

Jacob cleared his throat. He said, "A woman carries a child for nine months, then goes through pain to bring him into the world, and then spends years feedin' him, nursin' him when he's sick, makin' clothes for him, helpin' him with his school learnin'…then, he's taken from her. I just can't imagine how anyone can recover from that, Mr. Willis."

"I don't know that you recover, Jacob, only endure. During the funeral, my father spoke words of hope—*Blessed Hope*. Nevertheless, Julia Ann would later lie on David's grave and weep for hours at a time. I had hoped that maybe bringing new life into our family might help defer some of the grief. The next year we had baby Corine. She died a week after her birth. Weak heart and underdeveloped lungs, we were told. I knew I had to be strong and pray without ceasing.

"Father's Amiable Church prayed and fasted for days. I began to notice an evolution in Julia Ann. She no longer went to the cemetery and draped herself across David's grave. Instead, she sat alone, under a large elm tree, reading and studying specific passages from her Bible. I allowed her these private times of contemplation, prayer, and meditation by taking care of our other children.

"So it was, then, that a week or so after this altered behavior, Julia Ann walked into our kitchen, stood erect, and in a clear and confident voice told me that she had made a vow to the Lord that if we ever lost another child, she would never allow herself to grieve as she had for David Eugene and little Corine. She said, 'I owe that to our other children, and to you, too. Our God endured the death of His dear Son. He understands the hollowness we feel. But He also has more for us to do, and I will no longer shirk that responsibility.'

"The next day, we walked down to the banks of Barber Creek. I told her, 'We should have no more children. Surely it's not the Lord's will.'

"She responded, 'Daniel, I love you, but you may be wrong.

The Bible says to say, "If it be the Lord's will...." and that is how we will see how this works out in His grand plan for us. He will determine if other children are to come into our family.'

"Two years later, Daniel Oscar was born. When he reached twelve, we told him of his brother and sister's deaths. His response was, 'We will never be without a doctor again, no, never again. I will study as long and as hard as it takes to become one.'

"Then Robert Kenneth, Ruthey Madella, Julia Coatney, and young Ran were all born. And, yes, we lost another. Precious Stella, a victim of scarlet fever, lived only four months. But Julia Ann kept her promise to the Lord, and our family too.

"Daniel Oscar is almost finished with medical school. He will be the very first medical doctor, and a surgeon at that, in Vernon Parish. A child with appendicitis now will have a fighting chance. The Lord causes all things to work together for good!"

✦   ✦   ✦

"I should tell ya, Julia Ann was a Methodist, up till then. After hearing of Amiable Baptist praying and fasting for her, she insisted on joining their church."

Elwa added, "She still reads the Bible daily on the front porch while eating an orange and even its peel. We sometimes joke that she thinks there will be no one in heaven except Baptists. I told her that they might build a wall up yonder so that she won't have to know how many other folks made it into heaven, even not being Baptists."

That drew a chuckle and reminded Elwa of a funny story. "When I asked her what religion Jesus would be in heaven, she smiled with a twinkle in her eye. 'I reckon, son, it will be like the time a Catholic, Methodist, Presbyterian, and Baptist were fishing together down on Barber Creek.

"They got into an argument on what denomination Jesus would be in heaven. The Catholic declared, 'No doubt He will be part of our church, since we have the Pope." The Presbyterian said, "No, oh, no. When you consider all that John Calvin did for the Christian faith, He will be one of us." The Methodist then spoke, "Nope, no way, look at all that the Wesleys did for Christianity."

"The Baptist looked perplexed for a few minutes and spoke, 'Gentlemen, I don't think He's going to change.'"

The Stark Brothers, my boys, Rooster, and I all had a good laugh at that one.

"Boys, you can see Jesus in your sainted mother's eyes. Through it all, she still puts her confidence in the *Blessed Hope!*"

"The reports of my death have been greatly exaggerated." —*Mark Twain*

DAY 8

March 27, 1898
The Texas Road
Big Creek
Rapides Parish, Louisiana

We veered off the Beef Trail onto the Texas Road to Lecompte.

As we crossed Big Creek, a band of fifty or so Choctaw came riding up, hooping and hollering.

Jeremiah yelled, "Indians! Circle the wagons."

I told him, "We've only got two."

About that time, they circled him. Jeremiah was as white as rice.

I had to say something. "Now, Henry, you shouldn't scare Jeremiah like that. He's mighty good with a gun. You're liable to get shot. And what would I tell your children? Better yet, my godchildren?"

"You're right, Daniel. Did you get that candy in Texas for them? They love those sugar plums."

"Sure did. Now I suppose you want the steers I promised you. Pick out the best five or so, and invite me to supper sometime."

"You are a man of your word, and a good friend," said the Indian.

He and his braves turned and rode out among our herd, choosing the five head they felt would serve best in feeding their families.

Later, Jeremiah asked me, "You do that often? You know, show favoritism to injuns?"

"Every year."

"Why?"

"I figure I owe it to him and his people. They were here long before us, and, besides that, I'm not going to watch any child starve, godchild or not."

Jacob had listened to it all and asked me, "Mr. Willis, have you always been like this?"

"Like what?"

"A good man always doing what's right?"

I smirked and shook my head. "Not hardly. I've cut a wide path at times, not always good. Glad to say I learned a few lessons along the way, but sad to say that some came with a price."

"Sir?"

"I'll tell you and Jeremiah a story of when I was a boy. Like I told you before, my father was the pastor of Amiable Baptist Church. Once a month, we'd have a church conference under a large grove of cypress trees. The older men would testify with stories of their conversions. The womenfolk would sit by a pot-bellied stove, pray, and tell stories mostly about their husbands, children, and what the Lord had done for them all.

"There was singing, and shouting, and praising the Lord. And, there was plenty of food, but there was no fishing, swimming, or games of any kind for us boys. Now, don't get me wrong, that was all fine, but I had visions of a cane pole and me on the banks of Barber Creek with brim jumping into my lap. I thought surely that would not be a sin. After all, the Lord liked to walk on water and to make sure folks had plenty of fish to eat, right?

"Anyway, these meetings could and would go on for days. Being a preacher's son, I was required to sit on a log that had been cut in half on the front row. To a growing boy, it was about as exciting as watching paint dry.

"Now, my brothers offered me a quarter if I'd liven things up.

166

Do you realize how much money that was to a boy like me? I could buy two cane polls, with the line too. I needed that quarter.

"So, I got hold of my father's Bible the night before the conference and glued some of the pages together in the front of the big Book. I knew he'd never notice, much less preach a sermon that far back in his Bible. After all, we were a New Testament church.

"When Father stood the next day to deliver his sermon, he read the text for the day, 'And in those days, Noah took unto himself a wife.'

"I thought, *Oh, no, isn't that in Genesis*? All I could think of was another sermon of Father's, something to do with your sins finding you out!

"He then turned what he thought was one page and continued, 'And she was...fifteen cubits broad and thirty-five cubits long, made out of gopher wood, and daubed on the inside with pitch.' He held up the Book and added, 'My brothers and sisters, that's the first time I've ever read that in the Word of God, but if the Bible says it, I believe it! Amen.'

"The old men all joined in with an array of amens that echoed through the trees. I should know cause I was headed up one of them.

"Father continued, 'Just goes to show, we are wonderfully and fearfully made....'

"Now, boys, trust me, my father and a piece of hickory wood convinced me my Bible tampering days were over. And, equally as bad, my brothers reneged on the payment of the quarter, saying that what I did got me a whippin', but it didn't shorten the preaching and carrying on.

"Since then, I've never roped a crippled steer nor rode a sore-backed horse nor changed a Bible verse to suit me....

"In fact, every time I open a Bible, I swear I can detect a faint scent of hickory in the air."

"To write a good love letter, you ought to begin without knowing what you mean to say, and to finish without knowing what you have written."
—*Jean-Jacques Rousseau*

NIGHT 8

March 27, 1898
The Texas Road
Calcasieu River
Rapides Parish, Louisiana

After supper, Elwa stoked our campfire on the banks of the Calcasieu River. He asked me to tell the story he'd requested every year since his first cattle drive.

"Father, tell me again about your first cattle drive in '67? I never tire of hearing it."

"And I never tire of telling about it." I'll summarize here for you what I shared.

Just as I began trailing cattle, politics raised its ugly head. I'll give you an example of what I mean. I was once told a story of a woman who wanted to know what her son would become.

She put what little money she had on her kitchen table, along with a bottle of liquor and a Bible. As her son approached their home, she hid in a closet. She figured if he took the money, he'd be a gambler; if he drank the whiskey, he'd be a drunkard, and if he picked up the Bible, he might just become a preacher.

When the boy saw all this, he picked up the money quickly and stuffed it into his pockets; he then drank the entire bottle of the Devil's poison; and, finally, he put the Word of God under his right arm and staggered out the door. The mother exclaimed, "Oh, no, a politician."

★   ★   ★

After the war ended, I figured the best way to feed my family was to be a cowman. When I asked him for his daughter's hand in marriage, Robert Graham's words, "Can you feed her, boy?" kept haunting my mind.

Within a year, my wife was with child, and my first boy was on the way. I knew I'd better get to it since the meager money I earned from farming was not enough to feed a growing family.

The woods seemed to be full of unbranded maverick cattle that had greatly multiplied during the war, but I feared some of them might have once belonged to our neighbors, so I joined in "making the gather" in Texas. There were thousands of unclaimed cows roaming free in that vast land. We were able to rope and brand 300 head on my first cattle drive. I had already registered my brand, the Bar-D-K, in Rapides Parish.

The next year Henry Warmoth became Governor of Louisiana. Now, the last thing on earth I'd do is to speak ill of that low down Yankee scoundrel. Rooster's six mules dragging me across an alligator-infested swamp couldn't make me talk disparagingly of that worthless Carpetbagger. No, not me.

Where was I? Warmouth was a corrupt politician of the worst sort. He promised to help reconstruct Louisiana. It wasn't about Reconstruction, but about taking advantage of us after the war, punishing the South through fraudulent elections and outright thievery.

Out of all that came The Knights of the White Camellia. They said they would defend *our way of life*. I'm not sure if they were as crazy as the Ku Kluxers, for you see, our family, being part-Cherokee, never got an invitation to join either.

Wouldn't matter though, I've never cared for anyone who had to hide behind masks and robes to proclaim their beliefs. And, I certainly didn't need *our way of life* defended by whippings or a lynching. I trusted them 'bout as much as I did Louisiana's double-minded scalawag politicians.

My wife's brother William Graham has a few holes in his sheets to this very day, and is proud of it. He says he's going to have his sons engrave KKK on his grave marker in Butters Cemetery when his time comes. Can you imagine standing before the good Lord and explaining that, and all those burning crosses they've used to preach hate?

Listening to him talk, you'd think he was the One at Calvary. I told him to come down from his cross, cause someone might need the wood.

My friend from the war, Shanghai Pierce, told me a man could have all the cows he wanted in Texas with legions of Longhorns roaming free. He'd driven a herd from Texas to N'Orleans back in '55 on The Opelousas Trail. The only problem was they weren't worth spit after the war. I got the idea that might all change, and change it did as folks decided they preferred beef over pork about the same time as Warmoth was impeached. Our beginnings were humble, but with it, my wife and I fed our children.

And so, at this point, I launched into the tale Elwa had requested. "All right, son, let me tell ya about that first cattle drive again.

Demand began to change when a fellow named James McCoy established a cattle market in Abilene, Kansas, in '67. The Chisholm and Goodnight-Loving Trails in Texas headed north, but were too far from our home to make it worth our while. Even the easternmost Shawnee Trail was not a good choice because of Texas Cattle Fever and the many drownings of livestock in the dangerous waters of the Neches River, not to mention our cattle would lose too much weight on such a long hard drive.

"There was no railroad when I chose to drive our beeves to N'Orleans on the Opelousas Trail from East Texas. We crossed the Sabine at New Columbia, Texas. I could buy cattle then in Texas at $3 a head and sell them to the U.S. Army in N'Orleans for $20 a head. I never dreamed the selling price would double one day. We trailed cattle on the Opelousas Trail until 1882, when The Texas and Pacific Railway Company built a route from New Orleans to northern railheads. The next year, when you turned fifteen, you made your first cattle drive with me."

I assumed Elwa would find that much jabbering about the past to be adequate, but he cajoled me into carrying on a while more. The company was enjoyable, so I resumed my narrative, but first did some oral backtracking for some important family history.

"Now, I need to step back a piece to put things into perspective for you. It was on my own very first cattle drive that I met Etienne Fontenot. He owned a *stand* for cattle drives where The Opelousas Trail crossed the Calcasieu River. He once was good friends with Great-Grandfather Joseph's friend Jim Bowie, and Jean Lafitte, too.

"His waystation gave drovers access to cattle pens, a soft bed, and a hot supper. I was fascinated by him, for you see, Jim Bowie had introduced Fontenot to Great-Grandfather many years before. He had become one of the largest landowners in Louisiana and put the notion in my mind to buy land for our family and cattle. He had the crazy idea the ground they grazed on might be worth more than the cattle one day. The more I thought about it, the more I agreed with him.

"I knew much 'bout Bowie from Great-Grandfather, but I wanted to know more bout Lafitte. As a boy, I'd heard many a tale about his exploits. No-Man's-Land's early inhabitants held him in high esteem, and he reciprocated by showering them with gifts. He was considered a war hero rather than an outlaw because he helped General Andrew Jackson during the Battle of N'Orleans.

"Fontenot had furnished his men with beef and supplies when their ships sailed up the Calcasieu River. Laffite made his Louisiana headquarters at his home. They became best friends. Once, when he admired a diamond stud Laffite was wearing in his silk shirt, Lafitte tossed it to him and said, 'Here, it's yours!' I mean, that's just the kind of genuine camaraderie those fellows shared.

"Anyway, it was during this time that Lafitte fell in love with his best friend's sister, Madeline. The dark-haired, green-eyed beauty had a charm and grace that the pirate had never before encountered. He became smitten by her soft-spoken ways and fell hopelessly in love. But there was a problem, and it was a big one. She was already married. Her husband soon became jealous of Laffite, and accused his wife of having an affair with the buccaneer.

"One day, when her husband returned home from a trip, he discovered she was wearing an expensive brooch given to her by the pirate. The husband went insane with both jealousy and personal insult. 'I will not permit you to be unfaithful to me,' he scolded her as he snapped a small pistol from his hand. Without allowing his wife to explain or respond, he shot her across the room. She fell flat out on the floor, and when the husband saw her limp body, he knew he would be hanged for murder if he was caught.

"He vamoosed, leaving her to bleed to death. Oddly enough, by the act of a guardian angel or just fool luck, it wasn't her day to die. She survived, as I'll explain in a moment.

"Murderer or not, things didn't go so well for the husband, however. No, indeed. When the news of the shooting reached Lafitte, he vowed to kill the man. Whether he killed him or not will never be known, but one fact is for sure, and that is that the husband was never seen again—at least as anyone who knew him would recognize. Some folks surmised that he took a bad route in his hasty getaway and became food for the alligators.

"And that is possible. But others said Lafitte found him and made him walk a plank into the turbulent waters of the Gulf of Mexico. Knowing Lafitte's reputation, there may be some validity to that story, too.

"However, some lingering tales said the husband somehow made it to N'Oleans, grew a long beard, bought himself some silk vests and corduroy dress coats, and boarded a riverboat and spent nights at the gambling tables until he made it safely to the North. All of which goes to show you how legends are made and tall tales gain traction.

"More significant to the story, however, was the amazing fact that Madeline survived and swore she'd been faithful to her husband. Farfetched as it may be to hear, the bullet hit the brooch that she was wearing, and it saved her life. When she got shot, she fainted dead away, making it seem she had been killed. They say she had a mighty nasty bruise, and if her husband had not used a small-caliber pistol, it would have seriously wounded her. But within a few days, she was up and virtually back to normal.

"Feeling a debt of gratitude for indirectly saving her life by gifting her with the brooch that stopped the bullet, Madeline announced that she would travel directly to Lafitte's Maison Rouge mansion in Galveston to thank him personally. She did so, and she never returned to her prior home.

"Now, as I've heard it shared by more than one old-timer, one day Lafitte and Madeline sailed away with a ship loaded with treasure.

"What happened after that is left to speculation and rumor. They're those who believe they were lost at sea, but knowing Lafitte, I highly doubt that.

"Some speculated they settled on an island or found a distant port and took on new identities. Nobody has ever claimed to have seen any of the gold or other treasure, nor did anyone hear any more of the life of Madeline.

"To this day, some believe they have seen that ship on the Gulf of Mexico's horizon, not with a pirate's flag, but with one that has a pelican with three drops of blood on her chest feeding her young."

DAY 9

March 28, 1898
The Texas Road
Calcasieu River
Rapides Parish, Louisiana

We crossed the Calcasieu without incident. I knew the river like the back of my hand. But in the distance was a cowpoke I thought I recognized. He was watering his horse.

I asked Jeremiah if he'd care to take a little ride with me. He agreed, and we approached the cowpoke with our Winchesters out of their scabbards. He almost started to flee until Jeremiah drew a bead on him.

Jeremiah yelled, "Do you want to end up like your padna Scar Bartholomew?"

We tied him up in the big wagon with the calves, for the nearest jail was in Alexandria. We were not far from my home in Babb's Bridge.

I left Elwa in charge and rode home for the night, with the outlaw in tow. Julia Ann met me at the door of our Ole Willis Place.

How excited she was and asked, "Who's your *friend*?"

I told her that we shot this hombre's two sidewinding partners, but he made a getaway amidst all the gunplay. But, by fate, we came across him and got the drop on him.

"He will be sleeping tonight handcuffed to the foot of our iron bed cause he might get loose tied to a tree."

I told the outlaw, "I'd better not hear a sound out of you tonight. If I do, I'll do more than just tie you to a tree."

Jeremiah asked, "How'd you sleep?"

"Like a baby."

"Well, how'd your wife sleep?"

"Not a wink. I can't imagine what kept her awake."

I needed to get back to the herd, so I sent a wire from Forest Hill's telegraph station to the sheriff. They would need to pick him up when we got to Lecompte. I had no time to ride to Alexandria.

NIGHT 9

March 28, 1898
The Texas Road
Spring Creek
Rapides Parish, Louisiana

As we approached the trail's end Jeremiah asked me, "Mr. Willis, a ways back, you mentioned a story about the Texas and Pacific Railway that was for another time. We're almost there. Is that a story you'd be willing to share?"

"Not only willing, but if you're going to work with us, you'll need to know it. First, I want to tell ya, there are those that say there are no honest lawyers. That's simply not true. Don't you believe a word of it. Just last year, I met one in Mississippi and asked him to move to Louisiana so we'd have one. Here's that story."

Indeed, it was one of our last nights on the trail, but the boys didn't seem to have their fill of my recollections, so I indulged them with the story about the railroad.

"In Louisiana, the railroad is responsible for the health and wellbeing of our cattle once they are shipped north. That's the law, and it's a good one cause at the end of the trail, we can ride home and not worry 'bout our herd again. At least, that's what I was led to believe some time ago.

"In the spring of '83 I decided to trail 600 head of longhorn cattle from East Texas to Lecompte. Elwa was just a pup then, all of fifteen, but he'd told me he could rope and ride like one of those Mexican *vaqueros* he'd read 'bout. I'd read those stories, too, and told him, 'Good, cause they say they only dismount for a chance to dance with pretty girls. And since there'll be no pretty girls along the trail, you will have to sleep in your saddle."

☆   ☆   ☆

"The Texas and Pacific Railroad, called the T&P today, had finished a route from Shreveport to New Orleans the previous September. We would no longer need to trail cattle through the treacherous swamp country from East Texas to New Orleans. We never drove a single head on the Opelousas Trail again after the railroad came to Lecompte. From that day forward, we've always driven our cattle on the Beef and Texas roads.

"That year's cattle drive went well. I'd told Elwa he could dismount anytime he wished, pretty girls or not. After we drove the longhorns into the railroad's beef pens, we were eager to get home to a soft bed and our family's loving arms.

"However, to my total shock and dismay, two weeks later, I got word that sixty head of our cattle were dead. The herd was still in the railroad's beef pen cause of the large number of cattle being shipped from the railheads north of Lecompte. Or, at least, that's what they claimed.

"I rode over to investigate the matter. They informed me their lawyers had said the cattle were not their responsibility until they were loaded onto the train. I gave them the most educated response I could muster for their lawyers: "Hogwash." Trust me, a few other words came to mind, but discretion got the better of me.

"I rode straight from there to Alex and hired me a lawyer. He filed a lawsuit, and the judge ruled in my favor."

Jeremiah made a good point. "But, Mr. Willis, was not the judge a lawyer, too? Was he not honest?"

I stood corrected by Jeremiah. I apologized in sackcloth and ashes for falsely accusing all Louisiana lawyers of being dishonest. I was wrong.

"Let me begin again. Did I ever tell ya 'bout the time I was in Mississippi and met two honest lawyers?"

DAY 10

March 29, 1898
Trail's End
The Railroad Cattle Pens
Lecompte, Louisiana

I'd made a promise the day before to the mayor when I was at the telegraph station in Forest Hill. He saw me and suggested I drive the longhorns down the main street of Forest Hill. He said the kids would love it, and the not-so-young kids would, too.

As we approached the town, the streets were lined with people. The longhorns were as docile as kittens as we moved through the main street.

Of course, Ethel led the way. She looked as proud as a peacock. I asked Ran to join me as the point cowman. We could hear young boys tell their mothers, "I want to be a cowboy."

Now, the good mayor also suggested that we have a Willis Feast of Celebration after we drove our cattle to the beef pens in Lecompte. We were less than a day away, so I agreed. It would be a wonderful way to say thank you to our cowhands and our neighbors.

No neighbor of ours had ever "accidentally" put the wrong brand on a single head of our cows.

NIGHT 10

March 29, 1898
Trail's End
The Railroad Cattle Pens
Lecompte, Louisiana

"Father, being at the railroad again reminds me of that trip you and mama took to New Orleans," Elwa said.

"I suppose the others might want to know what you're talking 'bout. I can tell ya it was just six years ago on a hot August night in 1892. Your mother wanted to see N'Orleans. Being fetched up in Jackson Parish, N'Orleans was like a different country to her. I told her it would be that way even if she were from Baton Rouge.

"She'd never ridden a train either, so we boarded the Texas and Pacific Railway just across the tracks from here. I hid $2,000 on me just in case I was able to buy a few prized bulls at auction while we were there. I didn't trust the train's safe, and banks even less.

"After dinner in a fancy dining car, we watched with amazement the abundance of wildlife along the tracks. The old plantations reminded me of a time we'd never know again.

"It was in the dining car that we met a school teacher named Eugene Bunch. Julia Ann told him all about our Eugene. He got tears in his eyes. He was a Southern gentleman, except maybe when he found out I was a cowman and asked, 'You must be wealthy?' Now, boys, we have always been taught not to talk about such things and never do anything that was a show of wealth, so I replied, 'Not hardly, we're just trying to feed our children and pay half the rent.'

"He laughed and excused himself so fast you'd thought the train was on fire. Julia Ann said, 'Now Daniel, that's how I hope our boys turn out. What a polite Christian gentleman.'

"Then suddenly the train came to an abrupt stop when a dozen or so men appeared on the tracks heavily armed. As they boarded, Mr. Bunch stood and introduced himself as Captain J. F. Gerard to the passengers. Your mother looked like she'd just heard a dog talk. He then politely tipped his hat to the ladies, while refusing to take their purses, and he was very polite while taking all the men's wallets, all except mine. When he got to me, he told his gang, 'Don't waste your time here; he doesn't even have enough to pay half his rent.'

"I later heard he managed to steal $78 from the other passengers. That ended our trip, for your mother said, 'I've seen enough, take me home.' I knew I needed to find a fast horse with a buggy or a train headed in the opposite direction.

"I couldn't help but say, 'He was such a polite Christian gentleman. I hope our boys turn out that way.'

"She did not find the humor in my words, but after a brief hesitation, said, 'Daniel, do you have any idea how it feels to be thrown off a moving train?' I could see that twinkle in her eyes, which always meant it's all right. Still, why press my luck?

"A few weeks later, Pinkerton detectives tracked Bunch to a swamp near Franklin, Louisiana, and shot him dead along with all his gang. Hardly worth seventy-eight bucks, if you ask me.

DAY 11

March 30, 1898
The Willis Feast of Celebration
The Ole Willis Place
Daniel and Julia Ann Willis's Home on Barber Creek
Babb's Bridge, Louisiana

We had a huge bonfire to illuminate the celebration and take the chill out of the air. I also had decided to have fireworks. The kids were very excited. I was, too. You might say it was a day of *explosive excitement*, not cause of the fireworks, though. At least not the kind I lit with a piece of kindling from our bonfire.

The spark to these fireworks was kindled all the way back when I married Julia Ann. After we got married, my brothers started to marry Julia Ann's sisters. Not one, not two, but three of them. Four Willis brothers, in all, married to four Graham sisters.

The problem arose when my brother Matthew decided to make it five. He set out to win Julia Ann's youngest sister Lucy Ruth Graham's affection.

However, she made it clear that someone else had declared their affection for her, and she was pleased by that. She told Matthew, "Sorry, but no. I'm in love with James Moore."

Now, that was all right with Matthew. He then got word from one of the other sisters that what she told him was not the actual reason. She confided that Lucy had told the entire Graham clan that Matthew was just too ugly to marry.

That was all right with Matthew, too—until he commandeered a bottle of *Sweet Lucy*, no pun intended. The white lightning could peel the paint off Rooster's chuck wagon. If that was not enough, Lucy had asked our father if he would marry her and Mr. Moore. He had agreed!

Now the stage was set for the most exciting Willis Feast of Celebration ever. No sooner than father had said grace than here came Matthew on his horse hooping and hollering words that I've chosen to forget. I figured, *Let him ride through and sleep it off down on Barber Creek*, but he wasn't done. He had noticed Lucy and James's table on his first ride through.

Here he came again! Julia Ann cried out, "Do something, Daniel."

So, I did. Now grant it, I was a tad bit slower than I used to be when I could jump a four-rail fence with a bail of cotton on my back. But, I wasn't thinking 'bout that as I jumped on the back of the closest horse and rode like I was eighteen again. I grabbed Matthew's horse's bridle and turned the mare in a tight circle.

The circle was too tight for Matthew. He landed face down in a chocolate cake Lucy had baked. I figured it would be the last piece of cake he'd ever have of hers, so I told him, "You might as well eat the rest." He thanked her and told her he preferred her sisters' cakes, though. She did not get the gist of his remarks.

I felt at least the fireworks were over. Then I saw father. His opinion of anything more potent than dark roast Louisiana coffee was somewhere in the vicinity of the Devil, himself, playing the *Wedding March*, on Ran's fiddle.

I walked with Matthew down to the edge of Barber Creek to wash him up a little. When he cried, my heart broke for him, but I knew he'd someday meet another who would catch his fancy, albeit I also knew it would never be one of the Graham sisters, not even a cousin, not even a distant cousin. In fact, he might consider a different Parish where there were no Grahams.

I told him, "It's just puppy love."

He responded, "It's real to this puppy!"

What the healing hands of time could not mend, eventually the arms of another did.

Matthew never drank alcohol or ate chocolate cake again. At least not face down.

☆   ☆   ☆

"A Rider is coming on a magnificent steed,
a white horse, I'm told.

"He knows all the brands and earmarks,
for you see, He owns the cattle on a thousand hills.

"He will separate the goats from His sheep.

"If you listen carefully, you might even hear hoofbeats,
for you see He's mounted even as I speak.

"Not even a Louisiana Wind can change the fact that
He's coming—*coming again!*"

—*Daniel Hubbard Willis, Jr.* 1900

EPILOGUE

April 15, 1900
Easter Sunday
On Barber Creek
Babb's Bridge, Louisiana

Excerpted from Randall Lee "Ran" Willis's Diary

Father had taught me much about being a cowman, and about life, too. He encouraged me to write it all down on the Big Chief writing tablets he'd bought me. He said it was so that, "Those who come after us might not make the same mistakes."

I heard tell the crappie were biting down on Cocodrie Lake. But, this being Easter, they'd just have to wait to jump into my boat. Our Dominicker rooster's crowing reminded me I should start loading the wagon for church. I was genuinely excited, for Father had been asked to speak that day at Amiable Baptist. Father was frail but up to the task. There would be a big supper on the grounds after church.

I'd told Mama we should have Easter eggs. A friend of mine from Spring Hill Academy told me all about them.

He said, "When my folks lived in Germany, they decorated eggs at Easter."

Mama replied, "That will never catch on here. The hens would revolt, and me, too."

"Mama, they hid them, too."

She looked puzzled and asked, "Why in the world would they do that? Were they that ugly?"

"Not to worry, Mama, a rabbit then helps them find the eggs."

"Son, I'm going down to that school tomorrow to see if they've been into the cooking sherry."

I quickly changed the conversation. "Mama, what did you bake for the supper on the grounds?"

"Apple pie, of course. And, your father has butchered a hog, so we're taking a smoked ham from our smokehouse, too. You know, son, Baptists love to eat. Some I know are digging their grave with a fork."

Mother then added, "You know your Grandpa Daniel, Sr. was the pastor there for many years. He died a year and a week to the day after you were born.

"He was cut from the same cloth as his Grandfather, Joseph Willis, and even planted more churches than he did. He was the best man I ever knew. It was his words of wisdom from the Book that gave me the strength to go on after the deaths of your brother and sisters."

As our wagon rolled down the red dirt road, I could see the church steeple pointing toward Heaven. It would forever remind me of Father's words that day. As the folks gathered, father arose and slowly walked to the front of the crowd. Elwa held his arm to steady him. He spoke with a frail voice.

"Now, friends, as you know, I'm no preacher. But, I've been asked to speak a few words of my father, who is buried a few yards from here.

"But, then again, he's not there. Now, some of ya might be thinking that's not true. You might say, I was at his funeral. Others of you saw him in his open casket. A few of you helped lower his pine box in the ground, shoveled dirt on it, too.

"I can only explain why I believe that by using his own words about the loss of his Preacher. If you don't mind, I'll read them.

"'It was a sad day—the most tragic day ever, for you see our Country Preacher had died.

"I trusted him. I'd staked my future on him. But now he was extinguished like a flickering candle in the wind. The young Preacher's enemies, and there were many, had won.

"Success had eluded him, for you see, he didn't have enough money even for a grave, much less a marker. Fortunately, a kind soul gave him one. The womenfolk buried him on a Friday, for you see none of the men could be found, save one.

"'Oh, yes, he'd made some promises, big ones too. The kind no man could keep. But, he now had faded as the autumn colors.

"As victors, his enemies would surely exact revenge on his friends, so they hid like rabbits in a hole. One broke his promise and denied him. Still, another betrayed him. Many others even hated him. He was rejected by the religious folk of that day.

"'The women didn't seem to be afraid though, and three days later went to the cemetery to tend to him. But, he was not there, for you see the Country Preacher had risen, just as He said he would.

"One of the women told his followers He was alive. After seeing all He'd done, one of his friends even doubted that.'

"Today, many doubt that story, too, but I don't. Now, my friends, that's why I know my father is not in that grave cross the road. Because if it could not hold that Country Preacher, it cannot hold my father, or me one day in the not so distant future. He had taken death, the grave, and even Hell captive.

"I have but three words to say. They're the three greatest words ever spoken: 'He is risen.'"

As father ended his words, mother stood and began to sing, "Low in the grave he lay, Jesus my Savior."

We all joined in, "Up from the grave he arose; with a mighty triumph o'er his foes. He arose a victor from the dark domain, and he lives forever, with his saints to reign.

"He arose! He arose!

"Hallelujah! Christ arose!"

Yes, I was the first in line for Mama's apple pie—but first, I accepted the truth of my father's words when I walked to the front of that church and knelt and asked Christ to come into my life and take over.

For, you see, he arose for me, too, and you, also!

Suddenly watching paint dry was exciting to me....

Louisiana Wind's Characters

Daniel Hubbard Willis, Jr.–Great-Grandson of Reverend Joseph Willis. Cowman, Spring Hill, Rapides Parish, Constable, and Confederate veteran. He fought in many of the Civil War's great battles, including Shiloh, Bull Run, Perryville, Murfreesboro, Missionary Ridge, and Chickamauga.

An excerpt from his obituary in the *Alexandria Town Talk*, on June 23, 1900, stated:

"He participated in all the hard battles of that army and for bravery, soldierly bearing, discipline and devotion to duty, he was unexcelled in his entire Brigade. He was made Orderly Sergeant of his Company at an early period of the war. It has always been said by his surviving comrades that when any particularly dangerous service was required, such as scouting parties to ascertain the position and movements of the enemy, he was always selected for the place, and never hesitated to go, let the danger be what it may.

"He was for a long time connected with the famous Washington Artillery, and at the battle of Chickamauga so many horses of the battery to which he was attached were killed that they had to pull the guns off the field by hand to keep them from falling in the hands of the enemy.

"He was paroled at Meridian, Miss., in May of 1865, and brought home with him a copy of General Gibson's farewell address to his soldiers and of him it can be truly said that through the remaining years of his life he followed the advice then given by his beloved commander. His love for the Southern cause, and for the men who wore the gray, was not dimmed by years, but he lived and died firmly convinced of the justice of the cause for which the South poured out so much of her best blood and treasure.

"Before death he expressed a wish that he might see his children who were at home, especially Randall L., his baby boy, whom he had named in honor of his beloved Brigadier General, Randall Lee Gibson. He also requested that his Confederate badge be pinned on his breast and buried with him."

The writer of his obituary added, "During an intimate acquaintance, covering a period of twenty-five years, the writer never heard a vulgar or profane word pass his lips."

He was the first of four Willis brothers to marry four Graham sisters. He married Julia Ann Graham on January 5, 1867. He affectingly called her Julieann.

When he asked her father, Robert Graham, for her hand in marriage, he responded, "Can you feed her son?"

Daniel replied, "I have a horse, a milk cow, a barrel of corn, and a barrel of molasses."

Robert exclaimed, "My goodness, son, you have enough to marry several of my daughters." They were married at Robert's home, near Forest Hill, Louisiana, on Barber Creek.

Just a year after their marriage, on January 16, 1868, Daniel sold Robert Graham, 119 acres, "In the fork of Barber Creek," for $350. It was a sum that would have been almost a year's wages at the time.

When Daniel died in 1900, he left Julia Ann $35,000 in gold (the equivalent of $980,000 today), a home, land, and the woods full of cows, hogs, and horses on Barber Creek. She lived thirty-six years after his death. She never remarried and provided for her family, even though the Great Depression. Daniel had made good his promise to feed Julia Ann—and then some.

After being made Constable of the Spring Hill area, in Rapides Parish, Julia Ann often spoke of the time Daniel captured an outlaw from Texas hiding out in Louisiana's piney woods. She said it was too late to make the trip on horseback to the jail in Alexandria.

Therefore Daniel handcuffed the outlaw to the foot of their bed for the overnight stay. He then told the outlaw, "You better not make a sound."

Julia Ann added, "Daniel slept soundly, but I didn't sleep a wink all night."

He was a very successful rancher. He and his sons would buy cattle in East Texas for $4 per head and then drive them to the railroad's beef pens at Lecompte. They were then shipped by rail to the northern railheads to fetch $40 and more per head.

Once, on a cattle drive from Texas, in 1898, the cattle stampeded in the woods. His youngest son Randall Lee Willis, who was only twelve at the time and riding drag, thought his father had been killed. But then he saw his father's substantial white hat waving high in the air, in front of the cattle. He was the author's great-grandfather.

Reverend Daniel Hubbard Willis, Sr.–Great-Grandson of Reverend Joseph Willis and father of Daniel Hubbard Willis, Jr. He established more churches than Joseph Willis did. He is buried, along with his wife Anna Slaughter Willis, in the Amiable Baptist Church Cemetery. He was blind for the last twenty-two years of his life. His daughter would read the scriptures, and he would preach. He was the author's 2nd great-grandfather.

Reverend Joseph Willis–Preached the first evangelical sermon west of the Mississippi River in 1798. He was born into slavery. His mother was a Cherokee slave, and his father a wealthy English plantation owner in Bladen County, North Carolina. Joseph swam the mighty Mississippi River at Natchez, at the peril of his own life, riding a mule! He was the author's 4th great-grandfather.

Julia Ann Graham Willis–Wife of Daniel Hubbard Willis, Jr. Daughter of Robert and Ruth Graham. She would often read her red-lettered Bible, eat an orange, including the peel. When she looked at Daniel's Civil War photo, tears would come to her eyes.

When asked by her grandchildren about eating orange peels, she replied, "I don't know for sure, but I think they're good for you." She was bitten by a ground rattler, at age seventy-five, and survived with home remedies. She swam in Barber Creek twice a day until age ninety. She said that was what had prolonged her life. All her children and grandchildren loved to go swimming with her.

According to her granddaughter Ilie Close, "She always had food cooked for family and friends. There were lots of blackberries, huckleberries, and fruit of all kinds for good pies.

"She was raised as a Methodist but later joined the Baptist Church and was a devoted Christian. We use to joke she didn't think there would be anyone but Baptists in Heaven. Her hobby was making quilts, and she kept the family supplied with her handiwork."
She was the author's great-grandmother.

193

Randall Lee "Ran" Willis–Youngest child of Daniel Hubbard Willis, Jr. and Julia Ann Graham Willis. He was named after General Randall Lee Gibson. He married Lillie Gertrude Hanks. He learned to play the fiddle, by ear, after his father bought him one in East Texas on a cattle drive. He was known to be the best musician in the area. He was the author's grandfather, whom he was named after.

Henry Elwa Willis–Eldest son of Daniel Hubbard Willis, Jr. and Julia Ann Graham Willis. He is buried in the Paul Cemetery between Forest Hill and Lecompte, Louisiana. He named one of his eight children Kit Carson Willis after the famous frontiersman Kit Carson. He was the author's great-uncle.

Daniel Oscar Willis, M.D.–Son of Daniel Hubbard Willis, Jr. and Julia Ann Graham Willis. His father died at his home in Leesville while being treated for Bright's Disease, known as Kidney Disease today. He began his medical practice in 1904 and was the first medical doctor in Vernon Parish.

He owned the first automobile in the Parish. He served in United States Army Medical Corps in World War I. He owned the Hotel Leesville. After being slandered by a young lawyer in a trial, he bodily removed the lawyer from the man's room at the Hotel Leesville and then threw him into the street. The young lawyer's name was Huey P. Long. Daniel Oscar Willis was the author's great-uncle.

Ella Willis–Wife of Daniel Oscar Willis, M.D. Born Ella Elizabeth Lamberth.

Robert Kenneth Willis, Sr.–Son of Daniel Hubbard Willis, Jr. and Julia Ann Graham Willis. His wife Eulah (aka Eula) Rosalie Hilburn died February 6, 1919, at age thirty-four, during the influenza pandemic of 1918-1919. More people died in the plague than did in World War I.

His son Robert Kenneth Willis, Jr. was the first casualty from Rapides Parish in World War II. He's entombed in the *USS Arizona* at the bottom of Pearl Harbor. Robert Kenneth Willis, Sr. was the author's great-uncle.

Eulah (aka Eula) Rosalie Hilburn–Wife of Robert Kenneth Willis, Sr. Died February 6, 1919, at the age of thirty-four in the influenza pandemic of 1918-1919. She was recognized as extremely beautiful by everyone.

David Eugene Willis–Son of Daniel Hubbard Willis, Jr. and Julia Ann Graham Willis. He died of appendicitis at the age of eight. He is buried in the Graham Cemetery near Forest Hill. He was the author's great-uncle.

Stella and Corine Willis–Infant children of Daniel Hubbard Willis, Jr. and Julia Ann Graham Willis. Stella lived for 111 days and Corine for nine days. They are buried in the Graham Cemetery near Forest Hill. They were the author's great-aunts.

Lillie Gertrude Hanks–Wife of Randall Lee "Ran" Willis. They married on January 11, 1914. She was sixteen, and he was twenty-seven. They lived in the Ole Willis Place near Longleaf, Louisiana, on Barber Creek.

They had three sons: Howard, Herman, and Julian (the author's father), Willis. She and her three sons are buried next to each other in Butters Cemetery near Forest Hill, Louisiana.

She was the author's sainted grandmother and the wellspring of many of his stories.

Mary Stark Hanks–Mother of Lillie Gertrude Hanks Willis. She traveled with her parents John and Celina Marie Deroussel Stark, by covered wagon to Branch, Louisiana. After six children's birth and the premature death of her first husband, Charles Oliver, she married Arthur Allen Hanks. He was seventeen years younger than her.

Arthur Allen Hanks and Mary Stark Hanks owned a meat market in Lecompte, Louisiana. Their log home was located right in the middle of where IH 49 is today (approximately 500 feet south of Highway 112) near Lecompte.

They had five children, including Lillie Gertrude Hanks Willis. Arthur Allen Hanks disappeared with another woman and abandoned Mary Stark Hanks and their children. She was the author's maternal great-grandmother.

Arthur Allen Hanks–Husband of Mary Stark Hanks. He was seventeen years younger than her and the father of Lillie Gertrude Hanks.

He deserted Mary Stark Hanks and their five children for a twenty-three-year-old woman named Gertrude G. Jenkins. There was a forty-year age difference between his first wife, Mary Stark Hanks, and his second wife, Gertrude G. Jenkins.

They disappeared and fled to the Indian Territory and lived near Quay and Yale, Oklahoma.

He is buried in the Lawson Cemetery north of Yale, Oklahoma, in an unmarked grave. He was the author's maternal great-grandfather.

Jeremiah and Jacob Stark–Based upon Mary Stark Hank's brothers Rufus and Thomas Stark. Their stories in this book are purely fictional. Mary Stark Hank's was the author's maternal great-grandmother and the mother of Lillie Gertrude Hanks.

Matthew Willis–Brother of Daniel Hubbard Willis Jr. He fell in love with Julia Ann Graham Willis's sister Lucy Ruth Graham. She didn't feel the same way. He was the author's great-uncle.

Lucy Ruth Graham–Youngest sister of Julia Ann Graham Willis. She married James Moore. She died at age forty-two and is buried in the Moore Cemetery (aka Brewer Cemetery) near Forest Hill. The cemetery was located near Spring Hill Baptist Church. She was the author's great-aunt.

Boss Man Jake–Based upon Julian "Jake" Willis. He was the author's father. See Appendix D "My Father and Me" at the end of this book for more information on him.

Jimbo–Inspired by Randy Willis's three sons: Aaron Willis, Joshua Willis, and Adam Willis. Their strength of character has been demonstrated many times in how they treat people who can do nothing for them. They inspired the responses of the character Jimbo in three of the author's novels.

William Graham–Son of Robert and Ruth Graham and brother of Julia Ann Graham. His gravestone, in Butters Cemetery, near Forest Hill, has KKK inscribed on it. He was the author's great-uncle.

Gerald Duke–A cowboy's cowboy. He was known as Jerry Duke. His last horse was named Majestic. As boys, Jerry and the author would work as a team, roping, branding, and herding cattle. He was the author's half-brother.

Jim Bowie–Famous for his knife as well as fighting to defend the Alamo. He was a slave trader and a neighbor of Joseph Willis near Bayou Chicot, Louisiana.

Charlie Goodnight–The best-known rancher in Texas history. Historian J. Frank Dobie wrote, "Goodnight approached greatness more nearly than any other cowman of history."

Richard King–Riverman, steamboat entrepreneur, livestock capitalist, and founder of the King Ranch. Some believe his ghost wanders the halls of the Menger Hotel in San Antonio.

Ozeme Carriere–Leader of the most notorious band of Jayhawkers in Louisiana during the Civil War.

General Randall Lee Gibson– He served as a brigadier general in the Confederate States Army and as president of Tulane University administrators. He was a member of the House of Representatives and U.S. Senator from Louisiana. The author's grandfather, Randall Lee Willis, was named after him by his father, Daniel Hubbard Willis, Jr, after fighting in the Civil War under his command. The author was named after his grandfather Randall Lee Willis.

General Nathaniel Banks–Union general in the Civil War. After occupying Alexandria, he advanced up the Red River only to be halted by Confederate forces. In retreat, Banks and his men burned ninety percent of Alexandria.

Shanghai Pierce–One of the most colorful cattlemen in early Texas history. He trailed cattle to Louisiana in 1855. In 1900, Pierce lost more than $1.25 million in the Galveston hurricane. He died three months later. The Pierce estate imported Brahman cattle from India, which furnished Texas with the base stock from which large herds of Brahmans have grown.

Henry Warmoth–Governor of Louisiana, was widely considered a "carpetbagger," a northerner who moved to the South after the Civil War.

Jean Lafitte–French-American pirate and privateer in the Gulf of Mexico in the early 19th century. He supplied men, weapons, and his knowledge of the region during the battle of New Orleans, which helped General Andrew Jackson secure an overwhelming victory.

Captain J. F. Gerard–A school teacher in Louisiana, turned bandit.

Appendix A

The Wallfield Plantation in 1841
&
William Prince Ford, Solomon Northup, and James Bowie's relationship with Joseph Willis

As a child, Randy Willis lived near Longleaf, Louisiana, and Barber Creek.

As a teenager, he would work cows with his family on the open range, owned by lumber companies. Nine generations of his family have lived near Longleaf and Forest Hill, beginning with his 4th great-grandfather—Joseph Willis (1758-1854).

Randy would often ride his horse through his family's neighboring property on Hurricane Creek's banks between Butters Cemetery Road and Blue Lake Road near present-day Guillory Road, once William Prince Ford's Wallfield Plantation.

During that time, Randy Willis did not realize the significance of his ancestor Joseph Willis's connection to James Bowie, William Prince Ford, and his slave Solomon Northup.

After writing the biography of Joseph Willis, *The Apostle to the Opelousas*, Randy Willis got the idea for writing *Destiny*, *Twice a Slave, Louisiana Wind, Three Winds Blowing, Beckoning Candle*, and the play *Twice a Slave* from his friend and fellow historian Dr. Sue Eakin.

After reading an article that revealed Randy Willis had obtained the Spring Hill Baptist Church minutes, Dr. Eakin contacted him. The minutes had much information on two of its founders: Joseph Willis and William Prince Ford.

In 1798, Joseph preached the first Gospel sermon by an Evangelical west of the Mississippi River. Forty-three years later, he would establish his last church at age 83—Spring Hill Baptist. It would change American history—as far away as Hollywood.

A descendant of Spring Hill Baptist Church's last church clerk (in the late 1800s) refused to let anyone even read the minutes. When Randy Willis told his mother this during a casual conversation, she asked him, "What is her name?"

When Randy responded, his mother said, "She was my best friend at Glenmora High School." Randy and his mother soon drove to Lake Charles and acquired the minutes.

Ford bought the slave Solomon Northup on June 23, 1841, in New Orleans. He immediately brought him to his Wallfield Plantation near Forest Hill, Louisiana.

Just forty-six days later, Joseph Willis and William Prince Ford founded Spring Hill Baptist Church, August 8, 1841, near Wallfield Plantation.

The church was located between present-day Brewers Road and Jouette Road near Hurricane Creek. The church moved from one side of Hurricane Creek to the other after receiving a donation of land. The Brewer, aka Moore Cemetery, is near where the church stood.

Ford's slaves attended the church too, which was the custom in pre-Civil War Louisiana, but not during the Reconstruction era after the war.

One of the slaves, Judy, is listed as one of the church's sixteen founding members in the church's minutes. This fact was unprecedented in pre-Civil War Louisiana.

The minutes list many slaves by first name only.

Solomon Northup gave an account of Ford reading scripture to his slaves every Sunday in his book *Twelve Years a Slave*. William Prince Ford also allowed his slaves to own Bibles, which was unlawful.

Wallfield Plantation was located on Hurricane Creek, 1/4 mile east of present-day Forest Hill, Louisiana, on Guillory Road. It was on the crest of a hill, on the Texas Road that ran alongside a ridge.

William Prince Ford (1803-1866) built Wallfield Plantation in 1836. Land records show Ford purchased 558 acres in central Louisiana between 1836 and 1859.

Northup called this area, in his book *Twelve Years a Slave*, "The Great Piney Woods."

Northup refers to Ford as a model master saying, "Fortunate was the slave who came to his possession. Were all men such as he, slavery would be deprived of more than half its bitterness."

Solomon Northrup also wrote of Ford, "There never was a more kind, noble, candid, Christian man than William Ford."

Ford's wife during this time was Martha Tanner Ford. She was the sister of Peter Tanner. Both were founding members of Spring Hill Baptist Church. Martha Tanner Ford died in 1849.

Solomon Northup described Ford's Wallfield Plantation as "two stories high, with a piazza [porch] in front." The term piazza was not used in this area; therefore, it was probably added by Solomon Northup's ghostwriter.

Also on the grounds was a log kitchen, poultry house, corncribs, and several slave cabins. Northup mentions peach, orange, and pomegranate trees.

Northup lived at the plantation while working at Ford's lumber mill, north of Wallfield Plantation, until a 60% share in him was sold to John M. Tibeats in the winter of 1842. Ford's 40% share would later save Northup's life.

This remaining 40% was later conveyed to the cruel overseer and small plantation owner, Edwin Epps, on April 9, 1843, along with Tibeats' interest.

William Prince Ford was also the headmaster of Spring Creek Academy (later moved and renamed Spring Hill Academy). Ford's children and Joseph Willis's grandchildren attended school together at Spring Creek Academy.

Spring Hill Baptist Church and Spring Creek Academy were walking distance to Ford's Wallfield Plantation.

According to historian W.E. Paxton, in 1841, Joseph Willis entrusted his diary to his protégé, William Prince Ford.

Notes from the diary were arranged into a manuscript and later copied by Paxton, in 1858, for his book *A History of the Baptist of Louisiana, from the Earliest Times to the Present*, (1888). Paxton admits most of his facts concerning Louisiana Baptists are from Joseph Willis's diary and Louisiana Association Minutes.

William Prince Ford was not a Baptist preacher when he purchased Solomon Northup and the slave Eliza, a.k.a. Dradey, in 1841, like many books, articles, blogs, and the movie *12 Years a Slave* have portrayed.

The first part of the Spring Hill Baptist Church minutes is written in Ford's handwriting since he was the first church secretary and the first church clerk. The minutes reveal that on July 7, 1842, Ford was elected deacon. On December 11, 1842, Ford became the church treasurer.

It was not until February 10, 1844, that Ford was ordained as a Baptist preacher. A year later, on April 12, 1845, Ford was excommunicated for "communing with the Campbellite Church at Cheneyville." But, Ford's later writings reveal that he remained close friends with his mentor, Joseph Willis.

Dr. Sue Eakin asked Randy Willis if he would help her with her research on William Prince Ford. He also lectured in her history classes, at Louisiana State University at Alexandria, on the subject.

Dr. Eakin wrote Randy Willis on March 7, 1984, "We had a wonderful experience dramatizing Northup, and I think there could be a musical play on Joseph Willis. It seems to me it gets the message across far more quickly than routinely written material."

She added, "A fictional novel based upon Joseph Willis's life would be more interesting to the general public than a biography and would reach a greater audience."

Dr. Eakin is best known for documenting, annotating, and reviving interest in Solomon Northup's 1853 book *Twelve Years a Slave.*

At the age of eighteen, she rediscovered a long-forgotten copy of Solomon Northup's book on the shelves of a bookstore, near the LSU campus, in Baton Rouge. The bookstore owner sold it to her for only 25 cents.

In 2013, *12 Years a Slave* won the Academy Award for Best Picture.

"In his acceptance speech for the honor, director Steve McQueen thanked Dr. Eakin: "I'd like to thank this amazing historian, Sue Eakin, whose life, she gave her life's work to preserving Solomon's book."

Before all of this, Jim Bowie was a neighbor of Joseph Willis when they lived near Bayou Chicot.

Jim's brother, Rezin Bowie, was a neighbor to Joseph's eldest son Agerton Willis and his eldest grandson, Rev. Daniel Hubbard Willis Sr., for four years (1824-1827) in the village of Bayou Boeuf. The name changed to Holmesville in 1834. It is located near present-day Eola.

At Holmesville, on Bayou Boeuf, Edwin Epps enslaved Solomon Northup for almost ten years of his twelve-year indenture.

It was also here that Joseph Willis's eldest son and Randy Willis's 3rd great-grandfather Agerton Willis met and married Sophie Story.

Sophie Story was an Irish orphan brought from Tennessee to Holmesville (present-day Eola), Louisiana, by a Mr. Park. Agerton and Sophie's eldest child Daniel Hubbard Willis Sr., was the first to follow his grandfather Joseph Willis into the ministry and planted more churches than he did.

Bowie was famous for his knife at the Sandbar Fight (1827) and fighting and dying to defend the Alamo (1836).

Appendix B

Babb's Bridge and The Ole Willis Place
near present-day Longleaf, Louisiana

On the banks of Spring Creek, Babb's Bridge was the home of Joseph Willis in 1828, although it was not known by any name then, other than Joseph Willis's home.

The Ole Willis Place and Babb's Bridge were located three miles, as the crow flies, from Amiable Baptist Church (established by Joseph Willis, in 1828) and a little over a mile from present-day Longleaf, Louisiana. Longleaf is less than three miles from Forest Hill.

Babb's Bridge was a community of a few stores and homes. A pine bridge spanned Spring Creek (the headwaters to Cocodrie Lake) in the late 19th century and early 20th century.

It had a post office named Lucky Hit and a schoolhouse called Spring Creek Academy (later moved and renamed Spring Hill Academy). The author's grandfather, Randall Lee Willis, attended school there.

Not long ago, the water was so clear that you could read a book at its bottom.

Catharine Cole wrote, in 1892, in *Louisiana Voyages: The Travel Writings of Catharine Cole*, "There is a little thirty-year-old town by the name of Babb's Bridge. The bridge, Babb's Bridge you know is an affair of scented pine planks that steeply roof over a section of the lovely creek, so clear, so pure, that if one cast a newspaper on its shingly bottom I quite believe one could read its pages through the spectacles of the water."

She added, "I was told of an orchard at this place where the pears weigh a pound each." And, she said, "We put by the ponies at Babb's Bridge, and I went by invitation to the schoolhouse."

The site of the long-extinct community of Babb's Bridge is just off Highway 165, on Spring Creek, near Longleaf, Louisiana.

Babb's Bridge can best be found by traveling Boy Scout Road off Highway 165, three-fourths of a mile to a pipeline right-a-way on the left. Turn left on pipeline right-a-way and drive or walk down to the banks of Spring Creek, and you will be where the community and bridge once was.

☆　　☆　　☆

Daniel Hubbard Willis Jr.'s home, known as the Ole Willis Place, was located on Barber Creek.

The Ole Willis Place, near Babb's Bridge and present-day Longleaf, was Joseph Willis's great-grandson Daniel Hubbard Willis Jr. and his wife Julia Ann Graham Willis's home until she died in 1936. Daniel Hubbard Willis Jr. built the house soon after the Civil War.

After Julia Ann Graham Willis's death, it became her youngest son's home and the author's grandfather Randall Lee Willis and grandmother, Lillie Hanks Willis, until after World War II.

Today, there are a vast gravel pit and dunes next to where the house once stood. It was located on present-day John Meyers Road (aka Willis Gunter Road) near Boy Scout Road. Barber Creek flows into Spring Creek near the old community of Babb's Bridge and present-day Longleaf.

To find the location, drive past the pipeline right-a-way on Boy Scout Road, turn right onto John Meyers Road (aka Willis Gunter Road).

The Ole Willis Place was located just a few hundred yards from Boy Scout Road at the top of the first hill on the right. Barber Creek has been moved somewhat due to the excavation of the gravel pit.

In 1996, two Louisiana environmental groups, the Sierra Club and Louisiana Environmental Action Network, filed a lawsuit, in Federal Court, against the United States Environmental Protection Agency (EPA) to stop the destruction of Barber Creek. The environmental groups won, but the damage had been done.

☆ ☆ ☆

The Story of Joseph Willis
His biography by Randy Willis

Preface

My family's story in America does not begin here. It started in England in 1575. That year Nathaniel Willis was born in Chettle, Dorsetshire, a county in South West England, on the English Channel coast. The county borders another county to the west that contains my deep Willis roots, Devonshire. Why would my ancestors leave their homeland, England, for an unknown land fraught with danger? The answer was religious persecution!

In 1620 a small group of Separatists would flee England via Plymouth Sound, situated between the rivers Plym to the east and Tamar to the west, in Devonshire. Besides fleeing religious persecution and searching for a place to worship, they wanted greater opportunities.

The *Mayflower* was the aging ship that transported them. They sailed from Plymouth, on the southern coast of England, bound for the New World, seeking their new Plymouth. There were only 102 passengers and a crew of about thirty aboard the tiny 110' ship. They found their new home and named it Plymouth Colony. They became known as the Pilgrims. Five died during the voyage, and another forty-five of the 102 immigrants died the first winter. There, they signed the Mayflower Compact, which established a rudimentary form of democracy.

Nathaniel later moved to London, where his son John Willis was born in 1606, only fourteen years before the historic *Mayflower* voyage. Fifteen years after that voyage, at age 29, John may have sailed for St. Christopher (a.k.a. St. Kitts) in the West Indies on April 3, 1635, on the ship *Paul* from Gravesend. But there is no record the vessel stopped in New England.

Gravesend is an ancient town in northwest Kent situated on the south bank of the Thames River near London. The *Paul* was the ship John sailed on en route to the New World and carrying the dreams that would be passed to subsequent generations, including myself, he may have barely escaped death. The Great Colonial Hurricane was in August of 1635. It was the most intense hurricane to hit New England since European colonization. If John had sailed a month or two later, he might not have made it to America, and this story, along with his dreams, would have ended at the bottom of the Atlantic Ocean.

Nevertheless, John Willis first appears in America in Plymouth Colony, Massachusetts, in 1635, when his son John Willis, Jr. was born. He appeared again in Duxbury, in 1637, when he married Elizabeth Hodgkins Palmer, on January 2, 1637. She was the widow of William Palmer, Jr. Duxbury was first settled in 1632 by people from Plymouth Colony and set off from that town in 1637.

John Willis (a.k.a. Deacon John Willis) was later the first deacon in Plymouth Church. Reverend James Keith was the first settled minister in the area. The church parsonage, sometimes called the Keith House, was built for him. It is preserved and maintained by the Old Bridgewater Historical Society (OBHS) in West Bridgewater, Massachusetts. It is the oldest parsonage in America.

John also had brothers who were immigrants to the Plymouth Colony area. They were: Nathaniel Willis, Lawrence Willis, Jonathan Willis, and Francis Willis.

The population was about 400 in the 1630s. John Willis would have known everyone in the Plymouth Colony area, especially its Governor, William Bradford, the English Separatist leader of the settlers there. William was Governor of Plymouth Colony when John arrived in 1635. John Willis held offices in Duxbury in 1637 and at Bridgewater in the 1650s. Bridgewater was created on June 3, 1656, from Duxbury, in Plymouth Colony. In 1648, John was a juror at the murder trial of Alice Bishope, who was hanged for killing her daughter, Martha Clarke.

In 1623, Governor William Bradford proclaimed November 29, as a time for pilgrims, along with their Native American friends, to gather and give thanks. His proclamation contained these words:

"Thanksgiving to ye Almighty God for all His blessings." It would later be known as Thanksgiving.

A century later, John Willis's direct descendant, Joseph Willis, would marry a direct descendant of William Bradford, Rachel Bradford.

I'm the 4th great-grandson of Joseph Willis and Rachel Bradford Willis.

John and Elizabeth Willis had nine children: Sarah, John, Nathaniel, Jonathan, Comfort, Elizabeth, Joseph (1651-1703), Hannah, and Benjamin, Sr. John died August 31, 1693, in Plymouth Colony.

Benjamin Willis, Sr. was born in 1643, in Plymouth Colony, and died there, May 12, 1696. He married Susanna Whitman in 1681 in Bridgewater. Susanna Whitman was born in Devonshire. Benjamin, Sr. and Susanna Willis had six children: Abigail, Elizabeth, Susanna, Thomas, Benjamin, Jr., and Josie. Josie married John Council.

Benjamin Willis, Jr. was born in 1690 and died in 1779

in Bridgewater. Benjamin, Jr. married Mary Leonard in 1719.

Benjamin, Jr. and Mary Willis had five children: Agerton, Daniel, Benjamin, III, George, and Joanna. Joanna married James Council of Isle of Wight County, Virginia, in 1751. James was the son of John Council and Josie Willis Council, and grandson of Hodges Council. Hodges emigrated from Devonshire.

Benjamin, Jr. and Mary Willis's five children would all move to North Carolina. They would become the wealthiest plantation owners in Bladen County, North Carolina, with vast landholdings and many slaves.

One of these five children, Agerton Willis, and a Cherokee slave would have a son. He was born in 1758. He was their only son. As the son of a white man and a Cherokee, he lived as a slave on his own property. He was cheated out of his inheritance by an uncle and rejected by many in the family. He would fight for his freedom and change American history. He was my fourth great-grandfather.

This is his story. His name was Joseph Willis.

His Legacy

Joseph Willis preached the first Gospel sermon by an Evangelical west of the Mississippi River.

He swam the mighty Mississippi River, riding a mule, into the Louisiana Territory before October 1, 1800, the date Napoleon secured the Louisiana Territory from Spain. The Louisiana Territory extended from the Mississippi River to the Rocky Mountains. The territory was vast and mostly unexplored, with many hidden and not-so-hidden dangers.

He was born a Cherokee slave to his father. The obstacles intensified when his family took him to court to deprive him of his inheritance, a battle that involved the state governor. Never daunted, he fought in the Revolutionary War under the most colorful of all the American generals, Francis Marion, "The Swamp Fox." He would soon cross the most hostile country and enter land under a foreign government, while the dreaded Code Noir, the "Black Code," was in effect. In this territory, he preached a message that put him in constant mortal danger. All of this was done under a cloud of racial and religious prejudice of the most dangerous kind. At first, his denomination refused to ordain him because of his race. He lost three wives and several children in the wilderness, but he never wavered in his faith in Christ, nor in his calling to preach the Gospel of the Lord Jesus Christ.

Move to North Carolina

In the early 1750s, Joseph's father, uncles, and aunt moved to North Carolina.

The family traveled by sea and landed down the coast at New Hanover (now named Wilmington), North Carolina. New Hanover had North Carolina's most navigable seaport.

Even though it was not used often for transatlantic trade, this meant the area of the state was easily accessible from all other English settlements along the coast.

Wealthy North Carolina Planters

On December 13, 1754, Agerton purchased 300 acres in New Hanover County (in what is now southeastern Pender County) "on the East Side of a Branch of Long Creek." Pender was not established until 1874. New Hanover included what is now Pender and parts of Brunswick County.

Agerton Willis was taxed on this property the next year, 1755. There were only 362 white people taxed in New Hanover that year. About twenty families owned a significant number of slaves there during that time. Along with others like them in southeastern North Carolina, these families controlled the counties' affairs in which they lived and set the standards of morals and religion. The four Willis brothers and their sister Joanna were part of this small, socially elite group of families.

Between 1755 and 1758, Agerton moved to Bladen County, just to the northeast of Daniel, Benjamin, and Joanna. Joanna's husband, James, had been living there since 1753.

It was in 1758 that Agerton's only son, Joseph Willis, was born. Joseph would someday play a trailblazing role in early Louisiana Baptist history and blaze a path for the Gospel of Jesus Christ that still burns today.

Most of the early Bladen County deeds before 1784 were lost due to a series of fires; thus, we cannot find Agerton's first purchase of land in Bladen County. Nevertheless, a description of the bulk of his lands can be gleaned from later deeds. He purchased 640 acres from his brother Daniel on May 21, 1762, on the Northwest Cape Fear River's west side.

He then bought an additional 2,560 acres between October 1766, and May 1773, on both sides of the Northwest Cape Fear River near Goodman's Swamp. Altogether, Agerton's holdings formed a vast and nearly contiguous extent of land on both sides of the Northwest Cape Fear River, near the current Cumberland County line in present-day northwest Bladen County.

Agerton, Daniel, Benjamin, James, and Joanna were neighbors on the Northwest Cape Fear River. The other brother, George Willis, went first to New Hanover, obtaining a land grant on Widow Creek in 1761 and selling out in 1767. He then moved to Robeson County (formerly part of Bladen County), not far west of the rest of the family.

The four Willis brothers were all wealthy planters with extensive landholdings. As a planter, Agerton owned slaves, some of whom were Native American. At this time in North Carolina, many slaves were Native Americans; as late as the 1780s in North Carolina, a third of all slaves were Native Americans. The white plantation owners made native Americans slaves from the very beginning.

William Moreau Goins, Ph.D., wrote in the educational *Teachers Guide South Carolina Indians* in an article entitled *The Forgotten Story of American Indian Slavery* that "When Americans think of slavery, our minds create images of Africans inhumanely crowded aboard ships plying the middle passage from Africa, or of blacks stooped to pick cotton in Southern fields. We don't conjure images of American Indians chained in coffles and marched to ports like Boston and Charleston, and then shipped to other ports in the Atlantic world. Yet Indian slavery and the Indian slave trade were ubiquitous in early America."

Cherokee and other Native Americans were traded in slavery long before any arrived from Africa. The Indian slave traders of the Carolinas engaged in successful slaving among the Westo, the Tuscarora, the Yamasee, and the Cherokee.

Born a Slave

It was to a Cherokee slave of Agerton's that his only son, Joseph, was born. Agerton and Joseph's mother's relationship can only be speculation, but under the North Carolina laws of 1741, all interracial marriages were illegal. Since Joseph's mother was a slave, he was born to slave status. It is clear from Agerton's will, though, that he did not consider Joseph a slave but a beloved son—in fact, his only son. This fact did not sit well with some other members of the family.

Agerton's will reveals he intended to free Joseph, but this presented legal problems. "An Act Concerning Servants and Slaves," the law in North Carolina, stated, "That no Negro or Mulatto Slaves shall be set free, upon any Pretense whatsoever, except for meritorious Services, to be adjudged and allowed of by the County Court and License thereupon first had and obtained."

Joseph could not be freed solely by Agerton's wishes. In 1776, Agerton was only forty-nine but in poor health, and Joseph was still too young to prove "meritorious Services." Therefore, Agerton attempted to free him through his will written September 18, 1776, and also to bequeath to him most of his property. Just eighty days before this will was written, the Declaration of Independence had been signed, and times were very chaotic. Agerton would be dead within a year at age fifty.

The Race Card

Joseph's problem was that legal counsel advised the family that this part of the will could be overturned. This was a crafty legal maneuver by Joseph's uncle, Daniel Willis, for a slave could not legally inherit real estate at this time in North Carolina. Therefore, if Joseph was not freed, he could not be a legal heir. Since Agerton had no other children, this would make his eldest brother Daniel Willis "legal heir at law" under North Carolina laws of primogeniture in effect until 1784. Agerton had intended the trustee to obtain Joseph's freedom so he could obtain his inheritance, too. Still, Daniel ignored these wishes, as the following letter to the governor of North Carolina reveals:

Daniel Willis Senr. To Gov. Caswell Respecting Admtn. & C. (From MS Records in Office of Secretary of State.)

"Oct. 10th 1777.
MAY IT PLEASE YOUR EXCELLENCY
I have a small favr. [sic] to beg if your Excellency will be pleased to grant it Viz. as my Deceas'd [sic] Brother Agerton Willis gave the graitest [sic] Part of his Estate to his Molata [sic] boy Joseph and as he is a born slave & not set free Agreeable to Law my Brothers [sic] heirs are not satisfied that he shall have it. I am One of the Exectrs. [sic] and by Mr. M. Grice's Directions have the Estate in my possession as the Trustee Refused giving Security that the boy should have it when off [sic] Age If he Could Inherit it and now this seting [sic] of counsel some of them Intends to Apply for Administration as graitest [sic] Credittors [sic]. I am my Brothers [sic] heir at Law and if Administration is to be obtained I will apply myself Before the Rise of the Counsel and begg [sic] your Excellency will not grant it to any off [sic] them Untill [sic] I Come your Excellency's Compliance will graitly [sic] Oblige your most Obedient Humble Servt [sic] to Command
DAN. WILLIS, SEN.
Pray Excuse my freedm. [sic]"

Daniel's term "Molata [sic] boy" might indicate his attitude toward Joseph's mixed heritage.

Still, I suspect he used it more for a legal emphasis on the laws of North Carolina in the letter because virtually all Native Americans of mixed blood were known as mulattos in North Carolina at that time.

Later American history graphically illustrates the intense feelings of hate and prejudice toward Native Americans. More than seventy years after Joseph was born, President Andrew Jackson persuaded Congress in 1829 to pass a bill that ordered all Native American tribes of the South to be moved west of the Mississippi River. The Cherokees appealed to the Supreme Court, and Chief Justice John Marshall upheld their claim that there was no constitutional right to remove them from their ancestral lands. Jackson called this decision "too preposterous" and ignored the Supreme Court. He then ordered the army to "get them out."

The Cherokees were driven out to Oklahoma on what came to be known as the Trail of Tears. Along the way, a quarter of them died. The Cherokees were one of the so-called Five Civilized Tribes and were the most advanced of all Native Americans, with their own road system and libraries before any white person came into contact with them. They considered all men to be brothers, yet this was of little importance to many of that day. No doubt young Joseph Willis would draw from these character traits from his mother, as much as he did strength from his English father.

Daniel Willis's petition to the court also reveals that Joseph was not of legal age as of the date of the will, September 18, 1776. Legal age was then twenty-one; therefore, Joseph could not have been born before September 18, 1755, as some have supposed. It should also be pointed out that technically this case should have proceeded to the District Superior Court at Wilmington. Still, this court was in abeyance until 1778, following the court law's collapse in November 1772. Therefore, Daniel was writing to the governor and council instead.

The Bladen County tax list of 1784 indicates that the case had been decided by then since Agerton's property was taxed in that year under different family members' names. Even though Agerton's will had been probated and Joseph was living as if he were free, as he had always done, he was still technically a slave.

My Cousin's Keeper

In November of 1787, Joseph's first cousin John Willis, by then a member of the General Assembly of North Carolina and the eldest son of Daniel Willis, introduced a "bill to emancipate Joseph, a Mulatto Slave, the property of the Estate of Agerton Willis, late of Bladen, deceased." The bill passed its third reading on December 6, 1787, and Joseph was a free man by law at last.

The following quotes from the settlement listed in the final act are of interest:

"Whereas, Agerton Willis, late of Bladen County...did by his last will and testament devise to the said Joseph his freedom and emancipation, and did also give unto the said Joseph a considerable property, both real and personal: And whereas the executor and next of kin to the said Joseph did in pursuance of the said will take counsel thereon, and were well advised that the same could not by any means take effect, but would be of prejudice to the said slave and subject him still as property of the said Agerton Willis; whereupon the said executor and next of kin, together with the heirs of the said Agerton Willis, deceased, did cause a fair and equal distribution of the said estate, as well as do equity and justice in the said case to the said Joseph, as in pursuance of their natural love and affection to the said Agerton, and did resolve on the freedom of the said Joseph and to give an equal proportion of the said estate...Joseph Willis shall henceforward be entitled to all the rights and privileges of a free person of mixed blood: provided nevertheless, that this act shall not extend to enable the said Joseph by himself or attorney, or any other person in trust for him, in any manner to commence or prosecute any suit or suits for any other property but such as may be given him by this act...."

There is a lot revealed in this document. First, note that they call themselves the "next of kin" to the said, Joseph. The "fair and equal distribution" that is referred to turns out to be considerably less than the "graitest Part" [sic] mentioned in Daniel's letter ten years before. A later deed reveals that Joseph got 320 acres as settlement, and the above document indicates he also received some personal property as "consideration" for what "he may have acquired by his own industry."

The other real estate that Joseph should have received is described as "unbequeathed lands of Agerton" in later deeds because this part of the will was overturned. These deeds reveal that Joseph should have received at least 2,490 acres, and other deeds are no doubt lost. There was also a vast amount of personal property that Joseph did not get. There was also an additional 970 acres deeded directly to other members of the family. Sadly, Agerton's will is lost, and this information is gleaned from other recorded documents and later deeds.

Joseph Willis could undoubtedly relate to another Joseph from the Bible, who later in his life would say, "They meant it for evil, but God meant it for good."

Slavery and Native Americans in North Carolina

According to North Carolina genealogist and historian William Perry Johnson in a letter to Greene Strother, "In North Carolina, American Indians up until the mid-1880s, were labeled Mulattos..." In her book, *North Carolina Indian Records*, Donna Spindel writes about the Native Americans of this area of the state: "The Lumbee Indians, most of whom reside in Robeson County, constitute the largest group of

Indians in eastern North Carolina. Although their exact origin is a complex matter, they are undoubtedly the descendants of several tribes that occupied eastern Carolina during the earliest days of white settlement. Living along the Pee Dee and Lumber rivers in present-day Robeson and adjacent counties, these Indians of mixed blood were officially designated as Lumbees by the General Assembly in 1956. Most of the Indians have Anglo-Saxon names, and they are generally designated as 'black' or 'mulatto' in nineteenth-century documents; for example, in the U.S. Censuses of 1850-1880, the designation for Lumbee families is usually 'mulatto.'"

Joseph's mother probably was not related to the Lumbee Native Americans. She was also not a part of the indigenous peoples of this part of North Carolina since no Cherokees were living in Bladen County at the time of Joseph's birth in 1758. Therefore, Joseph's mother would have had to have been brought to Bladen County, North Carolina, by Agerton in the early to mid-1750s or by someone else.

Tony Seybert writes in *Slavery and Native Americans in British North America and the United States: 1600 to 1865* that "Because of the higher transportation costs of bringing blacks from Africa, whites in the northern colonies sometimes preferred Indian slaves, especially Indian women and children, to blacks. Carolina exported as many or even more Indian slaves than it imported enslaved Africans before 1720."

Nothing but a Horse, Bridle and Saddle

Many years later in Louisiana, Joseph would tell his grandchildren, Polk Willis and Olive Willis, who were tending to him in his last days, that he left North Carolina "with nothing but a horse, bridle, and saddle."

Polk and Olive later told their nephews, John Houston Strother and Greene Strother, this fact, and Greene Strother told me (also see Greene Strother's Unpublished Th.M. thesis *About Joseph Willis* and his book *The Kingdom Is Coming*). Different children and grandchildren also asked him from time to time about his heritage, and he would tell them his mother was Cherokee and his father was English, and that he was born in Bladen County, North Carolina. Family tradition is consistent among all the different family branches that I have traced and visited with starting in the 1970s. Every branch of the family, including some who had no contact during the twentieth century, had this same family tradition handed down.

After helping to emancipate Joseph, John Willis continued to have an incredibly distinguished career. He became a member of the General Assembly of North Carolina in 1782, 1787, 1789, and 1791; of the Senate in 1794; and of the House of Representatives in 1795.

In the same year that he helped obtain Joseph's "legal freedom," 1787, he was appointed as one of a committee of five from North Carolina to ratify the Constitution of the United States. This was done just in time for North Carolina to enter the Union as the twelfth state and to assist in the election of George Washington as the first President of the United States.

In 1795, Governor Samuel Ashe commissioned John Willis as a Brigadier General in the 4th Brigade of the Militia Continental Army. The land that the county seat of Robeson County, North Carolina (Lumberton), is located on was a donation from John's Red Bluff Plantation. A plaque remembering General John Willis stands there today. John Willis moved to Natchez, Mississippi, in about 1800 and died there on April 3, 1802. He is buried behind the Natchez Cathedral. His son, Thomas, later ran for and was almost elected Attorney General of Louisiana.

The Swamp Fox

It was during these trying times for Joseph that the Revolutionary War began in 1775. On June 14, 1775, the Continental Congress, convening in Philadelphia, established a Continental Army under the command of George Washington. Proclaiming that "all men are created equal" and endowed with "certain unalienable Rights," the Congress adopted the Declaration of Independence, drafted primarily by Thomas Jefferson, on July 4, 1776.

Joseph and a friend of his from Bladen County, Ezekiel O'Quin, left for South Carolina to join up with General Francis Marion, the "Swamp Fox." Marion operated out of the swampy forest of the Pedee region in the lower part of South Carolina. His strategy was to surprise the enemy, cut their supply lines, kill their men, and release any American prisoners found. He and his men then retreated swiftly to the thick recesses of the deep swamps. They were very effective, and their fame was widespread.

They took great pride in themselves. Marion's orderly book states, "Every officer to provide himself with a blue coatee, faced and cuffed with scarlet cloth, and lined with scarlet; white buttons; and a white waistcoat and breeches...also, a cap and a black feather...."

Joseph would later proudly tell the family and friends, "We were called Marion men." The lessons learned with Marion would serve him well his entire life. Joseph was proud of his service under Marion, for, at the time in Bladen County in 1777, it was estimated that two-thirds of the people were Tories. An oath of allegiance to the state was required at that time in North Carolina, and those refusing to take it were required to leave the state within sixty days.

Joseph Willis would not take this oath of allegiance, for he was a patriot loyal to his country, the United States of America.

Loyalty was a trait Joseph Willis would display throughout his life—loyalty to his country, loyalty to his family, and loyalty to his Savior, Jesus Christ.

"Patriots" was often used to describe the British Thirteen United Colonies' colonists who rebelled against British control during the American Revolution. Their leading figures declared the United States of America an independent nation in July 1776.

As a group, Patriots represented an array of social, economic, ethnic, and racial backgrounds. They included college students like Alexander Hamilton, planters like Thomas Jefferson and Joseph Willis's father and uncles, lawyers like John Adams, and just people who loved freedom, like 18-year-old Joseph Willis.

South Carolina

In South Carolina, with the Marion men, Joseph would befriend Richard Curtis Jr. Curtis was to play a significant role in Joseph's decision to go west. Later, in 1791, Curtis would become the first Baptist minister to establish a church in Mississippi. Ezekiel O'Quin would later follow Joseph to Louisiana as the second Baptist minister west of the Mississippi River in Louisiana. In 1786, part of Bladen County became Robeson County, and Ezekiel was listed as the head of a household in 1790.

Early Louisiana author W. E. Paxton, in his book *A History of the Baptists of Louisiana, from the Earliest Times to the Present* (1888), would write many years later that Ezekiel was born in 1781, and every prominent author who followed used that date. Of course, this could not be true if he fought in the Revolutionary War and was the head of a household in 1790. Ezekiel's son John also wrote that Ezekiel "grew up in the same area as Joseph." Perhaps the Ezekiel listed in the 1790 census was his father.

Joseph Willis's wife Rachel Bradford and Her Pilgrim Ancestors

Soon after the Revolutionary War, Joseph would marry Rachel Bradford. Rachel was born in about 1762. Their first child, Agerton, named after Joseph's father, was born in about 1785. I'm a descendant of this son of Joseph Willis and Rachel Bradford Willis. Mary Willis was born next, in about 1787. Both of these children were born in North Carolina. Later, Louisiana census records confirm North Carolina as their place of birth.

The last mention of Joseph in North Carolina was in the 1788 tax list of Bladen County. He was listed with 320 acres.

Taxed in the same district in 1784 was William Bradford, Rachel Bradford Willis' father. Rachel and her father descended from William Bradford (1590–1657). William Bradford had arrived in Plymouth in 1621 aboard the *Mayflower*.

On the death of the first governor of Plymouth, John Carver, he was chosen as the Pilgrims' leader in the same year. He served as governor for over 30 years. William Bradford is credited as the first to proclaim what popular American culture now views as the first Thanksgiving.

The Separatists' story of seeking religious freedom has become a central theme of the United States' history and culture. At an early age, William Bradford was attracted to the "primitive" congregational church in nearby Scrooby, England. He became a committed member of what was termed a "Separatist" church since the church members wanted to separate from the Church of England. By contrast, the Puritans wanted to purify the Church of England. The Separatists instead felt the Church was beyond redemption due to unbiblical doctrines and teachings. This Separatist view would greatly influence Joseph Willis over a century later.

By 1790, Joseph lived with Rachel in Cheraws County (now named Marlboro County), South Carolina, just southwest of Bladen County, across the state line. The 1790 census lists him as the head of the household with two females and one male over 16. In South Carolina, two more children were born to Joseph and Rachel: Joseph Willis Jr., born in about 1792, and Rachel's last-child, named after her, Rachel Willis, born circa 1794.

It was also here that Rachel died in about 1794. She would have only been about 32 years old. Rachel may well have died in childbirth.

Joseph was industrious and prosperous. By 1794, Joseph had moved to Greenville County (the Washington Circuit Court District), South Carolina, and bought 174 acres on the Reedy River's south side on May 3, 1794. He purchased two adjoining tracts of 226 acres on August 16, 1794, and 200 acres on May 8, 1775, on the Reedy River. These three tracts totaled 600 acres. The 226 acres had rent houses and orchards. Joseph Willis, at this time, was well-to-do.

These deeds also give us the name of Joseph's second wife, "Sarah, an Irish woman."

Two children were born in South Carolina to Joseph and Sarah: Jemima Willis in circa 1796, and Sarah's last child named Sarah after her, in 1798 (she later married Nathaniel West). Sarah is called Joseph's wife in a deed dated August 8, 1799, but she died after that.

Joseph lost two wives in only six years. Forty-five years old and alone with six children, he decided to venture west into a land full of uncertainty and danger. Joseph sold everything and spend it all sharing the Gospel of Jesus Christ. He would deliberately place himself in harm's way to share this message. Personal tragedies, prejudice, and rejection by his father's family would have disheartened most men from their calling to preach Jesus.

Baptist Beginnings

"Therefore, come out from them and be separate,
says the Lord." (2 Corinthians 6:17)

In Greenville County, South Carolina, Joseph joined the Main Saluda Church. He also attended the Bethel Association, the most influential Baptist Association in the "Carolina Back Country." He was a delegate from 1794 to 1796. Main Saluda was declared extinct by 1797, and Joseph became a member of the Head of Enoree Baptist Church. He was a member of Head of Enoree in 1797.

These churches were rooted in the Separate Baptists, which sprang from the First Great Awakening. This revival, the First Great Awakening, would be a driving force that would significantly influence Joseph Willis's determination to carry the Gospel of Jesus Christ where no preacher of the Gospel had gone before.

Head of Enoree (known as Reedy River since 1841) was also a member of the Bethel Association. Joseph was listed in the Head of Enoree chronicles and William Thurston as an "outstanding member." This same William Thurston would buy Joseph's 600 acres for $1,200 on August 8, 1799, after Joseph returned from a trip to Mississippi in 1798 with Richard Curtis Jr. It was also here at Head of Enoree that Joseph was first licensed to preach.

It is interesting to note that Richard Curtis Sr. was on a jury list in 1779 for the Cheraw's District. This indicates that the Curtis family lived in this area for at least a short while. Other historians have also stated that the family was living in southern South Carolina at this time.

After a 1798 trip to Mississippi with Richard Curtis Jr., Joseph returned to South Carolina to move his family to the Louisiana Territory and sell his South Carolina property. Never one to squander time, he helped incorporate the "Head of Enoree Baptist Society" in 1799 before leaving.

227

It seems that he tarried until the spring of 1800 to depart on his second trip west, thereby avoiding the winter weather.

The Separate Baptists strongly influenced Joseph's Christian background in North Carolina and South Carolina, although he came into contact with other influences in both states. The majority of Baptists who entered the South Carolina backcountry, which included Greenville County, were known as Separates. Another member of the Bethel Association in 1797 was William Ford. Later, in Louisiana, Joseph was closely associated with a William Prince Ford and entrusted his diary. William Ford was born in 1803.

An interesting side note is that just a few years before Joseph became a member at Head of Enoree, its pastor, Thomas Musick, was excommunicated in 1793 for immorality. This same man later organized Fee Fee Baptist Church in Missouri in 1807 (according to the church's history) located just across the Mississippi River near St. Louis. Fee Fee Baptist Church would be the oldest Baptist church west of the Mississippi River in the entire United States. Calvary Baptist Church at Bayou Chicot was not established until 1812. Nevertheless, Musick did not preach west of the Mississippi River until at least nine years after Joseph Willis did.

Spiritual Roots and The First Great Awakening

"Will you not revive us again, that your people
may rejoice in you?" (Psalm 85:6)

As a young man, Joseph heard and accepted the call to preach the Gospel of Jesus Christ. Joseph Willis's sermons were filled with the echoes of sermons and admonitions from First Great Awakening preachers like Jonathan Edwards, George Whitefield, and Shubal Stearns.

From 1734 to about 1750, the First Great Awakening ignited a fire for revival in the hearts of men called of God to preach the Gospel. The message of rejuvenation and life in the Spirit among stagnant churches, dying, or dead impacted the nineteenth century and the Second Great Awakening.

The results even can be seen today. In the late colonial period, most pastors merely read their sermons, which were theologically deep but lacked emotion and the call to repentance and salvation by grace through faith in Christ. The Great Awakening leaders, such as Jonathan Edwards and George Whitefield, had little interest in merely engaging parishioners' minds; they wanted to see evidence of true repentance and spiritual conversion. Colonists soon noticed a change toward more animated and passionate preaching styles, encouraging them to claim the joy of salvation and to share the love of Christ through action.

Joseph Tracy, the minister, and historian who gave this revival its name in his 1842 book *The Great Awakening*, even saw the First Great Awakening as a precursor to the American Revolution.

Whereas Jonathan Edwards sought to engage Native Americans, George Whitefield preached among the colonists. In 1745, Shubal Stearns heard Whitefield's cry for repentance and left the Congregationalist church. Stearns adopted the Great Awakening's New Light understanding of revival and conversion. This "new awareness" caused a division in the Congregational churches into Old Lights and New Lights groups. The New Lights claimed the Old Lights' religion had grown soulless and formal—no longer having the light of scriptural inspiration.

The New Lights were zealous in evangelism and believed in heartfelt conversion. Sadly, by the end of the 1740s, many fervent New Lights concluded that they couldn't reform established churches from within. Therefore, they felt the need to plant new churches to reach the lost and those who'd fallen away.

Whitefield said, "Mere heathen morality, and not Jesus Christ, is preached in most of our churches."

In 1755, Shubal Stearns moved from Virginia to Sandy Creek, Guilford County, North Carolina, believing that the Spirit urged him to do so. Three years after Stearns' arrival and less than seventy miles from Sandy Creek, Joseph Willis made his entrance into the world.

In Paul's second letter to the Corinthian church, he quoted, "Therefore go out from their midst and be separate from them, says the Lord...." As Stearns and the other New Lights left the Congregationalist church, they became known as Separatists, using

2 Corinthians 6:17 as their guide. Eighteenth-century historian Morgan Edwards wrote of Stearns, "Stearns's message was always the simple gospel," which was "easily understood even by rude frontiersmen," particularly when the preacher himself felt overwhelmed with the importance of his subject. Most of the frontier people of North Carolina had never heard such doctrine or observed such earnest preaching. The Separatists had great missionary zeal and spread at a rapid pace to the other colonies.

Stearns and his followers ministered mainly to the English settlers, and seventeen years after Stearns' arrival, forty-two churches were established from Sandy Creek. Baptist historian David Benedict wrote in 1813, "As soon as the Separtists [sic] arrived, they built them a little meetinghouse, and these 16 persons formed themselves into a church and chose Shubal Stearns for their pastor...." Stearns remained pastor there until his death, and from this "meetinghouse" the South felt the flames of revival, the fan of which was carried west by an unlikely missionary named Joseph Willis.

In 1772, Morgan Edwards wrote that Stearns's Sandy Creek church had "spread its branches westward as far as the great river Mississippi."

After courageously fighting in the American Revolution with Francis Marion, "the Swamp Fox," Joseph Willis was the first missionary and church planter to preach the Gospel of Jesus Christ West of the Mississippi River.

Mississippi Missionary

As mentioned before, Joseph was a member of Head of Enoree in 1797. Late that year or the next, he made his first trip to Mississippi with Richard Curtis Jr. This trip was made without his family, as it was the custom of the time to venture west, find a safe place, and then return for the family.

W. E. Paxton records the results of this first trip:

They sought not in vain, for soon after their return they were visited by William Thompson, who preached unto them the Gospel of our God: and on the first Saturday in October 1798, came William Thompson, Richard Curtis, and Joseph Willis, who constituted them into a church, subject to the government of the Cole's Creek church, calling the newly constituted arm of Cole's Creek, "The Baptist Church on Buffaloe" [sic].

This church, known as Woodville Baptist Church today, is located near Woodville, Mississippi, and the Mississippi River and is due east of Bayou Chicot, Louisiana, where Joseph would organize his first church west of the Mississippi River, Calvary Baptist.

Joseph returned for his family by 1799, but it would seem likely he might have made a trip across the river into Louisiana before this date since this is where he returned with his family.

Curtis had already made one trip to this part of the country in 1780. In that year, Richard Curtis Jr., along with his parents, half-brother, three brothers, and all their wives, together with John Courtney and John Stampley and their wives, set out for Mississippi. Mississippi Baptist historian T. C. Schilling wrote that "two brothers by the name of Daniel

231

and William Ogden and a man by the name of Perkins, with their families, most of whom were Baptists," were also on this first trip.

The late Dr. Greene Strother, maternal great-grandson of Joseph Willis and my cousin, told me that it was a family tradition that Joseph's first trip into Louisiana was in search of a Willis Perkins. Years later, in Louisiana (1833), a Willis Perkins was a member of Occupy Baptist Church while Joseph Willis was the pastor.

According to Occupy Baptist Church minutes, another member of the church during that period was Greene Strother's father, John Strother. Joseph Willis, Willis Perkins, and John Strother attended the same church meetings at the same time. Census records reveal that this Willis Perkins would have had to be the latter's son, though.

The Curtises were initially from Virginia. W. E. Paxton wrote: "The Curtises were known to be Marion men, and when not in active service, they were not permitted to enjoy the society of their families, but they were hunted like wild beasts from their hiding places in the swamps of Pedee." They were a thorn in the side of the British and their Tory neighbors."

Paxton continued:

"They left South Carolina in the spring of 1780, traveling by land to Tennessee's northeastern corner. They built three flat boats, and when the Holston River reached sufficient depth toward the end of that year, they set out for the Natchez country of Mississippi by way of the Holston, Tennessee, Ohio, and Mississippi Rivers. Those mentioned above traveled on the first two boats; the names of those on the last boat are not known. Those in the last boat had contracted smallpox and were required to travel a few hundred yards behind the other two boats.

"Somewhere near the Clinch River, on a bend in the Tennessee River near the northwestern corner of Georgia, they were attacked by Cherokee Indians. The first two boats escaped, but the third boat was captured. The price paid for this attack was high, for the Indians contracted smallpox from them and many died.

"Those on the first two boats continued on their voyage and landed safely at the mouth of Cole's Creek about 18 miles above Natchez by land. Here in this part of the state, they lived. They called Richard Curtis Jr., who was licensed to preach in S. Carolina, as their preacher. He would later organize the first Baptist Church in Mississippi, in 1791, called Salem. As time passed, the population increased. Some were Baptists, such as William Chaney from South Carolina and his son Bailey. A preacher from Georgia by the name of Harigail also arrived here and zealously denounced the 'corruptions of Romanism.'"

This, along with the conversion of a Spanish Catholic by the name of Stephen d'Alvoy, brought the Spanish authorities' wrath. To make an example of d'Alvoy and Curtis, they decided to arrest them and send them to Mexico's silver mines. Warned of this plan, d'Alvoy and Curtis and a man named Bill Hamberlin fled to South Carolina, arriving in the fall of 1795. Harigail also escaped and fled this area."

Paxton said that the country between Mississippi and South Carolina was "then infested by hostile Indians." It seems likely that Joseph knew at least part of the Cherokee language since he was half-Cherokee, an asset that could be of great help if the Cherokees were reencountered on the way to Mississippi.

For this reason and, more importantly, because Joseph was a licensed Baptist preacher, I believe Curtis brought Joseph Willis with him when he returned to Mississippi in 1798. Curtis was an ordained Baptist preacher also called to preach Jesus.

Besides, Curtis knew well Joseph Willis's courage under fire, since both were Marion men together in the Revolutionary War.

After the trip with Curtis to Mississippi in 1798, Joseph returned to South Carolina for his family and to sell his property. As mentioned before, he sold all of his lands to William Thurston in August of 1799, indicating his preparation to depart South Carolina.

The First Gospel Sermon Ever Preached by an Evangelical West of the Mississippi River

"Call to Me, and I will answer you, and show you great and mighty things, which you do not know"
(Jeremiah 33:3).

When Joseph Willis crossed the mighty Mississippi River into the Louisiana Territory, the Code Noir, the "Black Code," ruled the Louisiana Territory. This decree from King Louis XIV regulated, among other things, the condition of slavery and the activities of free people of color. It also restricted religion to Roman Catholicism, forbidding the exercise of any other religion. The Black Code was in effect by law until the Louisiana Purchase on April 30, 1803. In reality, it was a hindrance to the preaching of the Gospel for many decades after the Louisiana Purchase. Joseph Willis would be hated because of his defiance of it.

After crossing the mighty Mississippi, he would head first into the heartland of the Black Code, south Louisiana; that daring move would almost cost him his life.

In January 1797, the governing authorities issued regulations that made it mandatory for children of non-Catholic emigrant families to embrace Roman Catholicism and also forbade the coming of any ministers into the territory

234

except Roman Catholics. Joseph Willis defied this terrifying rule of law by traveling as far south as Vermilionville (Lafayette today) preaching the Gospel.

In 1798, Joseph Willis first preached in the Louisiana Territory.

Joseph Willis also helped establish Woodville Baptist Church near the Louisiana Territory in 1798.

He again crossed the Mississippi River into the Louisiana Territory in search of Willis Perkins in 1798.

Joseph returned for his family and sold all his property in South Carolina in 1799 and is not found there in the 1800 census.

In 1813, historian David Benedict wrote in his book *A General History of the Baptist Denomination in America and Other Parts of the World*, "Joseph Willis…has done much for the cause, and spent a large fortune while engaged in the ministry, often at the hazard of his life, while the State belonged to the Spanish government."

Before Napoleon Bonaparte acquired the Louisiana Territory from Spain on October 1, 1800, Joseph Willis was already preaching Jesus in the Louisiana Territory.

Baptist historian David Benedict confirmed in 1813; Joseph Willis had moved his family to the Louisiana Territory before October 1, 1800.

We know this because Joseph Willis had already spent a large fortune in the Louisiana Territory before October 1, 1800, according to David Benedict. Benedict was the premier Baptist historian in America at that time. We know this because Joseph Willis said it was 1798.

In 1854, the Louisiana Baptist Associational Committee wrote in Joseph Willis's obituary, "He proclaimed the Gospel in these regions before the American flag was hoisted here." That would have been before April 30, 1803.

David Benedict was a contemporary of Joseph Willis and wrote his book only fifteen years after Joseph Willis first preached west of the Mississippi River.

In violation of the Code Noir and at the risk of his life, Joseph Willis preached the Gospel west of the Mississippi even before Lewis and Clark began their historic journey by traveling up the Missouri River in May of 1804. He preached Jesus west of the Mississippi almost a decade before Abraham Lincoln was born. This would qualify as the first sermon ever preached by an evangelical minister west of the Mississippi River.

The Fiery Furnace

Joseph settled at Bayou Chicot between 1798 and 1805. In 1806, the Mississippi Baptist Association was organized. Though he was a licensed minister, a church had never ordained him. He believed that he should be ordained by the church. Some have questioned this and have asked why he did not just organize churches without his ordination. The answer is clear that he believed in the church's authority and that it was important to him to be accountable to that authority, as he had been in both North Carolina and South Carolina.

He also knew well the importance of banding together with other believers. Still, there had been no need for ordination before because the population at that time in Louisiana was very sparse—he had only six members in 1812 when he organized Calvary Baptist Church.

However, Louisiana was growing at a rapid pace. In 1812, the state population was slightly over 80,000. Eight years later, it was over 200,000, yet this section of the state was still thinly populated with churches twenty to fifty miles apart and have little communication with each other.

Therefore, in 1810, Joseph left for Mississippi to seek ordination. His son, Joseph Jr., would later often speak of Joseph Willis crossing the Mississippi River at Natchez and how dangerous it was.

Joseph Jr. said that his father would swim the mighty river riding a mule to take a shortcut and save time to preach Jesus.

After he reached Mississippi, once again, the race card would be played. Joseph took his letter to a local church stating that he was a good standing member in South Carolina. The custom then, as now among Baptists, was to transfer church membership by a letter.

The church to which he gave his letter objected to his ordination "lest the cause of Christ should suffer reproach from the humble social position of his servant."

Paxton wrote, "Such obstacles would have daunted the zeal of any man engaged in a less holy cause." Joseph's "humble social position" was certainly not his wealth but the fact that his skin was swarthy.

I'm often reminded when I think of Joseph Willis at this point in his life of the statement that, "The test of a man's character is what it takes to discourage him."

Once again, we see an essential personality trait of Joseph's that is recorded over and over again. He was longsuffering and willing to pay whatever price was necessary to proclaim the Gospel. After being betrayed by his father's family, losing two wives, and being rejected by his denomination, he never became embittered. In Joseph's mind and heart, no price was too high for the cause of Christ. His focus was not on the fiery furnace but the Fourth Man in the fire; he knew the safest place in life was in the fiery furnace because that was where the Fourth Man was—his Savior and Lord Jesus.

Paxton wrote, "he was a simple-hearted Christian, glowing with the love of Jesus and an effective speaker."

His youngest son Aimuewell Willis said before his death in 1937, "the secret of my father's success was personal work." He said that as a boy, he saw his father go to a man in the field, hold his hand, and witness to him until he surrendered to Christ.

Today, many generations later, his influence can still be seen.

One grandchild, Olive Willis, said Joseph would be reading the Bible and talking to them as a few of them would slip away, and he would say, "Children, you can slip away from me, but not from God."

According to Paxton, "Joseph was never 'daunted,' for his was a high calling, a single-mindedness of purpose."

The Churches

After Joseph's rejection in Mississippi, a friendly minister advised him to obtain a recommendation from the people he worked among. This he did, and he presented it to the Mississippi Association. The association accepted the recommendation, ordained Joseph, and constituted a church called Calvary Baptist Church at Bayou Chicot, Louisiana, on November 13, 1812. Calvary Baptist Church is still active today and celebrated its 200th anniversary in 2012. I attended the anniversary.

Louisiana had been a state barely seven months when Calvary Baptist was founded and was in a state of turmoil. Great Britain did not consider the Louisiana Purchase legally valid, and Congress had declared war on Great Britain the past June—The War of 1812.

Just a month and a day earlier on the Boque Chitto River, in what is now Washington Parish, Half Moon Bluff Baptist Church was organized. Located approximately eight miles from the Mississippi border, Half Moon Bluff was the first Baptist church organized in what is today Louisiana but was east of the Mississippi River. Some fifteen to twenty miles southwest of Half Moon Bluff Church, Mount Nebo Baptist Church was organized on January 31, 1813. Half Moon Bluff is extinct, but Mount Nebo is still active.

The Methodists had established a church even before these dates near Branch, Louisiana, but the first non-Catholic church in Louisiana was Christ Church in New Orleans. Its first service was held November 17, 1805, in the Cabildo, and it was predominantly Episcopal.

Paxton wrote, "The zeal of Father Willis, as he came to be called by the affectionate people among whom he labored, could not be bounded by the narrow limits of his own home, but he traveled far and wide."

Once when he was traveling and preaching, he stayed at an Inn. Several other men were staying there. One of these men was sick, and Joseph read the Bible to him, prayed with him, and witnessed to him about Christ. The next morning all of the men were gone very early, except for the sick man. He told Joseph that he had overheard the men talking about Joseph the night before and that they had gone ahead to ambush him. He told him about another road to take, and Joseph's life was spared. Joseph would receive warnings other times, too, just in time to avoid harm's way.

Paxton said those who loved Joseph called him the "Apostle to the Opelousas" and "Father Willis." According to family tradition, strong determination and profound faith were his shields. He would often walk great distances to visit and preach to small groups. He rode logs to cross streams or travel downstream. He would sometimes return home from a mission tour as late as one o'clock in the morning and awaken his wife to prepare clothes so that he might leave again a few hours later.

By 1818, when Joseph and others founded the Louisiana Baptist Association at Cheneyville, he established all five charter member churches. They were Calvary, 1812; Beulah, 1816; Vermillion, 1817; Aimwell, 1817 (also called Debourn); and Plaquemine, 1817.

Calvary was at Bayou Chicot, Beulah at Cheneyville, Vermillion at Lafayette, Aimwell about five miles southeast of Oberlin, and Plaquemine near Branch.

In 1824, he helped establish Zion Hill Church at Beaver Dam along with William Wilbourn and Isham Nettles.

He went far and wide, establishing Antioch Primitive Baptist Church near Edgerly, Louisiana, on October 21, 1827, just sixteen miles from Orange, Texas, and the Texas State line.

Joseph kept a diary. William Prince Ford arranged these notes in 1841, and Paxton copied them in 1858. Paxton admits most of his facts concerning Central Louisiana Baptists are from Joseph Willis's manuscript and Louisiana Association Minutes.

Ford also wrote about the manuscript. Paxton records one of Ford's observations made in 1834, and it is very revealing concerning Joseph's heart:

"Nearly all the churches now left in the association were gathered either directly or indirectly by the labors of Mr. Willis.

Mr. Ford wrote of this effort and Paxton quoted him: "It was truly affecting to hear him speak of them as his children and with all the affection of a father allude to some schisms and divisions that had arisen in the past and to warn them against the occurrence of anything of the kind in the future. But when he spoke of the fact that two or three of them had already become extinct, his voice failed and he was compelled to give utterance to his feelings by his tears; and surely the heart must have been hard that could not be melted by the manifestation of so much affection, for he wept not alone."

No church ever split while Joseph was its pastor. Baptist historian John T. Christian remarks in his book *A History of Baptists of Louisiana* (1923), "It must steadily be borne in mind that in no other state of the Union have Baptists been compelled to face such overwhelming odds; and such long and sustained opposition...The wonder is not that at first, the Baptists made slow progress, but that they made any at all."

Louisiana Property

The Opelousas Court House records that Joseph first bought land in Bayou Chicot in 1805.

On March 10, 1818, Joseph sold 411 acres for $2,000 to John Montgomery "in the neighborhood of Bayou Chicot." The deed reveals that Joseph had initially purchased this land from John Haye on September 21, 1809. This property had many improvements.

Other deeds refer to Joseph's property while there, such as 148 acres he sold for $351.00 to James Murdock on January 6, 1824. This land was part of a tract Joseph originally purchased from Silas Fletcher on April 20, 1818. He sold the balance of these lands to Thomas Insall on October 31, 1827, for $500. This was during the same time he moved to Rapides Parish.

Thomas Insall paid off a note he owed Joseph on October 11, 1833. These are but a few of Joseph's business transactions while at Bayou Chicot.

It was at Bayou Chicot that most of his children were born to his third wife.

The late Bayou Chicot historian Mabel Thompson of Ville Platte wrote to me that she had in her possession the diary of her great-grandfather, the schoolteacher in that area. In his journal, he listed the patrons of the children who attended school. Mabel Thompson later mailed me a copy. Joseph Willis is listed as a patron on July l2, 1814.

According to Mabel Thompson in another letter to me, "Chicot's chief attraction was it had an abundance of natural resources, such as timber, good water, wild game, good soil and friendly Indians...Chicot became a trading center for a large territory extending as far west as the Sabine River, serving Indians, trappers, frontiersmen, homesteaders, as well as plantation owners."

Third and Fourth Wives

Between 1799 and 1802, Joseph's second wife, Sarah, died. Joseph married a third time. This third wife was probably a Johnson and was born in South Carolina, but it would seem that Joseph met and married her in Mississippi or Louisiana. A son was born on January 6, 1804. He was named William Willis and is buried at Humble (formerly called Willis Flats) Cemetery next to the Bethel Baptist Church in Elizabeth, Louisiana.

Other children born to this union were: Lemuel Willis, born circa 1812 (died 1862); John Willis, born circa 1814; Martha Willis, born April 9, 1825 (and four females were listed in the 1830 census between the ages of five and twenty). A Sally Willis was listed in the 1850 Rapides Parish census as age forty-eight and living near William Willis.

The last two known children of Joseph were born to his fourth wife, Elvy Sweat. They were Samuel Willis, born circa 1836, and Aimuewell Willis, born May 1, 1837, died September 9, 1937, at age 100.

Joseph would have been about 79 years old when Aimuewell was born. The 1850 Rapides Parish Census also lists an additional four males in Joseph Willis's household: James, born circa 1841; William, born circa 1845; Timothy, born circa 1847; and Bernard, born circa 1848.

It would be unlikely that Joseph would have a second son named William. Aimuewell Willis always said he was Joseph Willis's youngest son. These last four males are most likely Joseph's grandchildren.

Historian Ivan Wise wrote in *Footsteps of the Flock: or Origins of Louisiana Baptists* (1910) that two sons of Joseph died, "poisoned on honey and were buried a half mile from the present town of Oakdale, Louisiana."

Joseph's third wife died and is buried at Bayou Chicot. The location of her unmarked grave is unknown, but I suspect she is buried near the original Calvary Baptist Church site located next to Vandenburg Cemetery.

One historian wrote that Joseph Willis had 19 children. Joseph's children, who were still living, would follow him when he would later move to Rapides Parish in 1827. Many were neighbors with him as late as 1850, as the census reveals, as well as several grandchildren, who were grown by then.

Joseph's eldest child Agerton married Sophie Story, an Irish orphan brought from Tennessee by a Mr. Park, who then lived near Holmesville below Bunkie, Louisiana. Agerton's son, Daniel Hubbard Willis Sr., was the first of many descendants to follow Joseph into the ministry. Paxton calls Daniel Willis, "one of the most respected ministers in the Louisiana Association." He established many churches himself and was blind for the last 22 years of his life. His daughter would read the Scriptures for him as he would preach.

He was pastor of Amiable and Spring Hill Baptist Churches for many years. He was my great-great-grandfather.

He settled on Spring Creek, near Longleaf, at a community called Babb's Bridge. Many of my cousins still live in that area today.

Joseph's daughter Jemima Willis married William Dyer, and they lived on the Calcasieu River near Master's Creek. The location is just west of Blanche, Louisiana, where Joseph died.

Mary married Thomas Dial (her first husband was a Johnson) from South Carolina, and they both were living in Rapides Parish in 1850.

Joseph Willis Jr. married Jennie Coker at Bayou Chicot and later moved to Rapides Parish and settled near Tenmile Creek.

Lemuel Willis married Emeline Perkins from Tenmile Creek and settled near Glenmora in Blanche, Louisiana. The late Dr. Greene Strother, Southern Baptist missionary emeritus to China and Malaysia, was his grandson.

William married Rhoda Strother on the "Darbourn" on the upper reaches of the Calcasieu.

Aimuewell married twice and settled in Leesville. His first wife was Marguerite Leuemche, and his second wife was Lucy Foshee.

Many of the descendants of these children live in these same areas today. At least nine generations have lived in the Forest Hill area, including Joseph himself. Oakdale, Louisiana, probably has more descendants of Joseph than any other region.

I visited with Aimuewell's daughter, Pearl, in Denver, Colorado, in December of 1980, and a short time later with Aimuewell's son Elzie Willis near Leesville, Louisiana. It was a strange feeling to talk with someone whose grandfather was born in 1758. Joseph was about 79 when their father was born, and Aimuewell was in his eighties when they were born.

No photograph exists of Joseph Willis. The photograph in Durham and Ramond's book, *Baptist Builders in Louisiana* (1934), is of Aimuewell, listed as Joseph in error.

In Service of America

Not surprisingly, many descendants of Joseph Willis are Baptists, but far from all are. Many have fought in the major wars and served America faithfully. Joseph fought in the Revolutionary War. Daniel Willis Jr., Aimuewell Willis, William Willis, Crawford Willis (killed at Shiloh), and Lemuel Willis served in the Civil War for the South.

Dr. Daniel Oscar Willis and Dr. Greene Strother served in World War I.

Dr. Greene Strother, Joseph's great-grandson, captured more Germans than any other soldier beside the famed Sgt. York, in World War I. He was awarded the French *Croix de Guerre*, the Distinguished Service Cross, and the Purple Heart.

Greene Strother also served as chaplain to General Claire Chennault's Flying Tigers while in China as a missionary. Like Strother, Chennault was reared in the Louisiana towns of Gilbert and Waterproof.

A host of descendants of Joseph Willis fought in World War II, including Robert Kenneth "Bobby" Willis Jr, the first soldier killed in World War II from Rapides Parish, Louisiana. Louisiana's Pineville American Legion post was named in his honor (the post no longer exists). The Japanese killed him on December 7, 1941, during the surprise attack on Pearl Harbor. His body is entombed at the bottom of Pearl Harbor, aboard the *USS Arizona*. I have visited the *USS Arizona* memorial twice and have marveled at his sacrifice and the others as I viewed their names carved in marble at the memorial.

Pioneer Church Life

Joseph Willis established a church on October 21, 1827, just sixteen miles from Orange, Texas, and the Texas State line near Edgerly Louisiana named Antioch Primitive Baptist Church.

After moving to Spring Creek, east of the Calcasieu River near Longleaf, Louisiana, around 1827, Joseph began to establish churches there, too.

The first was Amiable Baptist Church on September 6, 1828, near present-day Longleaf. He next established Occupy Baptist Church in 1833, on Tenmile Creek, near Pitkin, and then he established Spring Hill Baptist Church on Hurricane Creek in 1841, near present-day Forest Hill.

Joseph Willis was about 83 when Spring Hill was established.

The Baptist churches of that day did not necessarily meet weekly. Preachers would have to travel long distances. Those who met weekly might have a preacher only once a month or every other month.

Discipline was stern, with members being excluded (fellowship being withdrawn by the church) for gossiping, drinking too much, quarreling, dancing, using bad language, and in one case at Amiable, for "having abused her mother." But, the churches were also forgiving if you admitted you were wrong and promised not to do it again. Repentance along with salvation was emphasized.

A good example is found in the Spring Hill Church minutes. After twice promising not to "partake of ardent spirits" anymore, Robert Snoddy had the fellowship of the church withdrawn from him on May 31, 1851.

A month later, Snoddy sent this letter to the church explaining his actions:

"Dear Brethren, Having been overtaken in an error I set down to confess it. I did use liquor too freely, but did not say anything or do anything out of the way. In as much as I do expect to be at the conference I send you my thoughts. I did promise you that I would refrain from using the poison, but I having broken my promise I have therefore rendered myself unworthy of your fellowship and cannot murmur if you exclude me. I suppose it is no use to tell you that I have been sincerely punished for my crime in as much as I have confessed the same to you before, but I make this last request of you for forgiveness, or is your forgiveness exhausted towards me.

"It is necessary that I say to you that I sorely repented for my guilt, but my brethren if you have in your wisdom supposed that my life brings too much reproach on that most respectful of all causes, exclude me, exclude me, oh exclude me. But I do love the cause so well that I will try to be at the door of the temple of the Lord. Brethren, whilst you are dealing with me, do it mercifully, prayerfully, and candidly. I was presented by a beloved brother with a temperance pledge to which I replied I would think about it, but if I could have obtained enough of my heart's blood to fill my pen to write my name I would have done it. It is my determination to join it yet – and never taste another drop of the deathly cup whilst I live, at the peril of my life. Nothing more, but I request your prayers, dear brethren – Robert Snoddy"

Robert Snoddy was restored to membership. Four months later, he was once again reported drinking and once again excluded.

The Amiable Baptist Church minutes in 1879 declared their position in no uncertain terms: "On motion be it resolved that we as a church are willing to look over and forgive the past, and we as a church for the time to come allow no more playing or dancing among our church members. If they do, they may expect to be dealt with."

The Amiable minutes record that one dear member was admonished at a church service for dancing. He then stood in the church aisle, did a jig, and walked out.

Pastors were usually called to preach by the church for a one-year period. In 1857, Amiable voted to give Pastor D. H. [Daniel Hubbard Willis, Sr.] Willis $100.00 "to sustain him for the next twelve months...it being the amount stated by him."

In 1833, Joseph became pastor of Occupy Baptist Church near Pitkin, Louisiana. The church is next to Tenmile Creek. He served as pastor there for about 16 years. There he married Elvy Sweat, who was many years younger than he. She is listed as age 30 in the 1850 census; Joseph is recorded as 98 in the same census. He was only a mere 92. I suspect her age is listed wrong too. Joseph's son Lemuel and others said she was not good to him. As a result of this and Joseph's failing health, his son Lemuel and two men went and got him.

They took him to Lemuel's home in Blanche, Louisiana, where he lived the remainder of his life. Blanche was located three miles from Glenmora towards Oakdale. It is not on a present-day map, but GPS can still find it.

On a bed in an ox wagon used for an ambulance, he sang as the wagon rolled along to Lemuel's home. Joseph witnessed to the two men while lying in the back of the wagon. He preached to his last breath, either from a chair in the church or from his bed at home.

During this time, a man named John Phillips, from the government came by taking affidavits as to the population's race. Joseph signed this affidavit and stated that his mother was Cherokee and his father was English. This was registered at the courthouse in Alexandria, Louisiana. The courthouse was later burned during the Civil War.

Homecoming in Heaven

Joseph Willis died on September 14, 1854, west of Blanche, Louisiana, about three miles south of Glenmora. He is buried in the Occupy Baptist Church cemetery on Tenmile Creek, near Pitkin. Twenty years after he began his ministry in Louisiana in 1800, there were only ten preachers and eight Baptist churches with 150 members in the entire state. On January 18, 1955, just over 100 years after his death, 250 people, among them 16 ministers, gathered in freezing weather to unveil a monument in his memory at his grave.

I later interviewed many of the people that were there that day—including wonderful pastors such as J.D Scott, Grover Willis, and Theo Cornier. None of them knew why his year of birth was wrong on the monument. It should have been 1758, not 1764.

It took the most powerful hurricane (Laura) on record to make landfall in Louisiana to topple it in 2020. I contacted Charlie Bordelon, who repaired gravestones.

He (and others, including several of Joseph Willis's descendants) lifted the 1,586 pound stone with a crane. I thought of another resurrection to come at Joseph Willis's grave. But, this time, it will not be a gravestone but of an old-time country preacher!

The Louisiana Association published the following estimate of his work: "Before the church began to send missionaries into destitute regions, he at his own expense, and frequently at the risk of his life, came to these parts, preaching the gospel of the Redeemer.

"For fifty years, he was instant in season and out of season, preaching, exhorting, and instructing regarding not his property, his health or even his life, if he might be the means of turning sinners to Christ."

Louisiana Baptist historian Glen Lee Greene wrote in *House Upon A Rock* (1973, "In all the history of Louisiana Baptists it would be difficult, if not impossible, to find a man who suffered more reverses, who enjoyed fewer rewards, or who single-handedlyachieved more enduring results for the denomination than did Joseph Willis."

I will pour My Spirit on your descendants, And My blessing on your offspring. Isaiah 44:3 (NKJV)

Gatsby hesitated, then added cooly: He's the
man who fixed the World Series back in 1919."
—F. Scott Fitzgerald *The Great Gatsby*

My Father and Me

Julian "Jake" Willis was Boss Man Jake and Julian Willis, in my novels *Louisiana Wind* and *Destiny*.

Few years would have a more significant impact on my life than 1919 did.

In 1919, the third and final wave of the influenza pandemic occurred. The pandemic killed 675,000 people in the United States. That number included family members.

In 1919, President Wilson signed a proclamation commemorating the end of fighting in World War I as Armistice Day. My cousins and great-uncles returned home from the Great War.

In 1919, the Eighteenth Amendment was ratified, authorizing the prohibition of alcoholic beverages. It did not stop my namesake and Grandfather Randall Lee Willis. He would hide from my grandmother on Barber Creek and drink high-proof distilled spirits called Moonshine.

In 1919, Congress approved the 19th amendment to legalize women's suffrage. The next year my seven-year-old future mother, Ruth Lawson Willis, received the right to vote when she came of age.

In 1919, Norman Saurage discovered the secret of making my all-time favorite coffee in the home of LSU, Baton Rouge. He named it Community Coffee.

I lived three years in Baton Rouge near the campus off Dalrymple Drive, attended the games, sat in "Death Valley," and became a fan. Geaux Tigers!

In 1919, Arnold Rothstein paid members of the Chicago White Sox to lose the World Series deliberately. Babe Ruth said Shoeless Joe Jackson was "The greatest hitter I'd ever seen," Shoeless Joe admitted that he cheated. The quote, "Say it ain't so, Joc," became famous.

In 1919 my all-time favorite sports hero, Jackie Robinson, was born. He was an American professional baseball player who became the first African American to play in the Major League.

And in 1919, my all-time hero was born, my father, Julian "Jake" Willis.

Julian Willis fought in the South Pacific during World War II.

He joined the U.S. Army Air Corps (4 152 091, Technical Sergeant) in the 52nd Air Engineer Squadron, 330th Air Services Group, on October 14, 1941, at Camp Shelby, Mississippi.

In just 54 days, his training progressed to an accelerated fast-track when the Japanese attacked Pearl Harbor on December 7, 1941.

Two weeks later, Daddy received confirmation his first-cousin and close friend Robert "Bobby" Willis was KIA on the USS Arizona. Bobby Willis's is entombed at the bottom of Pearl Harbor.

He was the first casualty from Rapides Parish, Louisiana, in World War II.

After Bobby's death, the war became personal–very personal to Daddy.

It was the first in a series of wartime events that would mold Daddy's character and, at times, harden his heart.

Daddy was stationed at Keesler Field in Biloxi, Mississippi, for basic training when the Japanese attacked Pearl Harbor.

Daddy loved Western fiction. His favorite writer was Zane Grey. They both idealized the American frontier.

A few years ago, I received a phone call from the Sigma Nu (ΣN) National Headquarters in Lexington, Virginia.

I was a Sigma Nu Fraternity member in college at Southwest Texas State University (Texas State University today) around the time of the Lincoln-Douglas debate.

Little did I know Zane Grey had been a Sigma Nu, too, in 1894, at the University of Pennsylvania. Sigma Nu was calling to request a copy of all my books. They wished to place them in their library next to Zane Grey's novels. They are there today. I was honored for more than one reason.

Daddy was Trail Boss for many years of the Brazoria County Trail Ride and a board member of the Brazoria County Fair and Rodeo Association in Angleton, Texas.

Daddy loved to teach kids to ride horses, and he enjoyed seeing their excitement when they learned to enjoy horses.

He had more friends than anyone I've ever known.

He was a patriot.

He was the real deal–a man's man.

He was a cowboy's cowboy.

252

Author's Note

The Road Not Taken

One of my favorite poems is *The Road Not Taken*, written a century ago by Robert Frost. The last stanza contains my favorite words in the poem: "Two roads diverged in a wood, and I–I took the one less traveled by, And that has made all the difference."

My life began on a Louisiana red dirt road. We didn't have much money, but I never noticed because no one else did either—at least those whom my family knew.

As a boy, we lived near Willis Gunter Road and Barber Creek, near Longleaf, Louisiana. Barber Creek was as cold as ice.

One day, when I was just a pup of barely four, I decided to venture up the narrow red dirt road lined with longleaf pines to my Grandma's house. Her home was just a mile up Willis Gunter Road and overlooked Barber Creek. I remember stopping to pick some wild dewberries. Perhaps Grandma would be so happy to see me she'd bake me a pie while I swam in Barber Creek. No sooner had I arrived than Mama drove up in our Oldsmobile.

Now, Mama didn't seem to be happy with me. Visions of her making a switch by slowly cutting it from a tree—I mean very slowly—and removing the twigs one by one flooded my mind.

The drama of her cutting the switch was always worse than her use of it. But that did not occur that day, although I later wished it had.

She looked up and pointed to an old man driving a wagon down Willis Gunter Road. She then explained, "Ran, that old man drives up and down these red dirt roads looking for little boys. He then puts them in a gunnysack and hauls them off."

She did not say where he took them. I did not want to know. To this day, I've never run away from home again.

When I first shared this story with my eldest son Aaron, his response was, "He was driving a wagon? Who'd you vote for, Dad, Lincoln, or Douglas?"

I seldom get to walk those red dirt roads anymore.

Yet, there is another road, perhaps even less traveled than the red dirt road I trod as a boy in Louisiana or even the one Frost wrote.

Travel this road if you will. It will change your life. It will change your destiny.

In 1829, George Wilson was found guilty of six charges and was given the death sentence. However, Wilson had influential friends who petitioned President Andrew Jackson for a pardon. Jackson granted the pardon, and it was brought to the prison and given to Wilson.

To everyone's surprise, Wilson said, "I am going to hang."

There had never been a refusal to a pardon, so the courts didn't know what to do. The case went all the way to the Supreme Court, and Chief Justice John Marshall gave the ruling, saying, "A pardon is a piece of paper, the value of which depends upon the acceptance by the person implicated. If he does not accept the pardon, then he must be executed."

God loves you, and, yes, He has provided a pardon for you and me, paid for with Christ's life-blood, but you have the right to refuse the pardon for your sins.

Jesus was crucified between two thieves. One thief said yes to Jesus, but the other said no to Him. One accepted the pardon, and the other refused it.

The question to you and me today is the same as it was 2,000 years ago. Which thief on the cross are you? The one who said yes to God's pardon or the one who said no to His pardon? I have chosen to say yes.

You have the same choice.

Come

The last invitation in the Word of God is in Revelation 22:17: "And the Spirit and the bride say, 'Come!' And let him who hears say, 'Come!' And let him who thirsts come. Whoever desires, let him take the water of life freely."

Are you thirsty? Then come. Let him who hears come. And, whosoever will, come.

That invitation is to you—it is to me—it is to everyone!

Bring your disappointments, bring your failures, bring your fears, bring your heartaches. The Holy Spirit says come to Jesus.

He loves you. He wants to save you. He *will* save you. Come to Jesus, and drink the water of life freely.

He suffered, He bled, He died, because He loves you. Listen to the still small voice, of the Holy Spirit, bidding you come to Jesus.

Don't wait—come!

Look

"Look to Me, and be saved, All you ends of the earth! For I am God, and there is no other." (Isaiah 45:22)

"All you ends of the earth" includes the Aboriginal people of the Central Australian desert.

"All you ends of the earth" are those in darkest Africa.

"All you ends of the earth" are the isolated tribes in the Amazon rainforest in Brazil.

"All you ends of the earth" are presidents, world leaders, and kings.

"All you ends of the earth" is the polished lawyer, the gifted doctor, and the brilliant college professor.

"All you ends of the earth" is the prostitute, and the drug dealer, and the rapist, and the thief, and the murderer.

"All you ends of the earth" is you—and me.

God's Word, the Bible, states, "So Moses made a bronze serpent, and put it on a pole; and so it was, if a serpent had bitten anyone, when he looked at the bronze serpent, he lived."

Those who looked lived.

Those who looked were healed.

Those who looked were made whole.

Those who looked were saved.

They didn't wait until they were better people.

They didn't touch it.

They just looked.

Jesus tells us that this is a picture of Him being lifted up on the cross. "And as Moses lifted up the serpent in the wilderness, even so must the Son of Man be lifted up, that whoever believes in Him should not perish but have eternal life." (John 3:14-15)

That serpent represented the sin of the people. Christ was made sin for us.

Will you look to Jesus?—will you put your trust in Him?—the One who died for your sins.

Will you put your faith in Jesus?—the One who shed His life-blood for you—and me.

Some years ago, my eldest son, Aaron, was in an automobile accident. His back was broken so severely that the doctors said he might not ever walk again.

After fusing several vertebrae in his lower back, he was able to begin the long task of healing from the spinal fusion surgery. He was encased in a rigid plastic back brace from his neck to his waist.

Later, his doctor finally agreed to let him briefly remove the brace to take a shower, as long as someone was with him.

As I was driving to pick him and his brothers up for the weekend, unbeknownst to me, his brother, Josh, helped him removed the brace so he could take a hot shower in his shorts. Josh was with him but was much smaller than him at that time.

I decided to stop at the post office in Austin, when a still small voice spoke to me, saying, "You need to go now."

I passed the post office and drove as fast as I could to Wimberley, an hour away, wondering what that warning was.

There were no cell phones then. As I entered the house, I asked his mother where he was. She said in the shower.

I ran to it, and as soon as I entered the bathroom, he said, "Dad, I'm dizzy."

I stepped into the shower and placed my arms under his arms from his back. He immediately passed out.

.I told his younger brother to help me move him to a bed while their mother called 911. His dead weight was more than I could have ever imagined.

We got him onto the bed without reinjuring his back. I knew if he had fallen, he probably would have been paralyzed.

As I prayed, following the ambulance to the hospital's emergency room, I noticed the symbol on the ambulance's back.

It was the American Medical Association's (AMA) logo of a serpent wrapped around a staff.

The sign of healing medicine reminded me of the bronze serpent on the staff lifted up by Moses. Many Christians believe that's where the symbol originated.

But, more importantly, it reminded me of Jesus being lifted up on a cross for my son. God's son suffered in place of my son. I can't fathom love that great.

To this day, I cannot see that symbol without giving thanks to the Lord for that warning, and the shed blood of Christ lifted high upon a cross for my sins, for your sins, for the sins of the entire world.

Surely, there can be no greater love than God giving His Son's life-blood for us.

When we arrived at the hospital, the doctors gave him intravenous (IV) fluids and two bottles of Gatorade for dehydration.

The hot shower, along with pain medication and dehydration, had caused his blood to rush to his feet and thereby faint.

Will you look to the One who was lifted up on a cross for you? Will you look to the Great Physician—Jesus—to heal you of all your pain?

Will you look to Jesus, who took your place on a cross and died for your sins?

Choose

As I said before, Jesus hung between two thieves on a cross. One of them rejected Him, but the other one put his faith in Him.

"Will You remember me when You enter Your kingdom?" Jesus replied, "Assuredly, I say to you, today you will be with Me in Paradise." (Luke 23:43)

Both of those men were guilty. One put his trust in Jesus, and the other chose not to.

Again, the question is, which thief on the cross are you?

Now, there was the third cross that day. It was for another criminal named Barabbas, and he represents us.

Jesus was crucified on a cross meant for Barabbas—it was your cross, too—it was also my cross.

258

Jesus bore your cross and my cross. He took our place on that cross. The just for the unjust. The Righteous for the unrighteous. The sinless Lamb of God for the sinner.

Self-improvement will not qualify you for salvation, for God's Word says, "There is none righteous, no, not one." (Romans 3:10)

Comparing yourself to others will not work either, "for all have sinned and fall short of the glory of God." (Romans 3:23)

Doing your best cannot save you, for the Scriptures record, "But we are all like an unclean thing, And all our righteousnesses are like filthy rags." (Isaiah 64:6)

If you could be good enough to pay for your sins, ask yourself, why did Jesus have to die for you? The answer is you can't be good enough.

Come—come just as you are.

Will you say yes to Jesus—today?

There's a Scripture that I love, and it explains things very thoroughly.

"If thou shalt confess with thy mouth the Lord Jesus, and shalt believe in thine heart that God hath raised him from the dead, thou shalt be saved. For with the heart man believeth unto righteousness; and with the mouth confession is made unto salvation." (Romans 10:9-10)

You can settle this question right now in heaven and on earth by saying yes to Jesus—accepting His pardon, just as that one thief did on the cross.

There are no prescriptive or mandated words. Praying is just talking to the Lord.

If these words are how you feel in your heart, then pray:

"Heavenly Father,

I come to You in prayer, asking for the forgiveness of my sins.

I confess with my mouth and believe with my heart that Jesus is Your Son, and that He died on the cross at Calvary that I might be forgiven.

Father, I believe that Jesus rose from the dead, and I ask You right now to come into my life and be my personal Lord and Savior.

I repent of my sins and will surrender to You all the days of my life.

Because Your word is truth, I confess with my mouth that I am born again and cleansed by the blood of Jesus!

In Jesus' name, I pray. Amen!"

The most famous 25 words ever spoken: "For God so loved the world that He gave His only begotten Son, that whoever believes in Him should not perish but have everlasting life." (John 3:16)

"Whoever" is you—it's me—it's everyone.

Come to Jesus.
Look to Jesus.
Choose Jesus.
Today!

Yes

We moved to Clute, Texas, from Longleaf, Louisiana, when I was four-years-old.

All I remember of the trip was stopping at the Stateline in Deweyville, Texas. The pouring rain awoke my sister Marjorie, and she awoke me crying because her paper dolls had gotten wet.

Daddy had gotten a job at Dow Chemical in Freeport, Texas. A.J. Jeffers was the first from the Longleaf area to leave for a job at Dow. He returned and encouraged Daddy and others to do the same. A. J.'s brother Jimmy Jeffers and Daddy's brother Herman Willis soon followed. We all were close friends in Texas.

We also kept our home in Longleaf and often visited to work cows with my Uncle Howard Willis and his sons. I was always happy to return. I still am to this day.

Every Sunday morning, Sunday night, and Wednesday night, we were at Temple Baptist Church in Clute. It seemed to me that everyone attended church in those days.

One Wednesday night mother was unable to attend, so I walked to church with my twelve-year-old sister Marjorie. I was only eight-years-old. I had no intention of that night being any different from any other.

I cannot recall a single word Pastor Bill Campbell said in his sermon. But I do remember vividly another voice that spoke to my mind—to my heart. It was not an audible voice. It was a still gentle voice, tender but ever so clear, telling me to go forward and accept Christ as my Savior.

I recall my response to the Holy Spirit as if it was five minutes ago. "Lord, I'm too shy. I would if my mother was here to go with me."

I felt someone touch my arm. It was my sister Marjorie who was sitting in the back row with her friends. She could not have seen my face, for I was seated near the front.

She said, "I'll go with you if you want me to." I immediately walked with her to the front of the church and made my decision public.

I know you do not have to have an experience like that to be saved. Nevertheless, I'm so grateful for that experience, for it has never left my mind or my heart.

Oh, that I would today be more still and listen for that still soft voice. Oh, that I would speak less and listen more.

Listen, He is speaking.
Look, He has manifested Himself.
Choose—say yes to Jesus—today.
You will never regret that decision.

—*Randy Willis*

☆ ☆ ☆

"He is no fool who gives what he cannot keep to gain what he cannot lose." —*Jim Elliot*

In Appreciation

I'm thankful to the many people that encouraged me to write our family's history. My first-cousin, Donnie Willis, planted the first seed in my mind to write about our 4th Great-Grandfather, Joseph Willis. Donnie has been pastor of Fenton Baptist Church in Fenton, Louisiana, for over 50 years.

I'm also thankful to my sainted grandmother, Lillie Hanks Willis. She had a treasure chest of stories about Joseph Willis and insisted I write them down.

My Uncle Howard Willis was our family's master storyteller when I was younger. I sat for many hours, mesmerized by him. His granddaughter and my cousin Kimberly Willis Holt were inspired by him too. She is a National Book Award Winner, author of *When Zachary Beaver Came to Town*, *My Louisiana Sky*, and the *Piper Reed* series. *When Zachary Beaver Came to Town* and *My Louisiana Sky were* adapted as films of the same names.

I'm thankful to my late cousin and the maternal great-grandson of Joseph Willis, Dr. Greene Wallace Strother. His Uncle Polk Willis and Aunt Olive Willis tended to Joseph Willis in his final years, and they shared all that Joseph told them. Dr. Strother gave his extensive research to me in 1980. He served as chaplain to General Claire Chennault's "Flying Tigers" while in China as a missionary. He was a Southern Baptist missionary emeritus to China and Malaysia.

Karon McCartney, Archivist at the Louisiana Baptist Convention, has provided much help in organizing, cataloging, and protecting my research for decades, at the Louisiana Baptist Building in Alexandria.

My fellow historian and friend, the late Dr. Sue Eakin, asked me if I would help her research William Prince Ford. I learned much about William Prince Ford and Solomon Northup and their relationship to Joseph Willis from her. She encouraged me to have my research adapted into a play.

The play is entitled *Twice a Slave* and is based upon my novel of the same name. My books *Three Winds Blowing* and *Destiny* are partly based on the relationship of Joseph Willis with William Prince Ford and Solomon Northup.

Dr. Eakin is best known for documenting, annotating, and reviving interest in Solomon Northup's 1853 book *Twelve Years a Slave*. At the age of eighteen, she rediscovered a long-forgotten copy of Solomon Northup's book on the shelves of a bookstore, near the LSU campus, in Baton Rouge. The bookstore owner sold it to her for only 25 cents.

In 2013, *12 Years a Slave* won the Academy Award for Best Picture. In his acceptance speech for the honor, director Steve McQueen thanked Dr. Eakin: "I'd like to thank this amazing historian, Sue Eakin, whose life, she gave her life's work to preserving Solomon's book."

I am thankful for my three sons: Aaron Willis, Joshua Willis, and Adam Willis. Their strength of character has been demonstrated many times in how they treat those who can do nothing for them. The responses of the character Jimbo in three of my novels, was inspired by them.

And above all, I am thankful to the Good Lord. He has given me wells I did not dig, and vineyards I did not plant.

—Randy Willis

About the Author

Randy Willis is as much at home in the saddle as he is in front of the computer where he composes his family sagas. Drawing on his family heritage of explorers, settlers, soldiers, cowboys, and pastors, Randy carries on the tradition of loving the outdoors and sharing it in the adventures he creates for readers of his novels.

He is the author of *Destiny, Beckoning Candle, Twice a Slave, Three Winds Blowing, Carolinas Wind, Louisiana Wind, The Apostle to the Opelousas, The Story of Joseph Willis,* and many articles.

Twice a Slave has been chosen as a Jerry B. Jenkins Select Book, along with four bestselling authors. Jerry Jenkins is the author of more than 180 books with sales of more than 70 million copies, including the best-selling *Left Behind* series.

Twice a Slave has been adapted into a dramatic play at Louisiana College, by Dr. D. "Pete" Richardson (Associate Professor of Theater with Louisiana College).

Randy Willis owns Randy Willis Music Publishing (an ASCAP-affiliated music publishing company) and Town Lake Music Publishing, LLC (a BMI-affiliated music publishing company). He is an ASCAP-affiliated songwriter. He was an artist manager.

He is the founder of Operation Warm Heart, which feeds and clothes the homeless. He was a member of the Board of Directors of Our Mission Possible (empowering at-risk teens to discover their greatness) in Austin, Texas.

He was a charter member of the Board of Trustees of the Joseph Willis Institute for Great Awakening Studies at Louisiana College.

Randy Willis was born in Oakdale, Louisiana, and lived as a boy near Longleaf, Louisiana, and Barber Creek. He currently resides in the Texas Hill Country near his three sons and their families.

He graduated from Angleton High School in Angleton, Texas, and Texas State University in San Marcos, Texas. He was a graduate student at Texas State University for six years. He is the father of three sons and has five grandchildren.

Randy Willis is the fourth great-grandson of Joseph Willis and his foremost historian.

"Sow an act, and you reap a habit. Sow a habit and you reap a character. Sow a character, and you reap a destiny."—*Samuel Smiles*

To learn more about the author and the characters in this book, visit www.threewindsblowing.com

Randy Willis
PO Box 111
Wimberley, Texas 78676

512-565-0161
randywillisnovelist@gmail.com

Preach Christ at all times. When necessary, use words.

www.ingramcontent.com/pod-product-compliance
Lightning Source LLC
Chambersburg PA
CBHW032025240626
47154CB00003B/791